TO HAVE and TO HOWL

PARANORMAL WEDDING PLANNERS BOOK 3

A E J O N E S

AE Jones: To Have and To Howl
Copyright © 2017 by Amy E Jones

Publisher: Gabby Reads Publishing LLC

Cover Designer: http://theillustratedauthor.net/
Editor: http://www.demonfordetails.com/
Formatter: http://www.authorems.com

ISBN-10: 1-941871-18-6
ISBN-13: 978-1-941871-18-8

ACKNOWLEDGMENTS

First, I want to thank Melissa from the Illustrated Author for creating amazing new covers for my paranormal wedding planner series. Each one is better than the last and this one is my favorite so far!

Of course, I have to thank Faith for her amazing editing skills. This one was an emotional one for me and it took a while to get it right. Thanks for reading the many beginning chapters I struggled through.

To Sandra Owens who read an early version of this story and told me that I needed to let the readers know why Jack was struggling. Boy, were you right on that one!

And a special thank you to my beta readers: Becky, Sandy, Dyanne, Di, and Lara. Thanks for your suggestions, you guys are amazing!

As always, to my friends and family, thank you for your patience and understanding while I continue to hear voices in my head. At least I write them down in stories, right...right?

Di –

Thank you for being such a wonderful friend and supporter of my stories. I get such a kick out of your excitement when I have a new book come out. It just made sense that you also became a beta reader for my series. Even though I write alone, I edit with friends. Thanks for your suggestions and enthusiasm!

*Love and law are not so different
in their pursuit of truth.*

CHAPTER 1

Julia Cole entered the empty Tribunal chamber, her heart pounding in sync with the staccato click of her heels on the stone floor. She hesitated at the front of the gallery, resisting the urge to walk those few extra steps to the prosecutor's table.

She wasn't used to sitting in the audience when a trial took place, and if she had been able to convince the magistrates, she would have been prosecuting *this* case. But the magistrates shot down her request immediately. Not because she was a human wanting to try a supernatural case, or because she was normally a defense attorney, but instead they cited conflict of interest. Her husband was one of the victims. In her head, she knew they were right, but her heart was still kicking and screaming about it.

Today would not be a fun day. But then, fun had not been seen or had for a while now. Determination — yes. Single-mindedness — most definitely. Anger...well, anger had become her constant companion.

Julia sat in the front row and closed her eyes. She had been sitting in this same seat throughout the final week of the trial, absorbing every nuance, and staring the accused supernatural supremacist in the eyes. She would not be cowed. And since Thomas could not be here, she would be his representative, his presence, his voice. She would not allow her husband's message of tolerance to be silenced.

Today was the day. The verdict would be announced. And all the victims and their families would receive justice. There could be no other outcome.

The room filled up quickly. Throughout the trial, the magistrates had kept the chamber closed unless someone was called to testify or, in Julia's case, petitioned to attend. Now people crowded the benches and lined the sides of the gallery.

Jonathan Godfrey, the prosecutor, entered the chamber and nodded to her. He was a powerful foe in the courtroom, but in this instance, he had carefully considered her input and insights from the beginning.

Thomas's brother, Devin, arrived with his wife, Alex, who sat down next to Julia and squeezed her hand. Filing in behind them were Devin's teammates, the men who helped capture and bring the supremacists to trial.

She looked back at the four men and acknowledged each in turn, Charlie, Giz, and the twins, Connor and Jack. Jack had almost lost his life in the pursuit. She owed him and all of them for what they had been willing to sacrifice for this case. Even Alex was kidnapped and threatened. Julia wasn't sure if anyone would ever know the full extent of the crimes committed by these bastards.

And speaking of bastards—Tobin, the leader of the supernatural supremacists, swaggered into the room between two guards, his hands secured in glowing handcuffs. The supremacist gang had elected him as their representative in court. Why, Julia had no idea, but she also didn't understand why the idiots had followed him to begin with.

The room buzzed, anxiety jumping from person to person like static electricity. The guard at the front of the room gestured for them to rise. She stood with the rest of the crowd as the magistrates entered and sat at a raised bench in the front. There was no jury of your peers in supernatural court. Three magistrates heard the cases and rendered a decision.

The head magistrate raised his hand for silence and then motioned for everyone to take a seat. Julia pulled out her notes from the trial and the gold pen Thomas gave her. She gripped the pen so tightly she thought it might leave indentations in her fingers.

The head magistrate stood. "The case is concluded. In the matter of extortion, gunrunning, drug smuggling, kidnapping, attempted murder, and murder, we find Josiah Tobin and the Vipera gang guilty as charged."

The room erupted into shouts and sobs.

Julia's vision narrowed into a thin tunnel. The world tilted and went fuzzy...she shook her head hard, once, and deliberately slowed her breathing.

Had she heard the magistrate correctly? She turned to see Alex and Devin hugging beside her. It had actually happened. She wasn't imagining things. She had dreamed of this so many times, the reality was hard to believe.

"Order!" the magistrate yelled as he slammed his hand on the bench and the sound vibrated through the room as if amplified by a speaker. The crowd settled down, and everyone took their seats again.

"Normally we would pronounce sentence immediately. However, in human courts of law, we understand that victims and their families are permitted to speak before sentencing. Prosecutor

Godfrey has requested that this practice be followed here. We have decided to allow his request. The floor is yours."

Godfrey cleared his throat. "Thank you, your honors. Julia Cole has asked to speak on behalf of the victims."

Julia blinked. She blew out a breath and then inhaled, imagining herself breathing into a paper bag. She and Godfrey talked about the possibility of this happening, but he wasn't sure the magistrates would allow it. Now the time had come.

She could do this. Delivering closing remarks in a courtroom was second nature to her. She would speak for all the victims and their families today. Someone needed to be their voice, and she was more than ready to speak on their behalf.

She rose slowly, tested her legs, and when they didn't buckle, walked up to the podium. She froze for a moment. She'd forgotten her legal pad with her notes. But she didn't need it. She had practiced this speech over and over and over again for weeks. She looked each magistrate in the eye for a moment before uttering a word.

She cleared her throat and ran a thumb along her precious gold pen. "Thank you for allowing me to speak, your honors. Thomas Cole was an amazing man. He was a husband, a brother, a legal representative for the Elven Kingdom, and an attorney in human court. He fought his entire adult life for both humans and supernaturals alike. For him, there was no difference. He believed that everyone, regardless of race, gender, power, or lack thereof, deserved a fair trial. And all were equal in his eyes.

"Thomas was just one of the many victims of these supremacists." She looked back at the crowd, and gestured toward the small woman in the third row.

"Nina Murphy's only daughter, Carolyn, dared to love a human, and for that she was brutalized."

Julia cleared her throat to stop a lump of rage from stealing her voice. She turned to a large man leaning against the wall. "Steven Donald's wife supported mixed supernatural marriages, and as a result was beaten so badly she now refuses to leave her home. And the list of the Vipera gang's atrocities goes on and on." She held up her hands to encompass the room. "In this room alone, there are dozens of victims and their families, all deserving of justice, while they continue their fight to stop fear from taking over their lives.

"It has been seven months since the arrests were made. The correct verdict has been handed down. And now it's time to speak up for those who can't speak for themselves. We cannot let the crimes perpetrated on people who dared to love those different from themselves stand. These men need to be prosecuted to the fullest extent of supernatural law. If not, the victims cannot heal. Their families cannot heal. The entire community cannot heal." She paused.

"In a human court, murderers face the death penalty. I know this is not an option in your justice system. However, you can strip them of their powers and lock them away for life. Let the rest of us who aren't blinded by ignorance and hate feel safe again. Let the victims and their families begin rebuilding our lives with peace of mind. Thank you."

Julia turned and looked straight at Tobin, not blinking. Tobin's eyes tightened on her, and a chill spread through her, but she didn't turn away. She stared a moment longer before walking back to her seat and forcing herself to sit down slowly instead of flopping down, since her legs trembled.

The head magistrate spoke. "We need a moment to converse."

Instead of leaving the courtroom, the three magistrates closed their eyes. They had done this multiple times throughout the trial, speaking to each other psychically.

Julia closed her eyes and took a deep breath to calm her rat-a-tat heartbeat. *Please. Please. Please.* She chanted silently to herself.

After several agonizing minutes, the lead magistrate spoke. "Due to the severity of the crimes, we are in agreement with Mrs. Cole's request. Powers will be rescinded, and Tobin and the other members of the gang will be imprisoned for the rest of their lives."

Tobin's defense attorney surged to his feet. "Your honors—"

The magistrate held up his hands, palms out. "Enough, counselor. Our decision is final."

Maniacal laughter pierced the room. Julia turned, shocked to find Tobin on his feet, laughing hysterically.

"Calm your client, counselor," the magistrate warned.

"Or what," Tobin jeered. "What else will you do to me? You are fools." He turned toward the gallery. "All of you. You can't stop me, stop us. And if you think that human bitch holds any power over me, then you are mistaken." Tobin held his hands up, light exploded from them, and the handcuffs fell away.

Hands grasped Julia's shoulders and yanked her out of the chair, spinning her around, cocooning her against a hard body as if to shield her. *Jack.*

She wasn't sure how she knew immediately it was him, but she did. He tucked her head against his chest. Energy surged from his skin and buffeted her as he covered her body with his own.

People ran screaming in a panicked herd toward the back of the room. Jack half-led and half-carried her to the side. A chair flew by them, legs embedding in the wall.

She tried to peek around his chest.

"Stay down!" he hissed.

"Are Alex and Devin okay?"

"Devin's got Alex. They're fine."

A boom like thunder shook the room around them. Julia flinched, and Jack pulled her more tightly against him. Something growled close by, causing the hair on the back of her neck to stand on end.

The smell of smoke hit her nose at the same time someone yelled, "Clear!"

She squirmed in Jack's arms.

"Hold still for a minute and let me check you over."

"I'm fine. Let go!"

Jack frowned down at her. "You are nothing but trouble."

He let her go, but then caught her again when she stumbled slightly. She looked around at the chaos. Thankfully, most of the people had been able to get out of the room. Devin had Alex shielded in the corner. Both looked unhurt. Chairs were scattered, the prosecutor's table lay in pieces, and Godfrey held a handkerchief against the side of his head. The magistrates' bench smoked in several places where burn marks peppered the front.

In the middle of this scene, Tobin lay unconscious. A giant gray wolf stood with his front paws on Tobin's chest. A wolf that looked like he was grinning.

"Oh my God. Is...is that your brother in all his hairy glory?"

"Yeah," Jack sighed. "It's Connor. He's going to milk this story for months."

Julia had always known Jack and his twin, Connor, were werewolves, but *knowing* and *seeing* were two very different things. She gawked at the wolf as she tried to step away from Jack, but she couldn't move.

"Um, Jack. You can let me go now."

Jack looked down at his hands, still wrapped around her arms, and released her. She backed away, and, before she could thank him, he scowled at her.

"Stay out of the way while we get Tobin out of here."

The words of thanks stuck in her throat at his tone. "I'm not going anywhere near him. Besides, your brother looks like he's got it under control."

Connor tipped his head back and howled. Julia smiled at the perfect timing. She peeked back at Connor, who was looking right at her, his wolf grin back in place. Had his wolf hearing picked up their conversation?

Jack glared at his brother, grumbled "show-off," and then stalked toward Tobin and his cocky wolf brother before she could rethink thanking him for protecting her.

Alex made her way around the debris and wrapped her arms around Julia. "You're okay," she exclaimed. "Thank God it's finally over."

Julia stiffened in her arms as she tried to regulate her breathing. She had been doing so well just now. Flying chairs and show-off wolfs notwithstanding, she had held it together. Tobin and his gang would be punished, and she should be ecstatic.

But as the adrenaline drained away, happiness was not the emotion that remained. Instead, the familiar echoing emptiness returned.

No amount of anger or determination to see justice done could protect her from the realization that for her it would never truly be over.

Unlike a contract,
love has no expiration date.

CHAPTER 2

Jack stalked to the front of the Tribunal chamber, knocking a chair out of the way with a little more strength than necessary. He told himself his *enthusiasm* was due to wanting to secure Tobin as quickly as possible, although the Vipera leader wouldn't be going anywhere soon if Connor had anything to say about it.

It was *not* because of what just happened with Julia Cole. With her dark hair cut just below her chin to frame big, brown eyes and a gorgeous face, Julia screwed with his insides whenever she was within fifty feet of him. But that was his problem, and since it was one of a host of problems in his life, it would have to take a number and stand in line.

Even if Julia wasn't still mourning Thomas, she was so far out of his reach she might as well be on another planet.

"You okay?" Devin asked from beside Jack.

"Yeah. Are you and Alex okay?"

"Yes." Devin gripped his shoulder. "Thank you for protecting Julia."

Jack nodded. There was no need to thank him. The

second Tobin got free, Jack's first thought was to protect Julia. Actually, he'd grabbed her shoulders before he formed a thought, and the rest was his training kicking in.

Charlie and Giz joined them.

"Report," Devin said.

"No one was seriously hurt," Charlie replied. "A faery healer was in the crowd, and she's helping with the minor injuries."

Giz looked down at Tobin. "I want to look at those handcuffs before anyone else touches them."

Devin glared at the Vipera leader. "Let's get the crazy SOB secured first."

With the help of the guards, Charlie and Giz secured Tobin's hands and feet with new magic-imbued cuffs while Connor perched on his chest.

"Connor, get off him, already," Charlie said.

Connor climbed down from his perch. Light shimmered slightly around him.

Jack held up his hand. "Don't change now, bro. There are people here who don't need to see your naked ass."

Connor flicked his ears and whined before he sat and frowned at Jack. As much as a wolf can frown, that is.

Devin turned to Charlie. "Go with the guards and make sure Tobin is secured in his cell. And stand guard over him for now. I'm going to talk to the magistrates about who's assigned to watch him until he's transported to the Elven Prison."

"You got it," Charlie said, and followed Tobin and his guards out of the room.

"Giz, figure out what the deal is with those handcuffs, and how Tobin was able to get out of them."

Giz nodded before walking away.

"We've got a problem on our hands," Jack said.

"Agreed." Devin lowered his voice. "Someone had to help Tobin escape those cuffs. We've always known we didn't capture all the gang, but they've been lying low since the arrests."

"Until now," Jack said.

Connor growled, baring his rather large wolf teeth.

"My feelings exactly," Jack mumbled.

Devin glanced over at Godfrey, who sat in a slightly dented chair while a faery held her hand above the cut on his head, healing him. "I'm going to talk to Godfrey to get some more information. Jack, can you follow Julia home?"

Jack nodded and then frowned when he saw Alex standing alone. "Where's Julia?"

Devin's head whipped around. "Shit. Alex?"

Alex skirted around a broken chair and came over to the group.

"Where's Julia?"

"She just left. Said something about the wolf brothers having it all under control and she wanted to go home."

Jack sighed. Of course she did.

"Can you go catch up with her?" Devin asked Jack. "I want to be sure she makes it home safely."

Jack jogged toward the door and down the hall to the parking area, spotting the taillights of Julia's car as it pulled down the long driveway toward the gate. Jack ran to his SUV and followed her.

He wasn't surprised she wanted to escape and be alone. She had been all bluster and attitude with him just now, but earlier in court she was amazing. Without a doubt, Julia was one of the strongest people Jack knew. But even strong people had their limits, and she didn't need to have people surrounding her right now. Hell, Jack was an expert when it came to pushing people away. He recognized all the cues she threw off. And he couldn't blame her, not after what she'd been through.

After a few minutes, she merged onto the interstate, and Jack stayed behind her. He growled when she passed her exit and kept going. What was she doing now?

Jack clicked the call button on his dashboard screen and placed a call to Devin.

Julia traced her fingers over the letters carved in the cold headstone. Thomas Allen Cole. Almost three years had passed, but in moments like this the years faded away, and the wounds in her heart ripped open again, since they had never truly healed.

She wasn't sure why she felt the need to come to the cemetery. The casket was empty. Thomas was an elf, and his people believed his spirit should be released on a funeral pyre. The cemetery plot was for her human ceremony and sensibilities.

But right now, she wanted—no, *needed*—to be here, looking at her husband's name memorialized. It was the only permanent thing she had left of him.

"We did it, Thomas. After all this time, they'll finally pay. I looked your murderers in the eye. I want them to never forget what they did to you." She swallowed hard. "And what that did to me.

"I spoke for you, since you couldn't speak up for yourself. I'm sure I wasn't as eloquent as you would have been. You always told me to speak from the heart, but I couldn't do it in front of those bastards who killed you. I wouldn't let them see my pain. They would revel in it."

She clenched the fingers she had brushed over the

stone into a fist. "So I'll tell you what I wanted to say today, just for you." She closed her eyes. "I would have told them that since losing you, the past two years and eight months have been a waking nightmare. And if you were here right now, you would give me your signature stern look and declare I was being overly dramatic. But I don't think you can argue that losing the other half of your soul is life-altering. I've dwelled on the senselessness of it.

"I thought learning you died was the worst thing I would ever go through. I was wrong. When I found out you were murdered, my grief exploded out of me until it threatened to take over my life. And *that* could not happen.

"Instead I replaced it with anger, because anger was something I could manage. If I thought your death was senseless before the truth came out, I had underestimated what that word really meant. Meaningless, absurd, pointless. And to find out the reason you were murdered was because you loved me..." Julia paused for a moment as the tears finally escaped, "...that you died for what you believed in, is devastating for me and everyone else you ever fought for. Your murderers need to suffer for what they did to you, Thomas. And today was the final step in making that happen."

She wiped the tears away with an angry swipe. "So, how did I do, counselor?"

Choking silence.

She wasn't sure why she asked the last question as if he would respond to her. In all her conversations with him here, he never had, and he never would.

Because he wasn't here. She knew that. She was a practical, no-nonsense person.

But if she was honest with herself, she'd admit there was a little voice in her head that whispered, *What if...*

What if he spoke to her? Even if it was only one last time. And if he did speak to her, would the sound of his voice make her feel whole again?

Julia's phone rang, filling the silence. She looked at the screen and closed her eyes for a moment to collect herself.

"Hello, Devin."

"Where are you? Alex said you were going straight home."

"I'm heading home soon." She frowned. "Wait. How do you know I'm not home?"

"Jack called me."

"Jack?" She turned around, and her face heated when she saw Jack leaning up against an SUV parked on the lane behind her car.

"You had him follow me?"

"I wanted to make sure you got home okay. You can't blame me after everything that happened today."

She swallowed.

"Jules…"

He hesitated and she filled the gap. "I'm fine, honest."

"Do you want Alex and me to come over to the house?"

"I'm heading home right now, and I'll call you tomorrow, okay?"

"Call us if you need anything, even if it's just to talk. You did great today, Julia."

She disconnected and dropped the phone back into her jacket pocket. As she turned and faced Jack, anger surged along her skin like a rash. She did her best to not disturb the other graves as she walked toward the SUV. The closer she got to him, the harder her heart slammed against her rib cage.

He had to have heard what she said. She wanted to scream and then curl into a ball and never get up again. No one was supposed to hear what she said to Thomas. Least of all a man she would more than likely see again in the future.

She forced herself to swallow down her screams and looked him in the face. A face that showed no emotion, which was more than fine with her. She couldn't handle his pity. It would suffocate her.

"I'm going home now," she said, in what she thought was a relatively calm voice.

"That's a good idea. I'll follow you there."

She headed toward her car, but stopped and turned back to him. "You told Devin I didn't go home, but you didn't tell him I'm at the cemetery. Why?"

He gazed at her for a moment before responding. "He didn't need to know."

"Thank you."

She got into her car and drove slowly along the winding lane toward the cemetery exit.

*Matters of love
can't be resolved by a jury of your peers.*

CHAPTER 3

It had been five days since the trial. Five days for things to go back to normal. Or what Julia called her new normal since losing Thomas. And that new normal meant diving back into work again with a vengeance. Work was something Julia could control, something she was good at. As a defense attorney, she fought for her clients every step of the process.

But what many people didn't know about the law was that it included bursts of activity interspersed with downtime. Courtroom law was not the fast-paced, exciting drama shown on TV. And unfortunately Julia had *not* been born with a patience gene. It wasn't even part of her DNA strand. Waiting made her itch.

Whoever said patience is a virtue should be smacked. Or better yet, made to stand in line at the Department of Motor Vehicles. Yep, that would cure them of their virtuous opinions.

But even though she glared at her non-ringing, non-beeping, non-flashing phone for the hundredth time this morning, she knew her aversion to waiting would not convince a jury to hurry up and conclude their deliberations. Her arguments, cross-examinations, and closing remarks might exonerate her client, but couldn't speed up the process.

People were people. And a group of strangers with differing experiences sequestered in a room to decide on a man's freedom took time. She had to balance her sense of urgency with her hope that her client was found not guilty.

It was hard to believe only a few short days ago she was praying for a guilty verdict for Tobin and his gang. She shook her head to clear herself of the memory. This was not the time to dwell.

She needed to stay in the present. Even if it meant she was tethered to her phone waiting for the jury to reach a verdict. She stared at her computer screen. She had already cleaned out her emails, her file cabinets, and her office desk drawers. Before that she had given her paralegal, Tina, a stack of correspondence to work on.

A soft knock sounded at her door, and she looked up to find Alex standing in the doorway.

"Am I interrupting? Sorry to just walk back here, but Tina wasn't at her desk."

Julia beckoned for Alex to come in. "She's probably hiding. She knows what I'm like when a jury is still out."

"This has been a long deliberation. Is that a good or bad thing?"

"I'm hoping it's good. Often when the deliberations take longer, the jury votes in favor of the defendant." As well they should, since her client was innocent. But innocence didn't always win in court.

Alex smiled. "With you as defense, I can't imagine how the jury could go against you."

Julia chuckled. "What are you trying to tell me?"

"That you're my sister-in-law, but when you're in lawyer mode, you scare the bejesus out of me."

Even though Alex and Thomas never met, Julia was certain he would have adored her, and been happy his brother Devin found someone to love who would also keep him in his place. Thomas would have gotten a kick out of their relationship.

Alex reached over the desk and squeezed her hand. "I came to check on you since we've only talked on the phone since the trial. How are you doing?"

Alex was too observant. Julia had learned through her years of courtroom experience not to give too much away with her expressions, but she couldn't hide much from her friend.

"I'm fine."

Alex stared at her for a moment before continuing. "Okay. I'll let that be for now. In the meantime, I thought maybe I could entice you to go to lunch with me, my treat."

Julia's radar sounded an alarm. "What are you up to, Alex?"

Alex's eyes widened. "Who says I'm up to anything?"

Alex was always up to something. She couldn't help butting into everyone's lives, determined to help fix things. Julia stared at her with what she liked to call her lawyer glare, and Alex caved after a few seconds.

"Fine," Alex huffed. "I want your help with Jack and Connor."

No, no, no.

Julia had to admit they were both extremely handsome, if you were into tall, dark, and rugged. They were identical except their eye color: Connor's eyes were gem-green and Jack's sea-blue. Even if their eye color wasn't different, their dispositions set them apart. Connor was all grins and winks, while Jack was stoic and silent. There was something disconcerting about him — about both of them.

An image of Jack waiting for her in the cemetery flashed in her mind, and panic bubbled up close behind it. She would avoid Jack if she could, but he and Connor worked with Devin and the Tribunal to protect supernaturals. And now that she wrote the paranormal prenups for Alex's family's wedding planner business, and Devin's team provided security for high-profile weddings, she couldn't avoid them if she wanted to.

"Julia? Did you hear me?"

Julia blinked. "Sorry. What did you say?"

"I said I wish I knew what's wrong with Jack. He's always been quiet, but now he's downright surly. Devin says Connor can't get through to him at all either, even with the werewolf twin-speak thing they have."

"Werewolf twin-speak?" Julia asked.

"Yeah, they can sense when something is wrong with the other. When Jack was hurt a few weeks ago, Connor felt it. So what do you think?"

"Why are you asking me?"

"Because you were a witness to the twins' fight at Sheila and Charlie's wedding. Were words exchanged? Did Connor say something to provoke Jack? Give me *something*."

Julia nearly laughed at her friend's barrage of questions. "Are you cross-examining me, counselor?"

Alex blushed a little. "Sorry. I'm just trying to figure out what happened so I can help."

"I can't tell you much. I was sitting on the terrace with Connor after the wedding, and he was flirting with me."

Alex snorted. "Which doesn't surprise me."

"I don't remember exactly what he said. The next thing I knew, Connor jerked his head up and glared at Jack across the terrace. I could swear they were having an argument, but they weren't saying anything out loud. I didn't understand at the time, but maybe it was the twin-speak thing you're talking about. Anyway, Jack stomped over, punched Connor in the face, and then stalked off."

There was something going on with Jack, with both the brothers, but Julia wasn't going to get involved with their drama. Her plate was full with her job, and she already had enough trouble walking away from her cases. But she couldn't stop being a lawyer. Burying herself in the law had saved her sanity on more than one occasion, and it kept her linked to Thomas, who had been ten times the lawyer she could ever be.

Alex leaned forward. "We need to figure out what's going on with them."

Julia stopped herself from shaking her head. There was no *we* in this equation. Thank God her phone beeped, saving her from answering right away as she read the text message. "I'm going to have to take a rain check on lunch."

"Is anything wrong?"

"The jury's back; I've got to go."

Julia hugged Alex goodbye, relieved to have been summoned back to court. And as much as she wanted to say the relief was because the case was finally over—for her and her hopefully exonerated client—the truth was she wanted to stay far away from whatever drama Alex was about to dive into with both feet. Julia couldn't handle the emotions...or the twins, for that matter.

So she would not get involved.

Julia gave an encouraging nod to her client, Shawn, as the judge entered the courtroom and sat at his bench.

He turned to the jury. "Have you reached a verdict?"

The head juror stood in the box. "We have, Your Honor."

The bailiff accepted the paper from the juror and handed it to Judge Hastings. He reviewed the verdict with a poker face, and then gestured for the juror to continue.

"In the matter of manslaughter, we find the defendant not guilty."

Murmurs rippled through the courtroom until the judge called for quiet.

Judge Hastings turned to Shawn. "You're free to go."

A sob erupted behind her. Julia didn't need to look to know it was Shawn's mother, Deidre. Julia faced her client, and Shawn stared back at her in shell-shocked disbelief. After a moment, Shawn's face transformed before her eyes. A brilliant smile appeared to replace the stricken expression she'd seen throughout the trial.

"Thank you," he said, his voice rough.

She nodded, since her own throat clogged with emotion. *No!* She swallowed it down. Deidre grabbed her son and wept on his shoulder.

Time to go. Julia gathered her paperwork and stuffed it in her briefcase. Before she could escape, though, Deidre pulled her into a tear-drenched hug. Julia's arms went around the woman automatically, but what she wanted to do was run away screaming. The raw emotions bombarded her, her nerves stretched tight under her skin.

"Mom! Let Julia breathe. You're suffocating her."

Deidre backed up, wiping away her tears with the back of her hand. "Sorry about that. I'm just so grateful. You're amazing. Thank you so much."

"It's my job."

Deidre shook her head sharply. "Don't downplay your talent and dedication, young lady. Accept a thank-you when it's given."

"You're welcome."

Julia hurried out of the courtroom and down the corridor as fast as she could without seeming to run away, until she saw Godfrey ahead of her. She hadn't seen him since Tobin's trial. When he wasn't working for the Tribunal, he was the assistant district attorney in human court.

He was also a werewolf like the twins, but it wasn't common knowledge. She wasn't sure what the District Attorney's office would think if that tidbit ever got out.

She started toward him, and then paused when she caught sight of Devin. He met Godfrey in the hall, and they both headed toward Godfrey's offices. Had something come up regarding the Tribunal case?

Julia followed them down the hall and into the ADA offices. She knocked on Godfrey's closed door.

"Enter," Godfrey called out.

Julia opened the door. Godfrey and Devin both got to their feet when she walked inside. "Has something happened?"

Godfrey gestured to the second guest chair.

"What are you doing here, Jules?" Devin asked, as they both took a seat.

Godfrey sat back down as well. "I'll tell you what she's doing here. She just won a trial and kicked the prosecutor's butt in the process. You did a great job, by the way. Hastings only threatened you with contempt once. Normally he throws contempt threats around like confetti."

"How do you even know that already? Do you have secret cameras, or maybe minions in the courtroom?"

Godfrey grinned. "I'll never tell."

"Well I'm not used to compliments from the enemy."

"You're not my enemy. If I had my way, you'd be working as a prosecutor."

Julia shook her head. "Your boss has already tried to lure me to the dark side. It's not going to happen." She looked between the two men. "Are we done with the obligatory small talk now? Do you want to tell me why you both look so tense?"

Godfrey picked up a pen and tapped it against his desk. "Devin's team has been investigating what happened during the Tribunal sentencing."

"You mean when Tobin tried to incinerate everybody?" Julia asked.

Devin turned to her. "We've been trying to figure out how Tobin broke out of his handcuffs."

Julia frowned. "He used his powers, right?"

Devin and Godfrey glanced at each other.

Julia's nerves jangled under her skin. "What aren't you telling me?"

Devin sighed. "The handcuffs used on Tobin should have blocked his powers. He shouldn't have been able to get out of them. Unless they were malfunctioning."

"Or someone helped him," Julia choked out the words.

"Yes."

"And what have you found out?"

"Giz ran a number of tests on the cuffs, both magical and diagnostic. We can't figure out exactly what happened with them."

Julia bolted to her feet. "I want to be in on the investigation."

"Jules—"

"Don't *Jules* me, Devin! There are still supremacists out there, and we need to stop them. You didn't let me help with the case last time, but this time I want to know what's going on."

"I promise to let you know what's going on, okay?"

That wasn't the same thing as promising to let her help. He couldn't wordsmith his way out of this, not with a lawyer.

Godfrey zeroed in on her with a sharp gaze, as if reading her thoughts and waiting to see what she was going to say.

"You kept secrets from me before, Devin. Please don't do it again."

Devin grabbed her shoulders. "I don't know how many times I need to say I'm sorry for not telling you my suspicions about Thomas's death, but I am. And I promise not to keep any more secrets from you."

She took a deep breath while Devin held her shoulders and rubbed them lightly. Devin and his team had made it their mission to find Thomas's killers, she knew that. And she thought she had exorcised the anger about Devin's secrets, but apparently there was still a kernel left. It was time to let it go.

She met Devin's determined gaze. "Let me know what you find out. And I want to help."

Devin dropped his hands. "You can help, but in exchange, I want to update the security systems at your office and house. I also want to go through your day-to-day activities with you to determine if anything you're doing needs to be readjusted for the time being."

"Fine."

Devin gaped at her. "You agreed too quickly, Julia. I was expecting an argument."

"No point. I watched Tobin almost destroy a room by himself. This is out of my league. Besides, you would just harass me until I agreed anyway."

He smiled at her. "True. I'll have them go over everything to make sure you're safe."

Julia's warning signal went off again as she digested what he just said. Wait...*them?* Wasn't Devin going to do it? Before she could ask Devin who he meant, a knock on the door had Godfrey calling "enter."

Julia turned to see a smirking Connor saunter into the office, followed by a straight-faced Jack.

"Perfect timing," Devin said. "I want you two to check Julia's house and office."

Julia stifled her groan. She should have outlined ground rules before agreeing. She knew better than to jump in without hearing all the details. And now she would have to spend more time with Jack.

Julia frowned as she left the courthouse. Godfrey asked Devin to stay behind to talk for a minute, which meant Julia had been dismissed. She could help with the case, *damn it!* But right now it was the least of her worries. Steps sounded behind her, and she gripped her briefcase tighter as she hurried across the parking lot. She didn't want to face Jack again. Maybe if she ignored the two males trailing behind her, they would go away, or vanish…could werewolves vanish?

Her wish wasn't granted when Connor spoke up. "I'm not sure why she's acting like we aren't here, Jack. It's not like we can't follow her. Besides, we know where she lives."

She walked faster.

Connor chuckled. "You're going to twist an ankle in those heels, sweetheart."

She spun around. "Of all the Neanderthal—"

She stopped her eruption when she saw the grin on his face.

"You did that on purpose!"

"Got you to stop, didn't I?" Connor burst out laughing. "I love your spunk, Julia. You're one tough woman."

"I agree." She smiled at his infectious laugh.

"We're still going to spend some time with you, make sure you're safe, and your house and office are secure. We'll follow you to your house and check it over tonight. Are there any good takeout places nearby?"

Oh, no, not tonight. She avoided looking at Jack. She couldn't face him tonight. "I can't do this tonight. I have work to finish, and I have to prepare for a meeting with a client tomorrow."

Connor opened his mouth as if to protest, but Jack interrupted him. "We'll check your house tomorrow night." He paused. "But we'll be at your house in the morning to drive you to the office, so we can observe your routine."

"That works." She fumbled in her purse for her keys. So much for a graceful exit.

Connor reached for her briefcase. "Here, let me hold that for you." She almost protested until he flashed his ridiculous dimples at her.

She found her keys, clicked on the fob, and held out her hand to Connor.

"I'll put it in the back seat for you."

"Thank you."

He winked and she turned to reach for the car door, but Jack beat her to it. She looked up into his eyes for the first time. He gazed at her for a moment, as if he wanted to say something, but instead he opened the door and stepped out of her way.

"You are going home from here, right?" he asked.

"Yes. You don't have to worry about me." She slipped into the car, started it, and pulled out without looking back.

The farther she drove away from him, the more Jack's breathing slowed.

She was wrong. He did have to worry about her. He looked over at his twin, who had a shit-ass grin on his face. Never a good sign.

"You need to stay away from her, Connor."

Connor's grin fell away. "Excuse me?"

"I think I was pretty clear. Leave her alone," he demanded, sounding harsh to his own ears.

"What the hell is wrong with you?" Connor asked.

"Nothing is wrong with me."

"Right. You've been a cranky bastard for weeks, brother. What's going on?"

Jack ignored his question. "She's not a toy, Connor."

Connor glared at him. "I'm well aware of that."

"She's still in pain. She hasn't gotten over Thomas." Jack flashed on the memory of Julia running her hand over Thomas's tombstone.

Connor's eyes softened. "I know she's in pain, Jack. Why do you think I tease her? I want to see her smile. It's been almost three years since his death."

"There's no prescribed timeline to get over grief. Everyone is different. We thought the trial was finally over, and now we have to worry about other psychos out there gunning for her. Which makes it even worse for her."

"I get that, but I also don't want her to hole up in her house by herself tonight. It's not good to let things fester."

Why did Jack get the feeling Connor wasn't talking about Julia anymore? His brother could never be accused of being subtle. But Jack wasn't about to get into it with him.

"She has Alex, Sheila, and Peggy now. They won't let her hide away for long."

Connor grinned again. "You're right. Good thinking!

It's time to call in the troops."

What the hell was he talking about? "Connor—"

"Jack. Trust me. I know what I'm doing."

Jack knew his brother better than anyone. Scarier words were never spoken.

If a contract is bogged down in details, walk away.
But with love, the details matter.

CHAPTER 4

Julia rubbed her tired eyes. She had transcribed a legal pad full of scribblings to her laptop, and had been writing and re-writing the case notes for several hours now. It was time to stop torturing herself and take a break.

She set her laptop on the coffee table and climbed off her couch, stretching as she did so.

She had picked up her cell phone several times to call Devin and ask him how his meeting with Godfrey went, but she was bound to drive herself crazy if she headed down that rabbit hole. Plus, she was afraid he would ask her about Jack and Connor, and she didn't want to admit she hadn't let them come home with her. She felt a little guilty about it, but she couldn't handle the two of them tonight.

It was past dinnertime. If she remembered correctly, she had a shriveled-up peach and a couple of boiled eggs in her refrigerator. She wasn't sure how long the eggs had been in there, so the idea of experimenting with them for dinner wasn't very appealing. If she was lucky, there might be a can of soup in her pantry.

She hated to admit that she was a terrible cook. It all went back to her missing patience gene. Cooking took too much time. Then again, maybe if she was better at it, it wouldn't take so long.

The doorbell rang just as she headed toward the kitchen, and her heart stopped. Her friends always called or texted before dropping in. The last time someone unexpected knocked on her door, it was Devin. She had taken one look at his face and known something terrible happened. She'd zeroed in on his mouth and the words *Thomas* and *accident* before the world went black.

When she woke up, everything had changed. The world lost its crispness, its color. A fog settled around her, and nothing was clear to her anymore, except one thing.

Thomas was gone.

And when she finally, *finally*, started to rejoin the world again, to see glimpses of color around her, to let people in, Devin uncovered the truth. Thomas's death was not an accident. Someone murdered him.

And in that moment, she crammed all her emotions away. She would never let anyone near what was left of her heart. She couldn't risk it.

The doorbell rang again.

She went to her front door and looked out the peephole to see Alex and her friend Sheila beaming at her. Julia let out the breath she'd been holding and opened the door.

"What are you two doing here?"

They held up bags.

"We come bearing dinner!" Alex announced.

"How did you know I haven't eaten yet?"

Alex's eyes danced with mischief. "I've been in your kitchen before, dear. Your refrigerator is a bit of a lab experiment gone wrong."

Sheila giggled and then bit her lip as if to stop herself.

Julia smiled. "It's okay. She's right, which is why it's funny."

They walked toward the kitchen, where Alex and Sheila set the bags on her counter.

"What's for dinner?" Julia asked.

"We're making veggie tacos," Sheila replied. "Super easy and quick to make. I brought the recipe for you so you can make it in the future."

Alex snorted, and Sheila wagged her finger at her. "Enough, Alex. It's not like you're a gourmet cook yourself. I'm going to teach both of you how to do this."

Alex saluted. "Yes, madam chef."

"Where's Peggy?" Julia asked, surprised Thomas's sister hadn't come.

Sheila started rifling through the cupboard and pulling out pans. "She's stopping to get some wine and pick up Darcinda." She glanced over at Julia. "You don't mind us inviting her, do you?"

Julia shrugged. "The more the merrier." She didn't know Darcinda well, but the faery healer recently saved both Sheila and her husband Charlie's lives, so she was more than welcome to share tacos with them.

The doorbell rang, and Alex volunteered to get it. A few seconds later, Alex led Peggy and Darcinda into the kitchen.

Peggy gave Julia a big hug. "I'm sorry I was out of town when the verdict came down. I wanted to be there with you and Devin."

Julia squeezed her back. "I know."

Julia always got a kick out of her other sister-in-law. Peggy had her own personality, and wasn't scared to show it. Today she was dressed in a minidress à la the 1960s, with a hairdo that flipped up at the ends like Samantha from *Bewitched*.

But now that Darcinda had joined their merry group, Peggy's outfits looked downright sedate. Today Darcinda's long hair was dyed turquoise, and she wore a T-shirt that said *I don't need a stinking superpower, I'm a faery.*

The shirt was tucked into long cargo shorts that went to her knees, and she finished off the outfit with high-top black and white Converse tennis shoes. Even in that getup, she was gorgeous.

Darcinda smiled at her. "Thanks for letting me crash the party."

"The entire party was a surprise to me, so no problem."

Alex set wineglasses on the counter, and Julia found the corkscrew and made short work of opening the wine. Within minutes, they were sitting at the kitchen counter while Sheila worked on the tacos.

Alex poured more wine for Julia. "Devin told us about the handcuffs. I thought this was finally over."

Julia looked down at her wineglass and ran her finger around the rim. "Yeah."

"Devin and the guys will take care of it."

Julia wrenched away from her selfish thoughts. Alex had almost died at the hands of the supremacists as well.

"I know how scary this has been for you since your kidnapping," Julia said.

Alex's chin came up. "I'm not going to let them intimidate me. That's what they want. We took care of most of them, so now we find the stragglers and stop them, too. Besides, this isn't just about me."

"I'm fine," Julia assured them, in what she thought was a convincing voice.

Apparently she miscalculated, since seconds later she was enveloped in a hug with Peggy, and then Alex, and finally Sheila, who launched herself at them as well, her spatula still in one hand.

After a few minutes of sniffling, and hugging, and swearing on Sheila's part when she charred the onions in the skillet, the ladies finally calmed down.

Darcinda pulled the pan off the heat and dumped the charred onions in the disposal before turning back with a puzzled expression. "First order of business is teaching you guys how to throw a party. Just so you know"—her fingers waved to take in the four hugging women—"this ain't it. This is a therapy session, and I'm not dressed for a therapy session."

"You have a therapy session outfit?" Julia asked.

Darcinda nodded. "I have an outfit and hair color for every occasion."

Julia looked at the beautiful faery and couldn't stop the laugh from bubbling out, which set the other three off like dominos, giggles changing to guffaws.

Finally Sheila turned back to the stove. Alex set chips and salsa on the counter, and they snacked over laughter and topics of a less gut-wrenching variety.

Peggy regaled them all with a story about a recent date which almost made Alex shoot wine out through her nose, setting off their laughter again. Julia couldn't remember the last time she had laughed until her stomach hurt.

"When are Connor and Jack coming over to check your house?" Alex asked.

"Tomorrow. I'm surprised Devin let you come here tonight. How is he not here hovering over you?"

"He dropped me off and will be picking me up later. He thought the twins would be here. He was a little surprised not to see their car. They might be getting an earful right now."

Julia cringed. "They're going to check my office and house tomorrow."

"Well, I'm glad they're watching over you," Alex

said. "Plus, it's good Devin is giving Jack and Connor something to do. Maybe they can work out whatever is bugging them."

Sheila put new onions into the pan. "I'm worried about Jack, too. Ever since he was attacked by Dr. Williamson and he forced Jack to relive his shooting over and over again, he hasn't been the same."

"You're not to blame for that, Sheila," Peggy spoke up.

"Jack was protecting me when it happened," Sheila said. "I can't help but feel partially responsible."

Darcinda frowned. "Williamson is the bad guy here. The fact that he called himself a healer makes me want to turn him into a bug and smash him under my foot."

Alex's mouth fell open. "You're always so laid-back. Have you been hiding your violent streak all along?"

Julia set her wineglass down. "The more important question is *can* you turn him into a bug?"

Darcinda shook her head, though her eyes told a different tale. "No, it was just an expression."

"Remind me never to piss you off," Peggy said.

Alex snapped her fingers. "Ladies! Back on task, please. How do we help the twins?"

"Maybe they need mates," Darcinda said. "Those twins are incredibly easy on the eyes."

Alex laughed. "Sheila and I are married, so we probably shouldn't comment on that."

Sheila waved her spatula at Alex. "I seem to remember you ogling my husband after you were married to Devin and saying it was okay to look but not touch."

Peggy scrunched up her nose like she smelled something rotten. "I grew up with Jack and Connor. They're like brothers to me."

Julia smiled at Peggy's expression. "I've always wondered how you grew up with werewolves."

"The Elven Kingdom often employs werewolves as security. It's quite a lucrative business for the pack. Connor and Jack's father is the head of security for the pack, and it was his job to assign wolves to work security. He spent a lot of time meeting with our father, and the twins came along and ran the woods with Devin and me."

Alex's eyes lit up. "And now, with Julia spending time with the twins, it gives her the perfect opportunity to find out what's wrong and report back to us."

Julia gulped her wine. "I'm not going to be your spy, Alex." Time to change the subject. "Not that I don't appreciate the impromptu dinner party, but why did you decide to come over tonight?"

Alex, Sheila, and Peggy suddenly wouldn't look her in the eye. She turned to Darcinda, who shrugged.

"I'm the new girl. I have no idea what's going on."

"Alex?"

"Does there need to be a reason?"

"Alex! Did Devin send you over here to check on me?"

"Um. I may have gotten a call from Connor telling me to check on you."

"Really?"

"I was already thinking about it, and then when Connor called, he said you wouldn't let them in the house, and that you were working tonight and probably wouldn't eat."

Julia's chest tightened. "He doesn't know what he's talking about."

Sheila laughed. "What were you planning to eat, Julia? There's a box of crackers in your pantry that expired two months ago. And I looked in your refrigerator. There is some unidentifiable piece of fruit and two eggs that should not be touched."

"It's a peach. And that's what takeout is for."

"Well, I think it's sweet Connor's looking out for you," Peggy said.

"I'm not seeing sweet in this scenario," Julia responded. "Connor is a meddler. He just gets away with it because he has dimples."

She wondered for a second if Jack had dimples. She wasn't sure if she had ever seen him smile before. She shook her head. Between the supremacists and her clients, she had enough to worry about. She couldn't afford to worry about Jack Dawson too, no matter what his story was.

One misplaced phrase can impact a contract...
and a relationship.

CHAPTER 5

Jack stood on the edge of the cliff, staring at the full moon, high and bright in the heavens. The craters on the surface stood out against the darkened sky. He howled his frustration, his human voice weak and raspy as anger seethed under his skin.

Did he honestly think the man on the moon would help him? That anyone could?

He dropped to the earth, knees slamming to the hard ground. His hands landed on his thighs, palms up. He stared at them, his skin glowing in the moonlight. And then he stared some more.

Nothing.

He'd stripped naked after his second attempt, hoping to see some telltale sign. But no claws extended, no hair appeared on his hands, thighs, or chest. His head pounded a bass drumbeat, and his chest was heaving like he'd run a marathon. But nothing worked.

Jack couldn't shift.

His wolf was missing, or unhappy, or...something. Hell, he couldn't figure out what the problem was.

Could a wolf throw a snit? Take a time out? Whatever the problem was, he didn't know how to fix it. And as the days turned into weeks since he could communicate with his wolf, his anxiety had become a palpable presence, taking over his rational self.

It was as if he was a pre-teen again, before his first transition, but worse than that. At least when he was a child he could sense his wolf, its presence never too far from his thoughts or feelings. But now? Now he was alone. And he'd never been so completely alone before. Between his wolf and his mental link with Connor, he always had someone rattling around in his brain. But Connor's voice was also gone as well.

His solution so far had been to back away from everyone and everything, including Connor. From the looks Connor gave him, Jack could tell Connor believed he was purposely blocking him. If only it were that simple. Jack wanted nothing more than to hear his cocky-ass brother in his head again. But it was silent. And now that his wolf had abandoned him, his flight instincts were overpowering the fight.

But he couldn't hide anymore. The team was back on the supremacist case. And with Julia in the mix, the ante was raised. His father trained him to be a soldier, but his wolf gave him an advantage. Devin needed all hands on deck, and Jack wouldn't let his team down. They were more important to him than his pack ever was.

His pack. He couldn't afford to have them figure out he was having trouble. He never liked to get involved in pack politics, had abandoned the path his father mapped out for him, but Jack did know one thing: his pack would not simply pat him on the back and offer condolences if he couldn't shift again. At the very least they would exile him. At the worst? He didn't want to think about it.

Another reason he couldn't tell his brother. He wouldn't drag Connor into this. Jack was on his own for the first time in his life. He had to figure out something before the truth came out. And even though he couldn't hear his wolf or Connor in his head anymore, his own inner voice wouldn't shut up, asking the one question he didn't want to face.

If his wolf truly had abandoned him, would he ever be whole again?

Jack leaned against the fireplace in the team house. He'd locked his damn fears away two hours ago, while he was on that cliff overlooking the water, then dressed and made it in time for the meeting.

Now he looked around the room at his teammates. It was hard to believe the five of them got along so well, and worked together for the Tribunal, protecting supernaturals without exposing themselves to humans. Connor once joked, *What do you get when you add two werewolves, a nymph, an elf, and a witch together? A hell of a good team.* And he was right.

Their paths had been woven together as the Fates dictated. Connor and Jack grew up in the woods surrounding the Elven Kingdom. They met Devin and became thick as thieves, romping through the forest. Devin recruited both Jack and Connor for the team, as well as Charlie, sea nymph and former SEAL, who dragged along Gizmo, witch and techno-guru, for the ride. And a crazy ride it had been so far.

Now Devin paced in front of them, looking more anxious than Jack had seen him in months, which meant Jack couldn't—and wouldn't—let his own problems take center stage right now.

Charlie spoke first. "What's going on, Dev?"

Devin stopped. "Why aren't you two at Julia's checking her house?"

Jack replied. "She needed some time on her own. We're picking her up tomorrow to go through her daily routine at work, and then we'll check her house in the evening."

Devin frowned. "Apparently your brother didn't have the same impression."

What the hell does that mean? Jack looked over at Connor's way-too-innocent expression.

"So why did you call us here?" Connor asked, more than likely trying to change the subject.

"Now that we know someone attempted to free Tobin, I think we can expect more attacks from the supernatural supremacists."

"Damn," Connor said.

Devin continued. "We're going to increase the security at the wedding planner business, Julia's office, and our homes, but we should be prepared to go into full protective detail if necessary."

Jack straightened. "You think it will come to that?"

"I hope not. But we don't know who they'll retaliate against. Which means I'm not going to let my wife out of my sight. Tonight I'll tell her we're moving into the team house for the time being. The apartment can't be secured, and is surrounded by humans. We don't need anything to happen that can't be explained away."

Connor snorted. "Alex is going to *love* that."

Devin smiled. "I'll convince Alex she needs to be more cautious. It's for her own good. To a lesser extent, I'm worried about Peggy, since she's my sister, and they might want to punish me by hurting her, too. And after Julia's speech in court, they're most likely to go after her."

Charlie shook his head. "I don't see any of these women willingly accepting us as guards."

"I won't lose another family member," Devin stated as he started to pace the room again.

Jack didn't envy Devin. First these supremacist bastards killed his brother, Thomas, and kidnapped his wife. Now his entire family was at risk. And Julia— hell, could that woman take much more? Losing Thomas almost destroyed her. What if they went after her this time? Just the thought of it tightened his chest.

"What do we tell them?" Jack asked.

Devin frowned. "Nothing yet. Hopefully we won't have to resort to actual bodyguard duty. Right now I want us to outline our contingency plans so we at least get those in place. If we have to, we'll let the ladies know they're under our protection until further notice."

"Agreed." There would be no argument.

Oh, hell, who was Jack kidding?

The women would fight them with everything they had, but it wouldn't stop the team from protecting Alex, Peggy, and Julia with their lives.

Nothing is easy in law or love.

CHAPTER 6

Jack did not like the look on Connor's face *at all*. It was much worse than his normal cocky smirk. It was that damn cat-that-swallowed-the-canary grin, and it made Jack nervous.

"What's that shit-ass grin about?" he asked from the passenger seat.

"A guy can't smile without there being a reason?"

"Not when you're involved."

Connor gave him an even bigger smile. "Brother, I'm not planning to spend my life scowling like you. Why don't you try turning your mouth up at the corners before it forgets how?"

Jack gritted his teeth. He felt the familiar brush of Connor attempting to reach into his thoughts, but his twin was once again unable to connect with him. Jack wanted to welcome him in so damn badly, but it was as though he didn't remember how. They'd always been able to be there for each other through their connection. It wasn't until they were older that they realized not everyone had their ability to connect so directly, even in the supernatural world.

From Connor's scowl, Jack figured Connor believed he was blocking him on purpose. But ever since Jack was shot months ago, he'd been unwillingly pulling away from Connor bit by bit. And in the past several weeks, his brain had shut Connor out completely, much to Jack's frustration.

And now this case was forcing them to spend every waking moment together.

And then there was Julia. He wanted nothing more than to give her peace. He wasn't conceited enough to think he could make her happy, but if he could help stop the supremacists who were still out there, then maybe she could start over again.

As if in answer to his thoughts, Julia emerged from her house wearing a killer pants suit that fit her perfectly. Her hair today had a slight wave that curled right under her chin. Damn, she was a beautiful woman.

Jack didn't need to be in Connor's head to know what the new look on his face meant. He was looking at Julia with much more than friendship.

Anger crept into Jack's thoughts, and Connor's eyes widened at his brother. Huh. Maybe Jack's emotions weren't totally blocked from his twin after all. Jack climbed out of the car to greet her at the same time as Connor.

Connor leaned against the roof. She narrowed her eyes at him without acknowledging Jack. What had Connor done now? He hadn't uttered a word, and already she was irritated with his brother. He should be thankful those eyes weren't narrowed at him. He really should be...

"What's up, buttercup?" Connor asked.

Julia sighed before smiling. "I can't even pretend to be mad at you, even though you're a buttinsky."

"A buttinsky? Is that a legal term?" he asked,

although his smirk said he knew exactly what she was talking about.

"You called Alex and had her come to my house last night."

"Ah, yes, I did. Did you have fun?"

"Yes."

He nodded. "Well, then I'm sorry for causing you to have fun, Julia. I was way out of line."

"You are evil, Connor." She sighed. "We should probably get moving. I have a lot to get done at the office today."

Connor stepped toward the back.

"Where are you going?" Julia asked.

"When we run security, one of us sits in the back with you when we travel."

"Oh no. You drive, buttinsky. Jack can get in the back with me."

Julia climbed in the back seat, and Jack glared at his brother over the top of the car.

After a few seconds, Julia peeked her head out the window. "Are you coming, Jack?"

Connor shrugged. "You heard the lady, brother. I'll drive."

Jack climbed into the back of the car and took a deep breath, which he regretted instantly when Julia's scent hit him. It was spicy, with a hint of cinnamon. He was going to kick Connor's ass.

The plan had been for him to drive and Connor to be in the back. That way he could stay far away from the woman who tied his damn intestines in knots. Not that he told Connor why he wanted to stay away from Julia. Hell, he didn't understand it much himself.

In fact, he was surprised she wanted him to be in the back with her. She had been avoiding eye contact with him in general.

But Connor had to go and interfere. It was like the man ran hot and cold, with nothing in between. Connor either had women eating out of the palm of his hand, or he irritated the crap out of them. At least Julia hadn't fallen under his brother's spell. *Yet.*

But then why did Jack care one way or the other?

Because Julia was more than one of Connor's conquests. She was tough as nails on the outside, but he knew the same couldn't be said about what was on the inside. Ever since he kept watch over her at the cemetery, she was always in his thoughts. He couldn't forget her raw emotion. Emotion she concealed from everyone. She was embarrassed when she realized he had been a witness to it, but he would die before telling anyone what he saw.

"Earth to Jack."

He blinked and looked over at her.

"I've been talking to you, and you wandered off. Where did you go?"

He cleared his throat. "Nowhere."

Connor snorted in the front seat. Yep, he was going to kill his brother when he had the opportunity.

"Why did you guys need to pick me up today?"

"We need to see your route to work. You probably go the same way every day, right? From now on, try to mix the route up a bit, take some different roads on the way there and back. The idea is not to be predictable."

Julia nodded. "Got it. Has Devin said anything more to you about figuring out who doctored the handcuffs?"

"Not really," Jack answered. "Giz tried to trace the person magically, but the magical residue had dissipated."

"What do you mean?"

"It's kind of like DNA. If someone uses magic, it can oftentimes be traced back to the caster if they're tagged in our database. But there wasn't enough left to track. They made sure the magic didn't linger."

"Then what are the next steps?" Julia asked.

"First, we make sure you're safe at work and in your home. That should take a day or two. Then we'll move on to the investigation to bring the rest of the gang down."

"Which we all want, including you."

He frowned at her.

Julia continued. "They shot you and you almost died. You were impacted as well."

His stomach twisted. "I want the supremacists to pay for what they did to Thomas, and everyone else they harmed."

"Well, I want them to pay for what they did to you, too," Connor added from the driver's seat.

Jack had almost forgotten Connor was in the car.

"No one asked for the chauffeur's opinion," Julia replied.

Jack resisted the urge to laugh. Connor was right about one thing. She was a spitfire.

She tilted her head and looked at him. "Was that a smile I just saw on your face, Jack?"

"Not possible," Connor blurted. "Must have been a figment of your imagination."

"You heard what the lady said," Jack bit out. "Just drive."

"Yes, Miss Daisy. Anything you say, Miss Daisy."

Julia burst out laughing, and Jack gaped at her. He had never seen her laugh before. Her dark brown eyes sparkled, transforming the sorrow he normally saw in them. It was breathtaking.

The tightness in his chest returned. This woman was dangerous to his sanity. What little he had left. The only way he could cope these days was to remain in total lockdown, and Julia had the key...and no idea what could happen if she unlocked him and set the panic free.

"Oh, come on, Jack. That was funny. You have to admit it."

He wouldn't admit anything of the sort. It was petty and ridiculous, but he wanted to be the one to make Julia laugh. Not Connor. But this wasn't a competition for her affections. And he had never been the funny twin, even before his wolf deserted him to fend for himself.

He had a job to do—protect Julia—and that was what he was going to do. He couldn't get involved with her, emotionally or otherwise. He was too screwed up to even consider the idea. End of story.

There is a civil way to handle conflict resolution...

or not.

CHAPTER 7

Within minutes of arriving at Julia's office, Jack learned that, in addition to her tenacity — oh hell, who was he kidding? In addition to her *stubbornness*, Julia was also a workaholic.

Her paralegal Tina had her messages and her calendar printed off for the day. Julia asked Tina to come into her office and then shut the door without a backward glance.

While the two women were behind closed doors, Jack and his brother looked over the front office space, with Connor checking for bugs using one of Giz's toys while Jack used another one of Giz's gadgets to confirm there was nothing mystical in the room. Everything checked out fine for today.

After a few minutes, Tina came out of Julia's office, closed the door, and sat down at her desk.

Connor smiled at her. "So, Julia told you we're here to help?"

"Yes, but she also told me not to let either of you steamroll me."

Connor tried to look innocent. "Steamroll?"

"Well, she actually used the word charm for you and steamroll for Jack." She looked over at Jack. "I can't believe there are two of you."

"That's what our momma said too," Connor quipped.

Jack barely managed not to roll his eyes. Tina didn't want to know the truth about what their mother and father said when she had twins. It was *not* a happy moment.

"How many appointments does she have today?" Jack asked.

"Five."

"Are any of them new clients?"

Tina glanced at her computer screen. "Yes, her two o'clock is new."

"Was the appointment made in the past couple days?"

"No, he's been on her calendar for a week." She frowned. "Why would anyone want to hurt Julia?"

"That's what we're here to find out," Jack answered. They had advised Julia to tell Tina that she had been threatened, so her paralegal would be more careful over the next few weeks. It wasn't like they could tell Tina the truth about the supernatural supremacists, since their primary mission was to protect supernaturals from exposure to humans.

Tina nodded. "Julia told me to stand my ground with you two, but I'm worried about her." She hesitated for a moment. "I'll help you if I can. I want Julia to be safe."

"Then we're on the same page," Jack said.

Connor leaned over the desk and winked at her.

Tina blushed. "Julia's right. You two are trouble."

Trouble or not, Jack would do whatever it took to protect Julia.

They pulled chairs closer to Tina's desk and had her

walk them through Julia's daily activities so they could understand when she was in potential danger. The one thing Julia insisted on was they couldn't be in her office when she was consulting with clients.

Logically, Jack understood why, but it didn't stop him from arguing the point with her on the ride in. He lost. After all, she was a lawyer.

Later, Connor typed notes on his phone while he and Jack talked through her normal workday.

"Tina, can you pull together Julia's calendar for us for the rest of the week?" Connor asked. "We need to know if she has to appear in court, and anywhere else she may need to be outside this office."

"Yes. Her court schedule is light this week. I'll get you something in a few minutes."

Connor lowered his voice. "At least our wolves can tell if her clients are supernatural or not."

Jack's nerves popped. *Shit.* Would he be able to tell? This was the worst possible time for his wolf to abandon him.

Julia stretched. She'd already done three back-to-back meetings this morning, and needed to catch up with her emails and other work she didn't do yesterday. A light knock on the door interrupted her thoughts.

"Come in."

Jack opened the door. "Is it okay if you leave this open when you don't have client meetings?"

"Unless I'm making a phone call discussing a case, that should be fine."

"It's lunchtime soon. Connor went to get some food."

"Tina could have just ordered us something. We have food delivered all the time."

"She told us. But you shouldn't be predictable. If you don't bring food from home, someone should go to a restaurant and order the food and wait for it. That way they don't know it's coming here."

She tapped her pen on the desk. "I'm worried about Alex. She's the one who testified against the supremacists."

Jack stepped into the room. "Devin is watching over Alex."

"Even your testimony was more damaging than my speech was."

His eyes tightened. "Connor was the one who testified. I don't remember much from the shooting."

"I'm sorry about what happened to you."

He looked at her for a moment. "There's nothing for you to be sorry for. I'm fine."

His defensive posture—arms crossed—told her he was far from fine. But before she could comment, Connor's voice came from the front office. "Food's here."

Jack backed toward the door. "Come get some before it's cold."

He didn't strike Julia as someone who would back away from anything, yet he was retreating. Nope, he was far from fine.

Lunch was awkward in spite of Connor's attempts at humor. Jack glowered at his food instead of eating it. If memories of the shooting had put Jack in this snit, she was sorry for bringing it up, but she didn't think bringing it up yet again to apologize was going to help matters. After she choked down some of the food, it was a relief to escape back to her office to get more work done.

She hung up the phone an hour later. Her one o'clock conference call meeting had run eight minutes over. She hated keeping people waiting, and her two o'clock appointment today was a new client. She skirted her desk and opened the door.

Jack sat in the waiting room with no Connor...and no client.

She turned to her assistant. "Tina, did my appointment not show?"

Tina cleared her throat. "Yes, he was here, but he left."

"Left? Did you explain I was on a call?"

"Yes."

Tina straightened papers on her desk instead of looking her in the eye.

"Did he reschedule?"

"No. He's decided to find another attorney." Tina glanced meaningfully at Jack, who sat scowling with his arms crossed.

Julia turned to him. "Did something happen?"

"Nope."

She crossed her own arms to mirror his. "What did you say to him?"

"Nothing."

"Did you glare at him like you're glaring at me right now?"

He didn't say anything. Julia looked back to Tina, who nodded slightly.

"You scared away my client!"

"I'm here to protect you, Julia. If he was that jumpy just because I was staring at him, it makes me wonder what he's hiding."

The door opened and Connor strolled in, stopping mid-stride as he took in the room. "What's going on?"

"Your brother scared off my client!"

Connor's eyes twinkled. "I was gone for ten minutes. What the hell happened?"

"Nothing. The guy was squirrely as hell. I didn't

even say anything to him. If I had, he probably would have wet himself."

Julia stared at him. It was one thing for them to protect her. It was another for them to interfere with her business. "You will not bother my clients again, Jack. Either you agree to that, or you're out of here."

Jack got to his feet and uncrossed his arms. "If I think anyone is a threat to you, client or not, I *will* be bothering them. And I'm not going anywhere."

Shit, shit, shit. Jack looked down at the woman glaring up at him. What the hell was he thinking? She was going to do whatever she wanted to do, *especially* if someone told her not to.

Logically, he knew that. But it didn't stop his stupid mouth from spouting before his brain could put a stop to it.

"You have no say over what I do here. This is my business. My clients need my help."

"I know this is your business. But you need to be rational about it."

Stupid, stupid mouth.

Julia's pupils flared, almost swallowing her brown eyes. Jack braced himself for an earful, but instead Julia turned away from him and marched toward her office.

"I don't have time for this. I need to get back to work." She closed her door with a resounding thud.

Connor mumbled something about him being a dipshit before walking over to Tina's desk.

Jack sat back down and closed his eyes. He spent twenty minutes listening to Tina talk to Connor. They didn't try to engage him in the conversation, which was more than fine with him. He apparently needed to put his mouth in check.

Two hours later, Julia came out of her office with her briefcase. "I'll see you tomorrow, Tina." She ignored Jack and walked with Connor to the SUV, sitting in the front passenger seat. That wasn't security protocol, but at this point he wasn't about to say a damn word. When they pulled out of the parking lot, Julia turned to Connor.

"We have a stop to make before we head to my house."

"Where to?" Connor asked.

"The team house. Devin is expecting me."

Jack stopped himself from groaning. The shit was going to hit the fan, all right.

A short time later, Connor pulled into the driveway and parked. Before they could unbuckle their seatbelts, Julia spoke.

"If you don't mind, I'd like you two to wait here. I'm sure Devin can protect me while I'm in the house."

Connor chuckled as they watched her walk up the sidewalk. Devin waited at the door for her. He frowned slightly at the two of them in the SUV and then closed the door.

Connor turned to him. "Damn, Jack. I can't believe you actually used the words 'be rational' to a woman. And not just any woman! Julia Cole. What were you thinking?"

"I was doing my job. We are supposed to make sure she's safe. She isn't taking this seriously."

"Oh, she's taking it seriously, all right. She's feeding your ass to Devin right now. You should have known she wouldn't take this lying down. You can't antagonize her."

Jack snorted. "Really? And what about you planning a party with the girls without her knowledge?"

"That was for her own good."

Jack was also looking out for her good too. What was so bad about wanting to protect her? Wasn't that what he and Connor were assigned to do? Wolf or not, Jack was going to do his job, regardless of what a gorgeous, spitfire of a woman had to say about it.

An arbitrator can help resolve issues
of the legal and love variety.

CHAPTER 8

Time to set some ground rules.

Julia sat down at the dining room table across from Devin. She hadn't told Devin anything specific during her call to him earlier, which probably freaked him out even more. They were the only two people in the house that she could see. She was surprised he let his wife out of his sight.

"Where's Alex?"

"She's upstairs. I asked her to give us some time alone."

Julia opened her mouth, and Devin held up his hand. "Something's wrong. You called and asked to see me. Connor and Jack are sitting out in the SUV like you've put them in a time out. So spill."

"I agreed with you when you suggested I should have my house and office secured. But what I can't agree to is Jack scaring away my clients. They need me. And while I want to be safe, I'm not convinced the supremacists will target me. I'm more worried about Alex."

Devin sat back, settled his forearms on the table,

and clasped his hands. "I think you underestimate the power you have, Julia. Like it or not, you're a symbol of everything the supremacists are against. If they have their way, they'll destroy you to prove their point, especially after your speech in court the other day. I will not let anything happen to you. I gave my oath to Thomas."

Julia clasped her own hands under the table to stop them from shaking. "When did you do that?"

"The day you two married. Thomas made me promise to protect you if anything ever happened to him."

Julia shut her eyes. "Devin, Thomas is gone. Alex is your priority."

"I would die for Alex, and for you. I swore another oath over his funeral pyre that I would protect you. You are my sister now, and I will not let anyone hurt you ever again."

Julia willed the tears away. She would not cry. Devin had enough to worry about.

"Please, Jules, let them check your house and keep an eye on you for another day, so we can be sure you're being safe. I trust them both. They will do anything to protect you."

She blew out a harsh breath. "You have to tell Jack to back off then. He's being a Neanderthal right now, and it's impacting my job."

"It's probably his wolf. They can be pretty bossy at times." He placed his hands palms up and she grasped them.

"That's what I'm afraid of. Is there some sort of Xanax for werewolves? Because I think Jack needs one."

Devin cleared his throat to cover his laugh. "He's been strung a bit tight lately. Once we get through this, I'm going to order him to take some time off. In the meantime, I'll talk to him."

"Thank you."

"But understand this, Jules. If they think something is wrong, you have to listen to them. I know you're used to taking care of yourself, but for my own peace of mind, please listen to them."

"As long as they're truly looking out for my well-being, I'll listen."

"Spoken like a lawyer." Devin pulled her up with him. "Why don't you go visit with Alex while I talk to Jack and Connor?"

Julia nodded. She needed some time away from the twins. Alex would understand where she was coming from. It wouldn't hurt to get her up to speed so she could work on Devin if things got too bad with Jack. A good lawyer always had a contingency plan, and whether Jack believed it or not, she was a damn fine lawyer.

The front door opened and Devin appeared, beckoning for them to come into the house.

Connor opened the car door. "Time to face the music, bro."

Jack bit back an expletive and climbed out of the car.

They headed into the house and sat down at the dining room table with Devin. Jack peered into the living room, but it was empty.

"Julia is upstairs with Alex. Tell me what's going on," Devin said, jumping right into things.

Jack opened his mouth, but Devin shook his head, stopping him.

"Nope. I want to hear what happened from Connor first."

Connor shrugged. "I went to the bathroom, and

when I came back, Julia and Jack were toe-to-toe in the waiting room."

Devin's eyebrows went up as Connor continued. And as the story unfolded, Jack tried not to flinch. In hindsight, he could have dialed it back with jumpy client-guy, but the guy was acting so damn weird, and Jack couldn't rely on his wolf to tell him if he was supernatural or not. And maybe that was when he really started scowling at the guy.

He didn't like being out of control.

But Connor wasn't done, and when he got to the part where Jack told Julia to be rational, Devin placed his hand over his heart.

"Holy shit, Jack. You're lucky you still have your balls."

He gritted his teeth before responding. "I might have gotten a little carried away."

"Ya think?" Devin blurted. "No wonder she called me."

Jack stood up and paced beside the table. "She's worried about everyone else. And *I'm* worried that if a true threat happens, she's going to run headlong into it instead of away."

Devin sighed. "I agree. Which is why you're both protecting her and will continue to do so."

Connor smiled. "You convinced her not to give Jack the boot?"

"For another day. But Jack, you have chill out a bit. Julia is fiercely independent and doesn't like anyone telling her what to do. You guys have to give her space, or she's going to bolt, and that will make all our jobs harder."

"And if we run into trouble?" Jack asked.

Devin looked up the stairs before speaking and then lowered his voice. "Then all bets are off. You do whatever it takes to keep her safe. I'd rather deal with her wrath after the fact than have something happen to her."

Jack nodded. He would have taken matters into his own hands even if Devin hadn't given him permission. And he had no problem facing Julia's wrath, either. Not if it meant keeping her safe.

Julia knocked on the bedroom doorjamb while she watched Alex perched on the bed reading on her tablet.

"Come in."

Julia hovered in the doorway and looked around the room. Suitcases were lined up against the wall, and one was open. Belle was curled up inside it in a furry white ball taking a kitty nap while the ugliest cat she had ever seen lay on the floor next to the suitcase as if on guard duty. There was a chunk missing out of his ear, and his fur looked like someone had splattered gray paint across it. This had to be Giz's cat, Monster, although Julia had not met him before.

"Are you guys staying here at the team house?" Julia asked.

"Yeah. Devin thinks it will be safer for now, until we find out who helped Tobin. He can't be with me twenty-four hours a day, so he wants me to be here with the rest of the guys."

Alex set down the tablet and patted the bed next to her. "Come sit down and tell me what's going on. Devin shooed me out of the downstairs so you two could have a talk. Now I need details, my friend. What did the twins do?"

Julia plopped down next to her. "All kidding aside, I think you would have been a great lawyer, or maybe a detective."

"Tell Devin that. He never wants me to help with any of his cases. Now stop trying to distract me and tell me what happened."

Julia summarized her earlier discussion with Devin.

"So Jack's being a bossy jerk?"

"Yes."

"I'm surprised. I thought for sure you were going to tell me Connor did something to set you off. Jack is normally so even-keeled."

"You were right. Something's troubling him, and it makes him angry. I can relate."

Alex stared at her without speaking, and Julia wished she hadn't said anything.

Finally, Alex spoke. "I'm going to suggest something, and I don't want you to get upset."

Starting off a conversation like that usually was doomed to failure.

"Go ahead."

Alex hesitated for a moment before speaking. "Maybe it would help if you see Dr. Jennings."

"Your psychologist?" Julia's voice rose.

Alex held up her hands. "Before you nix the idea, will you at least listen?"

Julia nodded, even though her flight mechanism had kicked in.

"Dr. Jennings helped me with my anxiety. I haven't told you much about the way I used to be, Julia, but I couldn't participate in the wedding business. Heck, I couldn't even talk about a wedding without breaking out in a cold sweat. Dr. Jennings is a big reason why I'm functioning normally now." Alex smiled. "As normal as a human-faery hybrid can be, that is. She's also an expert in grief counseling."

Julia took a breath.

"I can't imagine what you've been going through, losing Thomas, and then finding out he was murdered.

Now we're still dealing with a threat of other supremacists out there. I think it would help you to talk to a neutral party."

"I'm fine."

Alex looked at her.

"Besides, she doesn't know about supernaturals, right? What if I slipped up and talked about something I shouldn't in front of her?"

Alex shook her head. "Nice try. You're a lawyer. I doubt you're going to divulge anything you shouldn't."

"Thanks, but I don't think it's necessary."

Alex squeezed her hands. "Okay, what about this? You can make one appointment, and if you don't think it's working, then you don't have to go back. I'll even call and let you have my appointment if it will take a while to get on her calendar."

Julia opened her mouth to protest, but stopped herself. "Let me think about it."

Alex's eyes widened and then her face lit up with a smile. She clearly had been expecting Julia to refuse, but Julia didn't want to argue with her tonight. It was easier to tell her she'd think about it. But the truth was, she didn't want to talk to Dr. Jennings or anyone else about her feelings. She had locked her feelings away again after her outburst at the cemetery, and wasn't about to let them out.

If only Jack hadn't been there to witness it.

Ask for counsel.
Doing everything alone is a recipe for disaster and loneliness.

CHAPTER 9

As Connor pulled into her driveway, Julia wanted nothing more than to take a long, hot bath while sipping a glass of wine. But before she could open the car door and say her good nights, Jack spoke.

"I know it's late, but I want to do a quick check of your house. We won't stay long. Tomorrow we'll bring Giz over to review your security alarm, if that's okay."

She nodded before her brain told her to argue. Jack was speaking to her in a reasonable voice, and asking her opinion. Maybe Devin actually got through to him, or hit him over the head with a baseball bat and he was concussed right now. Either way, she could deal with this semi-laid-back Jack. If he started acting up again, she would concuss him herself.

Jack held his hand out, and she looked at him in confusion.

"Keys?"

She rummaged in her purse before she located them and placed them in his palm.

Jack got out of the car, and she sat with Connor in awkward silence for a moment.

"Sorry Jack got a bit carried away today."

"You don't have to apologize for your brother."

"Maybe not, but I'm going to anyway. He's not normally this…"

"Snarky, bossy, cranky?"

"All of the above."

"Everyone's a little worried about him."

Connor frowned. "I'm worried about him."

"He won't tell you what's going on?"

"Nope. Been there, tried that, have the verbal scars to prove it."

Julia could speculate with the best of them on what could be the problem, but she reminded herself she was not going to get involved. She had a hard enough time suppressing her own emotions. She didn't have time to help Jack deal with his.

"I think I'll be okay with driving myself to the office tomorrow."

"I agree."

She blinked at his acquiescence. "You're not going to follow me around anymore?"

"Not tomorrow, at least. We've got to interview some people. We'll come check your house with Giz later in the day."

"For the supremacist case?" She sat up straighter. "Who are you interviewing?"

Connor hesitated.

"Don't think about holding back from me, Connor. I told Devin I want in on this. I'm going to be part of this investigation, because I need to find out how Tobin got out of those cuffs, and to help stop the other supremacists who are still out there."

He sighed. "We're going to talk to the guards who transported Tobin to the Tribunal chamber."

"I want to be there."

"Not a good idea."

She wasn't having any of that. "You're being shortsighted right now. I'm an asset to you."

Connor's eyebrows rose. "How do you figure that?"

"I know how to interrogate witnesses. I can spot a lie a mile away. A witness isn't much different from a suspect. Plus, I'm the voice of reason. Your charm and Jack's bossiness aren't going to convince those guards to tell you the truth."

"Don't you have to go to work?"

Julia shook her head. "Tomorrow morning's calendar is light. I'll call Tina and let her know I'm working offsite."

"You've got this all figured out, huh?" Connor asked before smirking.

"Absolutely," she responded.

"Absolutely not." Jack shook his head for emphasis.

Connor waited to drop this bomb until after they left Julia's house. Jack glared at his brother, although it didn't help, since Connor was driving instead of looking Jack's way.

"Sorry, bro, but you've been outvoted. She's coming with us for the interview."

"Why would we put her in that type of danger?"

"I think you're underestimating Julia Cole, Jack. She is not going to let this go. She was kept in the dark on the first investigation, and now she's determined to be involved."

"Fine. But that doesn't mean that she should come with us into the field!"

"We're going to take a page from Devin's book."

"What the hell does that even mean?" Jack growled.

"It means, Devin learned not to let Alex investigate

on her own. If he kept her close, he knew what she was up to."

Jack hadn't thought about that. His brother actually might be on to something.

Connor looked over at Jack and grinned. "I can tell I'm right from your expression."

"You can't tell that by my expression."

"Oh, but I can. You look like you've been sucking on lemons. And that always means you don't want to admit I'm right."

Jack scowled at him. "You don't know me that well."

Connor's smiled dimmed. "That may be true now."

Shit. Jack closed his eyes.

They drove in silence for a few minutes until Connor broke it. His brother didn't do well with silence.

"It's been a crazy couple of days. Let's go for a run in the woods. Chase some rabbits."

Jack flinched at the words. "This isn't the time for jokes, Connor."

"I'm not joking. When was the last time you let your wolf out? You're so damn uptight, it would probably help."

"I didn't ask for your advice."

Connor didn't respond. Instead he sped up and made it to the house in record time. He pulled into the driveway and slammed his way into the house. Connor was definitely the calmer of the two of them, but when he got pissed, everyone stayed clear of him. Normally Jack was the one to calm him down, not set him off.

By the time Jack made it into the house, Connor was already halfway up the stairs.

"Wait, Connor. I'm sorry."

Connor turned and looked down at him. "Just tell me what I've done."

"You haven't done anything."

"Right. Well then, you're just being an ass because you feel like it? 'Cause that's worse than if I had done something to deserve it."

"It's not you—"

"If you finish that sentence with 'it's me,' I'm going to puke. You're not breaking up with me. I'm your brother."

"I know."

"That's it?"

"I don't know what else to say, Connor. I have some crap I have to work through. Give me some space, please."

Connor closed his eyes for a second before nodding. "Fine. I'm here when you want to talk." He didn't wait for Jack to answer before heading up the stairs.

Jack swore under his breath and walked into the living room.

Gizmo sat on the couch with wide eyes. "Didn't mean to eavesdrop, but it was kind of hard not to."

"No worries."

Jack dropped down in a chair. Living in a house with the team seemed like a good idea when they first moved to San Diego to work for the Tribunal, but maybe it was time to find his own place. Devin and Charlie had moved out when they got married.

Since Jack sure as hell wasn't walking down the aisle anytime soon, a small studio apartment would work for him. All he needed was a bed to sleep in. Although he hadn't been doing much sleeping lately.

"It's none of my business what's bothering you, Jack. But if you ever want to talk, just let me know. I'm not going to take sides, unless whatever is going on between you and Connor starts affecting our jobs. Then I will speak up, loudly."

Giz was as laid-back as anyone he'd ever met. For

him to say what he did meant Jack needed to get his shit together soon. He shouldn't have bitten Connor's head off earlier. Hell, Connor asking him to let out his wolf was an innocent enough suggestion, and one they'd enjoyed doing together a thousand times before.

Jack would give anything to run with Connor. But Jack's wolf was AWOL, and he had to figure out how to fix things before anyone found out, especially his twin.

If there was one thing Jack knew about Connor, it was he would do anything to protect Jack, as Jack would for him. Which meant the less Connor knew, the better. Because if the pack found out he had lost control of his wolf, then the shit would definitely hit the fan.

Jack would not take Connor down with him.

Interrogation works in the courtroom,
not the bedroom.

CHAPTER 10

Julia held her breath while Connor slowed the SUV, pulled up to a tall gate, and spoke into a communication device. Apparently the Tribunal was serious about security at their holding facility. A camera swung toward the car to look at Connor before moving slightly to pan across the back seat. As Connor drove through the gate, Julia shifted in her seat as the air seemed to thicken with static that played along her skin.

"The feeling will pass in a moment," Jack said, his first words of the morning. "It's a magical barrier."

Connor came to a stop in front of a large building that looked like an ancient fortress.

Julia gaped up at it. "That looks medieval."

"It's been here for a thousand years," Connor said. "Of course they've made upgrades since it was first built."

Julia glanced over to see if he was joking. "A thousand years? Nothing was here a thousand years ago."

"There might not have been much human population other than some indigenous tribes, but supernaturals have been here for millennia."

Julia swallowed hard. Even after marrying Thomas and learning about his elven heritage, she still didn't know the full history of the supernatural population.

A large guard met them at the front entrance. He nodded to the twins before looking at Julia.

"We weren't expecting three of you today."

Connor shrugged. "Change of plans. Can you tell us where Warden Schuler is?"

"I'm here to escort you."

He ran his hand over a monitor at the front door, and the door clicked open. They entered a closed vestibule, and the guard motioned for them to stop.

A buzzing filled the air, and glowing blue lights descended from the ceiling. Or, more accurately, flew down from the ceiling toward them. The lights were alive! They looked like lightning bugs on steroids, and flew around them at a dizzying pace.

"Close your eyes," Jack said.

Julia did as instructed, and the dizziness subsided. After another minute, the buzzing stopped, and Julia opened her eyes.

"What was that?" Julia asked.

"Silviam," the guard responded. "They check for supernatural weapons."

The inner vestibule door opened, and the guard led them through the door.

"Please stop at the desk. The guard there will need to check your briefcase while you walk through the metal detector."

Julia looked around. What an amazing mix of magical and technological safeguards. After her briefcase was checked, they followed the guard down a hall to a double door with various symbols engraved in its frame.

The guard held open the door, and Julia stepped inside first. She hadn't known what to expect, but the room looked like a normal office, including a desk, an old-fashioned wooden filing cabinet, and chairs. What she didn't expect was Warden Schuler, who stood and walked around the desk.

The warden was a she. A very beautiful she, with flowing black hair, and robes that reminded Julia of a Greek goddess. Sexist of Julia to be surprised, but she was used to physical strength being so important in the human world's penal system. It obviously wasn't the case with supernatural prisons.

Warden Schuler shook her head. "This technically isn't a prison. It's a holding facility for supernaturals awaiting trial or transport to penal facilities."

Julia jerked. "How did you..."

The warden smiled. "I apologize. It's rude for me to mind-dip, but you are projecting quite loudly, my dear."

"Sorry," Julia muttered. But should she really be sorry for thinking too loud?

The warden paused as if she was listening to her thoughts again before nodding to the twins. "It's good to see you both again, even under these circumstances. Attorney Godfrey informed me you were going to be visiting us today to interview the guards."

"Yes," Connor replied. "We want to interview the guards who were assigned to watch Tobin."

"Of course. And who have you brought with you today?"

"You didn't read my mind to figure it out?" Julia blurted.

The warden shook her head. "I just caught your thoughts earlier, I don't delve into a person's mind on purpose unless I am given permission. I'm Warden Schuler, but I'll not stand on formalities with you. Please call me Alina."

"I'm Julia Cole."

Alina's eyes tightened on Julia. "Thomas's wife." She didn't wait for a response, or maybe she simply heard Julia's thoughts and continued on. "I worked with him on several occasions in his capacity as Elven Counsel. He was an amazing defense attorney. He is sorely missed."

Julia swallowed. "Thank you."

"I also heard about your speech at the trial. Our people are still talking about it. You created quite a stir."

"Until Tobin decided to blow things up."

Alina frowned. "And he shouldn't have been able to do that."

"We agree, which is why we're trying to figure out who helped Tobin with the cuffs," Jack said.

"What is the normal process for prisoners here?" Julia asked.

"Prisoners in general cell areas are overseen by rotating guards. Higher-profile prisoners like Tobin are kept in individual cells. Three guards were assigned to him while he was awaiting trial. Solan and Cartman escorted Tobin to his sentencing hearing, and were there when he attacked."

Connor nodded. "Charlie interviewed them once they had secured Tobin."

"And you wish to interview them again?"

"We want to talk to everyone who had access to Tobin."

"Just the guards, as I said before."

Julia leaned forward. "Can you think of anything that happened out of the norm?"

"More out of norm than day-to-day in a supernatural holding center?" Alina asked. "No, I am not aware of anything out of the ordinary. We have actually been hyper-vigilant since Tobin was placed here."

"What about food?" Julia asked. "Who prepared his food? Was there anything they could have hidden on his tray to help him escape the cuffs?"

Alina shook her head. "No, the food is examined before it is taken into the cell."

"Clothing? Bedding? Custodians? Was anyone allowed in his cell?"

"No. All clothing and bedding is scanned. However, if you would like to talk to anyone on my staff, I can make them available."

"I think it's a good idea," Julia said as she pulled her notepad out of her briefcase and ripped out a sheet. "I have a list of people we would like to interview."

The warden reviewed the list and looked up with wide eyes. "You have been very thorough. I'll take you to one of the rooms we reserve for lawyer/client discussions. I'll have the guards meet with you first, and then I'll send the other staff members you have listed here to see you as well."

Julia tucked her notepad away and looked up to meet the warden's amused gaze.

"I'm surprised you don't have me on your list of suspects."

Julia shrugged. "We're talking to you now, aren't we?"

Alina's eyes widened for a moment, and Julia worried she had gone too far until the warden tilted her head back and laughed. "I like you, Julia Cole. If anyone can get to the bottom of this, you can." The warden acknowledged the twins with a brief nod. "No offense, gentlemen."

"None taken," Connor said with a grin.

Julia took a peek at Jack, who wasn't enjoying the conversation half as much as his twin. A few minutes later they were settled in a meeting room waiting for their first suspect to interrogate, and Jack was still scowling.

"What's wrong, Jack?"

"I think you need to be a bit more careful who you antagonize, Julia. You don't want to make the warden mad. She could make this process difficult for all of us."

"She didn't appear irritated to me. Did she seem irritated to you, Connor?"

"Nope."

Before Jack could respond, there was a knock, and Connor escorted in a guard to interview. And so began the first of many question and answer sessions that got them nowhere closer to the truth. After the last interview, the warden came to see them.

"Well?" Alina asked.

Julia tapped her gold pen against her pad of scribbled interview notes. "We're missing something. I don't see how anyone could have tampered with the cuffs once they were here."

"Exactly what I said before," Alina agreed.

"Right. So if someone was unable to tamper with the cuffs after the fact, then maybe something was wrong with them to start with. Who places the spell on the cuffs?"

Alina laced her fingers together. "It's more complicated than that. The magic is imbued in the cuffs while they are being forged. McHenry is one of the best magical metallurgists we have. He wouldn't make a mistake like that."

"Unless he did it on purpose?" Julia countered.

The warden pursed her lips. "I hope you're wrong about that."

"We should talk to him next," Connor said.

"He doesn't work here."

"How are the cuffs transported?" Jack asked.

"McHenry places the cuffs in a magically sealed box that cannot be opened until it arrives in my office. But he doesn't bring them himself. His forge is in the Demon Burrows in the Elven Forest, and he doesn't leave there."

"Why not?" Julia asked.

"He is what you would call a throwback to simpler times."

Julia leaned forward. "Enough of a throwback that he doesn't like humans?"

"I...I don't know the answer to that. If we can't trust McHenry right now, then I don't know how we can trust any of the security measures we would use to transport Tobin from the center."

Julia's chest tightened. "Wait. Tobin is still *here*?"

"Yes. We didn't think it made sense to move him until we could guarantee he can be secured during his transport. For now, we have him in his own wing under solitary confinement. The Tribunal stripped him of his powers yesterday, and now he should be ready to go once we get the security measures under control."

"Then we need to get this resolved ASAP so he can be moved to his new forever cell. I think we need to pay McHenry a visit."

"No!" Alina and the twins all said at once.

Julia set down her pen on the desk. "What am I missing here?"

"We can't enter that part of the forest without permission, and we won't get it easily," Connor said.

"Even if Devin tells them it's about Tobin?"

"Yes. Parts of the forest are not completely under elf control. To enter them without permission could cause problems between the elves and the demons."

Julia wasn't going to give in that easily. "Then how do we get permission?"

Jack ran his fingers through his hair. "We petition the Elven Council, who will then speak to the Demon King."

Julia gulped. "The council run by my former father-in-law."

"Yes."

The same father-in-law who might not have said it out loud, but the haunted look in his eyes as he stood over Thomas's funeral pyre told her he blamed her for his son's death.

And she couldn't really defend herself, since she agreed with him. If it hadn't been for her, Thomas would be alive right now.

Even lawyers need a break from the law.
But can the same be said of love?

CHAPTER 11

How was it possible that Julia kept impressing him again and again? She had been a dynamo during the interviews, asking the right questions at the perfect moment. Then, after each person left the room, she would succinctly review her notes and address any concerns she had about the interviewee. Her thoughts about the cuffs being tampered with beforehand was right on the damn money too.

Now Jack watched Julia with concern. She was sitting next to him in the back seat, silent. And Julia was never silent. Even if she wasn't speaking, she was thinking loudly. But since they left the holding center, she had folded in on herself.

"Are you okay?"

She blinked and turned to look at him. "I'm just going through today in my mind."

It was more than that, but Jack wasn't going to argue with her.

"Do you think Devin can get a petition in front of his father?" Julia asked.

"Yes, but there are protocols to follow, and they'll take time."

She frowned. "Bureaucracy. It isn't much different than human law."

"Do you want us to drop you at work?" Connor chimed in from the driver's seat.

"No. I told Tina I would probably work from home this afternoon."

Connor turned the corner and pulled onto the highway. "That works for us. We can check the security at your house while you work."

Julia's eyes widened. "Shouldn't that be in the form of a question rather than a statement?"

Connor shook his head. "Nope. You agreed we could check your house today. I'm not giving you the option to back out."

"Fine," Julia said before pulling out her pad of paper and flipping through her notes.

Jack wanted to reach over and yank the paper out of her hands. She was going to burn herself out. In the past two days she hadn't taken a break. If Connor hadn't convinced the ladies to visit Julia, she would have worked that night as well.

Which was no way to live. But then Jack had no room to talk. And he didn't have the right to give her advice.

Twenty minutes later they arrived at Julia's house, and she headed straight for the office next to her bedroom. Two hours later, she still hadn't emerged from the room. Jack stopped in front of her office door and watched her hunched over her computer, typing away. He knocked on the doorjamb.

Julia looked up from her computer screen, and blinked. "How's it going?"

"Okay. We've checked your house and made sure everything is physically and magically secure."

"Where's Connor?"

"He went to grab some takeout. Your pantry is bare, and Connor took one look in your refrigerator and mumbled something about what he imagined the apocalypse would look like before heading out the door."

Julia's eyes widened. "Did you just make a joke, Jack?"

Jack could feel the corners of his mouth start to turn up before he controlled himself. "Those were Connor's words, not mine."

"He didn't need to get food for me."

"He didn't just do it for you. Giz is working on your alarm system. If we don't feed him, things will get ugly."

"Giz is here?"

Jack entered the room. She hadn't even heard Giz? It wasn't like they were being quiet. She was so immersed in whatever she was working on, she blocked out everything else.

"Why don't you call it quits for the night? It's after six, and Connor should be back in a few minutes with the food."

She glanced down at her paperwork. And from the small frown on her face, Jack could tell she wasn't going to stop.

"Do you ever slow down?" he blurted.

"What do you mean?"

"You've been going nonstop for the last three days. When do you take a break and relax?"

She opened her mouth and then closed it again.

"Exactly. It's time to call it a night, counselor."

Julia's eyes tightened on him and he waited for her argument.

"Fine. If you want me to relax, then you have to do something for me."

He should have known she'd want to work some sort of deal. "What?"

"You have to sit down and have a conversation with me."

He opened his mouth, and she rushed on before he could speak.

"Not a conversation about the case, or security. An actual, honest-to-goodness discussion between two adults."

He didn't like the idea one bit, but he couldn't expect her to be more flexible if he wouldn't be. "Okay," he said, sitting down slowly across from her desk.

Julia smiled. "I'm not going to cross-examine you. It's just a talk. I'll start with something easy."

He leaned back in the chair.

"Tell me your deepest desire."

Holy shit. He jerked upright like he'd been shocked with a cattle prod.

Julia burst out laughing. "Oh, the look on your face just now."

"Very funny."

"I'm sorry. You bring out the worst in me. I'll be good, I promise. Let's start over. Tell me how you came to work for the Tribunal."

Jack calmed his breathing down. This was safe territory. "Connor and I grew up with Devin. When Devin started to put his team together, he asked us to join him."

"Because of your security training?"

Jack's eyebrows rose in surprise.

"Peggy told me the pack's business is security, and you used to provide security for the Elven Kingdom. Is that where you learned how to do all this?"

"Yes, although we've learned a lot since then from the team."

"Are you happy the team settled in California? You're close to your pack again."

Jack managed not to cringe. Even before the problem with his wolf, Jack avoided his pack. Now? He didn't want to go anywhere near them. But that wasn't exactly something he wanted to get into with Julia. "It's nice to be back near the forest."

She looked at him for a moment without speaking. Was that her lawyer look she was using on him right now? Time to deflect.

"What about you? Are you originally from California?"

"No. I'm an East Coaster." Julia picked up her pen and rolled it between her fingers.

Jack nodded. "Not surprised about that one, Ms. Workaholic."

She rolled her eyes. "Thanks. I grew up in Philadelphia and came to California for law school, which then turned into a job with a large law firm."

"And now you're on your own?"

"I learned a lot at the law firm. I worked seventy-hour weeks and helped with all the grunt work. And that helped me become a better lawyer. It also told me that I wanted to choose what cases I took on, instead of being stuck with what the firm assigned to me. Which meant I had to be my own boss."

"Doesn't look like your workload has slacked off."

She shook her head. "It ebbs and flows. You're like a broken record. If you're going to chastise me for working too hard, then I get to chastise you for being such a damn cranky-pants."

He chuckled at her choice of words and cocky grin.

"Dear God, it's a miracle. Jack just laughed. I'm going to write the date and time down in my calendar."

Jack reached over and shut her laptop lid. "Enough work for now."

"Hey!"

"It will be there later. Time to take a break."

"Food's here!" Connor called out.

"No fair! You knew your brother was back through your twin-speak, didn't you?"

Jack shrugged, even though his twin-speak, as she called it, had abandoned him. "You'll never know for sure."

She rounded the desk, then paused to look up at him. "You never did tell me your deepest desire."

"You won't get the truth from me anytime soon, counselor." And she never would. He couldn't tell her that, if he was honest, she was his deepest desire. It was a good thing he wasn't being honest with her or himself right now.

Honesty would not set him free.

Julia finally pushed Connor, Jack, and Giz out the door an hour later, after swearing to turn on her security alarm. Her stomach hurt from too much laughter and Thai food. Listening to the three men squabble had been a treat. She looked around her kitchen to see if anything needed cleaning, but the guys cleaned up after themselves. Julia turned out the lights and headed down the hall to her office.

Everything was still piled on her desk where she left it earlier. She plopped down in her chair, opened her laptop, and clicked on the keyboard to take it out of sleep mode.

The screen lit up with her partially typed notes. She reached for her notepad and stopped. Jack would scold her for working any more tonight. She saved the file and then powered off her computer. Stuffing her notes and laptop in her briefcase and then closing it with a resounding snap, she sat back in her chair.

Julia smiled at the idea of a free night. It was Friday night, after all. When was the last time she had taken a night off that hadn't been foisted on her?

What should she do?

She threw in a load of laundry and then dove into her closet and pulled out clothes she could donate, folding them and placing them in plastic bags. The bags went into her garage, and she grabbed her vacuum cleaner and cleaned the entire house.

By the time she was finished, Julia was sweaty and exhausted. She sat down on her couch and shook her head. What the hell was she doing?

She hated to admit Jack was right. She didn't know how to relax. Or rather, the truth was she was afraid to relax. If she didn't stay busy, then she had time to think, and that was too dangerous.

Jack would be giving her crap right now if he was there. She thought back to her earlier conversation with him. He had actually been fun to talk to once he got the stick out of his butt. And she...

Julia jerked upright on the couch. How had she not seen it? Sure, she had given him a hard time, but her comments had almost been like she was flirting with him. Her stomach rebelled, the Thai food threatening to come back up.

No! There would be no flirting. She was married... Julia's hand covered her mouth. She wasn't married anymore. Damn it. This was what happened when she let her mind wander.

And this sure as hell wouldn't do anymore.

Julia picked up her cell phone off the coffee table and typed a quick text to Alex.

Are you awake?

Seconds later, the phone rang. She should have known Alex wouldn't settle for a quick text conversation.

"Hello. What's up?"

"I've been thinking about our conversation yesterday. I'd like to schedule some time with Dr. Jennings."

"Good. I'll text you her office number. I'll also call her office on Monday and let them know I referred you." Alex hesitated for a moment before continuing. "Are you okay?"

"Yeah. I just think it's time to move forward."

"I think you're right. Hopefully Dr. Jennings can help."

Julia needed to do *something*. She didn't much like the person she'd become in the past two years. If she was going to be on her own for the rest of her life, she needed to learn how to like herself again. And if she couldn't be alone with her own thoughts for even one night, then she wasn't any good for herself or anyone else.

Do not treat your lover like opposing counsel.

CHAPTER 12

Julia's heart galloped in her chest as she typed the appointment with Dr. Jennings in her calendar and hit save. Her breathing sped up, which was ridiculous. She had faced down prosecutors, judges, and juries in the courtroom. Making a simple phone call shouldn't cause anxiety. But then in the courtroom she wasn't talking about herself and her feelings.

Yes, she made the speech at Tobin's sentencing, and it had flayed her insides even if she hadn't let anyone see it. But she would do anything for Thomas, even if he wasn't here anymore.

Her fear was that her meetings with Dr. Jennings would be much worse. She shook her head to dislodge the negative thoughts.

It turned out that the office had a cancellation tomorrow afternoon and was able to fit her in...or maybe Alex had persuaded Dr. Jennings to see her so quickly. Either way, it was a blessing. If Julia waited too long for the appointment, she might change her mind.

She reviewed the rest of her calendar. The twins weren't hovering over her anymore, but they had asked Tina for her schedule, so they knew where she was at any point in time. And now that she looked at it and remembered what Jack said, she realized how pathetic her schedule really was. She was either at the office, the courthouse, or the wedding planner business. Or at home working. Which meant work, work, and—oh, yeah—more work.

Which also meant Julia was a very dull girl.

And that made her mad. But then everything made her mad. Mad was her perpetual state of being. She didn't have the right to call Jack out on his crankiness. It truly was the pot calling the kettle and all that.

Julia called Alex, who answered after the second ring.

"Hi, Julia."

"Hey, am I interrupting anything?"

"Nope. I finished up at work and am headed back to the team house. Are you at work?"

"I'm thinking about heading home."

"Why? Are you sick?"

"No. I'm trying not to be a workaholic."

"Wow. Well, if you're turning over a new leaf, why don't you help me with a wedding tomorrow morning?"

"Tomorrow is Tuesday. Who gets married on a Tuesday morning?"

"A witch and a warlock. Their coven leader reviewed the couple's charts to determine the best day and time for the wedding to take place."

"How is working a wedding not the same as working at my office?"

"Oh, come on. It'll be fun. It's about time you got a glimpse of this part of the business. All you do is write those stuffy paranormal prenups. This way you can be there for the celebration."

"Let me think about it."

"One of these days I'm going to convince you."

"Maybe."

Alex sighed. "That's better than no. If you're leaving early from work—and I'll believe it when I see it—come over to the team house. The guys are starting a meeting, so we can spend time together."

Julia's alarm bells went off. "Are they discussing the supremacist case?"

"Yes."

"I'll be over in a little bit. I want to hear what they've found out so far."

Julia shut off her computer and packed up her briefcase.

Tina glanced up in surprise when she walked into the waiting room. "Do you have a meeting I didn't note on your calendar?"

"No. I'm leaving for the day."

Tina frowned. "Are you not feeling well?"

Wow, she really was pathetic if everyone jumped to the conclusion she was sick. "I'm fine. I just decided to leave early. Why don't you take the rest of the day off too?"

Tina looked at her like she just said aliens had landed.

"I'm fine. Have a good night," Julia called as she headed out the door. It was time to shake things up a bit.

Frustration had become Jack's constant companion. Why was there no break in the case? Because they didn't have much of a case to begin with. A pair of handcuffs that had been tampered with, and no one to trace it back to, unless you counted a recluse supernatural who was impossible to get close to.

He sat down at the dining room table and rubbed

his hand over his eyes while Connor, Giz, and Charlie talked.

"How's it going, Jack?"

He removed his hand from his face and stared across the table at Charlie. His teammate was studying him a bit too closely. Charlie was up to something.

"I'm fine. Why do you ask?"

"I'm supposed to work the witch wedding tomorrow morning. There are a couple of high-ranking supernaturals in attendance, so they wanted some security at the ceremony. Can I convince you to switch with me and work it?"

Jack shook his head. "Sorry, man, I've got something else going on."

Again with the staring. It's a good thing Charlie wasn't psychic, or he would have gotten a mind-full right then.

Devin walked in and sat at the end of the table, stopping any further discussion.

"Let's talk through what we know about the case."

Connor snorted. "We don't know much. We've spoken to the guards and the staff at the detention center, and Julia didn't miss a trick. Still, no dice. We have no leads except McHenry."

Giz leaned forward in his chair. "I think the cuffs were tampered with, but there isn't enough of a magical signature left to determine if it was done during the creation of the metal or afterward."

"So it comes back to McHenry," a female voice announced.

Jack turned toward the door to see Julia.

Devin looked at his watch. "It's early, Julia. Is something wrong?"

Julia sighed. "No, nothing is wrong, and I'm not sick. If one more person asks me that…" She let her rant trail off. "I left work early, okay?"

She glared at Jack, as if to dare him to say anything. He bit his lip to stop a grin.

"Sure," Devin said softly, as if he was trying not to set her off again.

Alex came into the room from the kitchen with a pitcher of iced tea and a stack of glasses. "Julia and I decided to attend the meeting. More minds, and all that." She set the pitcher and glasses on the table and sat down next to Charlie, who winked at her.

Julia stared at the empty seat next to Jack, and he pulled it out for her. Her eyes widened slightly before she took her seat.

"Okay, what did I miss?" Alex asked.

"Not much," Julia answered in her blunt but truthful way before looking to the side and frowning.

"What did you just come up with, Julia?" Jack asked.

"How did you know I came up with something?"

"Your facial expression. You do that when you're thinking through something."

"I didn't know I was so transparent."

He shrugged.

"Have you come up with something?" Alex pushed.

"Sometimes, when I get stuck on my court cases, I back up to the beginning and try to look at it in a different way. I was just thinking that we need to ask ourselves *why* the cuffs were tampered with."

"To set Tobin free?" Connor said.

Julia shook her head. "Yes, but he didn't get away. If they truly wanted to set him free at that time, wouldn't they have had others in the courtroom to help him?"

"And why try to break him out in a room full of people to begin with?" Jack asked.

Julia nodded. "Exactly. So, what was the purpose, if not to break him out?"

"To send a message," Devin answered. "Tobin blustered on about us not being able to stop them. If they're able to help him when he's in the holding center, then they demonstrate how powerful the supremacists still are."

"Fear and intimidation," Charlie said, "like terrorists."

"Which means they'll strike again," Jack said.

"But why haven't they done anything yet?" Alex asked.

Devin frowned. "Maybe they're simply trying to throw us off. Anticipation of something else happening is often worse than the actual event."

Julia tapped her index finger on the table. "Which makes it all the more important to talk to McHenry."

"I can't speed up the bureaucracy," Devin responded.

Alex sat up straighter. "But we do have an in."

Devin shook his head. "No, Alex."

"What do you mean?" Julia asked.

"Stuart Sutter is on the Demon Council. He reports to the Demon King, and he's going to be in attendance at tomorrow's wedding. I told Devin he should approach him to see if he can get permission to go see McHenry."

Julia clasped her hands together. "That sounds like a plan."

"I can't approach Sutter. Elves and demons have a precarious relationship. Any interruption of the established protocols, and I could jeopardize the treaty between the two races."

"But I don't have to adhere to those protocols."

"What are you up to, Jules?" Devin asked, fortunately before Jack blurted it out.

"Nothing. I'm scheduled to help Alex with the wedding tomorrow. I can approach Sutter."

Julia didn't help with the weddings. She was up to something, all right. If Jack hadn't been looking at Alex, he would have missed her surprised expression when Julia said she was helping. An expression that changed to satisfaction, like a cat stretching in the sun. The team had dealt in the past with Alex's mischievousness. Teaming up Alex and Julia was a disaster in the making.

Devin stood up. "You can't bulldoze him, Jules. You have to talk to him civilly. I can't even be there, or it will look suspicious."

Jack stood up as well. "We'll watch Julia and Alex. Connor and I were just talking to Charlie about working the wedding."

"We were?" Connor asked with a shit-eating grin on his face.

"Yep. We were just hammering out the details before Devin came in," Jack said, glaring at this brother and daring him to deny it. For once, his brother didn't fight him, which meant Jack would owe him. But it was a small price to pay for being able to watch over Julia.

There is no standard template for love.

CHAPTER 13

Dear Lord, really? The bride was decked out in bows, with miles of elaborate train whispering along behind her as she floated down the aisle.

Literally.

Julia watched at the back of the church and bit her lip to stop the huff of exasperation from escaping.

Alex leaned over and whispered, "I know that look."

"It's a bit over the top," Julia whispered back.

The music swelled, and Alex leaned closer. "She's a high-powered witch, and she's in love. Plus, we're just the wedding planners, and she's our client. We mustn't forget what my grandmother always says…"

Julia bumped her shoulder against Alex's, and they both recited, "'What the client wants, the client gets.'"

The music faded, and the bride dropped to the floor like a tulle-wrapped hovercraft. Julia and Alex moved into the back vestibule and watched through the door while the couple exchanged their wedding spells.

"Thanks for helping today," Alex said with a suspiciously innocent expression. "It was so nice of you to volunteer."

"Cut it out."

"What?" Alex shrugged. "I can appreciate when a girl is given an opportunity to get something done."

"Which one is Sutter?"

"He's sitting at the side of the church, two rows up from where the twins are standing."

The twins watched over the crowd to make sure nothing went wrong. They were both so intense when they were in bodyguard mode it could be intimidating, especially for a wedding.

Julia blinked, concentrating on the ceremony. The coven leader held her glowing hands over the bride's and groom's heads, chanting a blessing.

She motioned for them to face each other, then looked up at the audience and raised her voice to say, "If anyone objects to this union, speak now, or forever hold your peace."

"I object!" rang out a voice. Followed by a collective gasp from the audience.

Was this actually happening? Julia had only ever seen it in the movies. But real life had a tendency to be much more interesting than fiction.

The bride and groom spun to face the crowd as a woman leapt to her feet in the third row.

Alex cursed under her breath. Connor and Jack split up and headed around the room, Connor walking toward the woman and Jack toward the bride and groom.

The coven leader's eyes narrowed on the woman. "Why are you interrupting this ceremony, Marissa?"

"Because it's a sham!" she shouted. "I should be standing up there!"

The bride's face went pale.

"Go home, Marissa," the groom hissed.

Heartless, much?

Alex hustled into the room. "Let's remain calm, everyone. We can talk this through rationally."

Marissa glared at her. "You're the flippin' wedding planner. Stay out of this."

So much for a fun, uneventful wedding. Julia's lawyer mode clicked in as she hurried to the front of the room. "It's time to take this conversation elsewhere. Let's go into the side room to discuss it."

"And who are you?" the bride demanded.

"I'm a lawyer. I've arbitrated disputes in the past. How about I listen to both sides of this so we can reach an agreement?"

Marissa slashed her hand through the air. "There is no resolution to this unless it involves me in front of that altar."

Julia walked toward the bride and groom. "I don't think you want to continue this conversation in front of your family and friends, do you?"

"We don't mind," spouted a woman in the back of the church. "This is the most fun I've had in years."

Julia knew laughing at the sheer ridiculousness of the situation would not help. "Audience excitement aside, I still think it would be better if we took this to a different room."

"No!" Marissa shouted, her skin starting to glow as she glared at Julia.

Thoughts of déjà vu gripped her along with strong hands on her shoulders. Jack once again spun her around and sheltered her from danger. His heat wrapped around her, and she melted for just a moment into his embrace. It had been so long since she had been held. But he shouldn't be touching her.

"Coast is clear," Connor said.

"You just can't seem to stay out of trouble, can you?" Jack mumbled in her ear.

Julia jerked away from Jack, and his eyes narrowed

on her for a moment. She turned away from him to find Connor holding Marissa's arms.

"Don't hurt her!" the groom growled. "She wouldn't have hurt anyone, she's just upset."

Now he was worried about her? Julia couldn't keep up with this train wreck.

"You've ruined the wedding," the bride sobbed.

"It should have been our wedding," Marissa sobbed back.

Our, as in, the two women? Julia blinked. Yep, real life was *so* much more interesting than fiction.

"How do you think I feel?" the groom shouted. "I love you both."

Silence.

Deafening, shocking, silence.

Broken by a giggle in the middle of the room. "This is way better than my soaps."

"It's a menege," exclaimed a blue-haired matriarch in the front row on the groom's side.

"It's pronounced ménage," said the other blue-haired woman, who was on the bride's side.

"What's that?" asked another lady a row behind them.

"A relationship with three people."

"If you three truly love each other, then why is she not standing up on that altar with you?" Julia asked.

The bride glanced guiltily at her elderly matriarch in the front row.

Julia spoke to the bride's grandmother, who was decked out in a pink pillbox hat reminiscent of the old Jackie O photos. "Do you object to this?"

"How can I object to something I know nothing about?"

Julia gestured to the bride and groom. "I think you need to have a conversation with your families before anything can be resolved."

The bride and groom rushed over to their respective grandmothers.

"I'm so sorry, Nana," the bride cried.

The older woman patted the bride's face. "Sweetie, all I care about is that you're happy. If these two make you happy, then why cover it up?"

The bride rested her cheek against her grandmother's hand. "It isn't exactly normal."

Her grandmother laughed. "Honey, we're witches. Since when has normal been part of our gene pool?"

The bride's grandmother turned to face the groom's grandmother. "You got a problem with this, Gloria?"

"Nope. I'm thinking it means more grandbabies to love."

The groom-grandson's face turned crimson.

These grannies were enlightened ladies. Julia glanced over at Alex, who was biting her lip and struggling to keep a straight face. Apparently, Connor didn't fight hard enough, and he barked out a laugh.

Julia couldn't help smiling, but her smile dropped away when she caught sight of Jack staring at her. His eyes seemed to penetrate her skin, searching for something. But she didn't have anything to give him. Her emotions were on lockdown.

And the barrage of intense emotions bouncing around the room exhausted her. She backed up, and Alex wrapped her arm around her shoulder.

"Good job, counselor. Is it bad to want to drink this early?"

"Not after this wedding," Julia said. "By the way, I won't be volunteering to help oversee another wedding again any time soon."

Alex grinned. "Got it. Wait till the office hears about this one. Everyone is going to be jealous they missed it."

Julia glanced over at Jack, who had his arms crossed and a scowl back on his face. "I'm not sure Jack would share your opinion."

"He'll get over it. Now, are you going to help me salvage this wedding?"

Julia nodded, and Alex took charge again. Within minutes, the trio stood in front of the altar. Marissa was wearing the other bride's veil so she felt part of things. The brides exchanged vows with their groom and with each other.

The trio walked to the back vestibule, and a line of guests formed to offer their congratulations. Julia made her way over to the side of the church where Sutter waited his turn. She could feel someone staring at her from behind, and she didn't need to turn to know Jack watched her closely.

Julia smiled at Sutter. "That was a bit more excitement than I'm used to at a wedding."

He shrugged. "I once went to a wedding where the bride put a hex on her mother-in-law and the woman started to oink like a pig."

What the heck was she supposed to say to that? "Wow. That is fascinating."

"Exactly. What I also find fascinating is why a lawyer would be in the wedding planner business."

"To be honest, I normally don't work the ceremonies. I'm behind the scenes mostly, working on prenups and wedding contracts."

"What brought you here today?" he asked.

Julia decided to go with the truth. "You."

His eyebrows rose. "Me? And why is that?"

"I hoped to talk to you. You work for the Demon King, and a recent communication from the Elven Kingdom requesting access to the Demon Burrows should have arrived for review."

"I highly doubt the king will allow access."

Julia straightened her shoulders. "Even if it's to stop the supremacists?"

Sutter's eyes tightened on her face.

"You're the lawyer who spoke at the supremacist sentencing."

"Yes, Julia Cole."

"Your reputation precedes you. Even in the forest, news of your impassioned speech is still being talked about. The story grows with every telling."

"It probably didn't hurt that Tobin tried to blow things up afterward."

Sutter barked out a laugh. "Precisely. I think in the latest version I heard, you fought him off yourself with your bare hands."

Julia held up her hands. "No, I can't claim credit for stopping him."

"But you think granting access to the Demon Burrows could stop the supremacists still out there?"

"Not stop them necessarily, but we might be able to find out who helped Tobin. Or, if you can convince McHenry to come see us instead, the request won't be necessary."

"McHenry! Oh, my dear, you have no idea who you're up against. McHenry is one of the most powerful beings in the kingdom. And he will not leave the forest for anyone or anything."

"Not even his honor?"

Sutter's gaze sharpened on her. "What do you mean?"

"I mean that, based on what I've heard, McHenry is extremely powerful, so how can he have created a defective product? Unless he's doing it on purpose. Either way, McHenry's reputation and the reputation of the Demon Kingdom will suffer."

He bowed slightly, taking Julia by surprise.

"You, my dear, are a true master. I will relay this to the king."

"And McHenry?" Julia asked.

Sutter shook his head. "I will send a missive to him. I don't want to be anywhere near him when he gets it. His temper is legendary."

Sutter bowed again. "It was a pleasure to meet you, Julia Cole. And I thought the wedding was the most exciting event of the day...until now. If you'll excuse me, I'm going to congratulate the trio before I take my leave."

As Sutter spoke to the brides and groom, Alex joined Julia.

"Well? How did it go?"

"Pretty good. He's going to speak to the king."

"So now we wait."

Julia huffed out a breath, and Alex laughed. "And I know how much you looooove waiting." Alex bumped her shoulder. "As soon as the receiving line is done, the guests are going next door to have brunch. Do you want to go somewhere afterward and drink our lunch?"

"I can't. I have an appointment with Dr. Jennings this afternoon."

Alex nodded. "So soon? That's good."

"You didn't have anything to do with that, did you?"

Alex's eyes widened in her infamous mock-innocence face. "I have no idea what you mean."

Julia narrowed her eyes. "You better hope I never have to cross-examine you in court. You would collapse like a house of cards."

Alex shrugged. "Maybe or maybe not." She reached for Julia's hands and squeezed them. "I care about you."

Julia swallowed around a lump in her throat. "I know you do."

Alex blinked several times and then withdrew her

hands. "I better get moving and make sure there isn't anything I need to take care of."

Alex walked away, and, after a moment, Julia glanced over her shoulder at Jack. The heat of his unceasing gaze ran along her neck. In a few long-legged strides, he was standing in front of her.

"You seem to be acting like my human shield a lot lately."

"If you didn't aggravate people, I wouldn't have to."

Julia laughed. "Well, thank you…I think."

The corner of his mouth turned up slightly. "It's in my job description."

She knew he had spoken in jest, but she was surprised to realize this being simply part of his job stung a bit. "Well, I'll try to not aggravate anyone else."

He grinned. "I'm not holding my breath."

She plunked her hands on her hips. "I think I liked grumpy Jack better. At least he didn't talk."

He ignored her barb. "How did it go with Sutter?"

"I threw down the gauntlet. We'll see if McHenry takes the bait."

Jack's grin evaporated. "You need to be careful, Julia."

She shook her head. "We need to stop the rest of the supremacists before they come out of the woodwork. Now Tobin is out of commission, I think it's a matter of time before a new leader of the Vipera emerges. Once that happens, we'll be in trouble again."

"Agreed, but it doesn't mean you have to be the one leading the charge."

"I'll be careful, Jack. But I'll also do what I have to. And if I get in trouble, that's what you're here for, right? It's in your job description."

He scowled at her.

"I'll see you later. I've got to go," she said as she turned for the door.

"Work, work, and more work makes Julia a dull girl," he called out.

Julia's heart seized. She had thought the very same thing about herself.

She almost blurted out that she wasn't going back to work, but he didn't need to know she was going to see a therapist. Even though he hid it fairly well, she caught glimpses of his concern, and if the therapy didn't work out, she didn't want him to know she failed. Didn't want his look of concern to turn to pity.

Relationships should not revolve around
opening and closing arguments.

CHAPTER 14

Julia stood in the hall staring at the name Dr. Olivia Jennings on the glass door. She reached for the doorknob and hesitated. *Suck it up, girl!*

She squared her shoulders, opened the door, and marched into the waiting room, which was empty except for a receptionist sitting to the side. Julia spoke to the young woman, who had her complete the requisite forms and then directed her through the side door before Julia was able to take a seat in the waiting room and muster her courage.

Julia straightened her suit jacket and glanced around the room. The office she entered was tastefully decorated in neutral beiges and blues. Definitely feminine, but in a way that wouldn't turn men off.

Behind the desk were several framed diplomas from various colleges. Dr. Jennings was one smart cookie. Julia pulled on her cuffs and then told herself to stop fidgeting. She hadn't been this nervous since her first trial.

The door opened and Dr. Jennings walked in. Hair

in a bun, glasses perched on her nose, and an air of seriousness in place.

"I'm sorry to keep you waiting, Ms. Cole."

Dr. Jennings held out her hand and shook Julia's hand with a no-nonsense grip.

"No problem, Doctor. I'm happy you were able to fit me in on such short notice."

Dr. Jennings gestured to the guest chair while she sat at the desk. "Alex called and asked if it was okay if she referred you to me. She was worried, and I was happy to schedule an exploratory session."

"So we can find out if this is going to work out."

"Exactly. We need to be able to interact well with each other in order to make any headway with therapy. Personalities can get in the way, so the first session is more of a get-to-know-you session."

"Like a blind date."

Dr. Jennings smiled. "So to speak. Why don't you tell me why you're here?"

Julia flinched at the question. "You're cutting to the chase. What happened to the get-to-know-you session?"

"Oh, that's coming next, but I want you to tell me what made you seek out counseling."

Julia paused and then decided to jump right in. Otherwise what was the point of being here? "Two and a half years ago my husband died. He was an amazing man. Funny, gorgeous, brilliant. And before I make him out to be perfect, he was also stubborn, egotistical at times, and very overprotective of me. When I lost him, I..."

Dr. Jennings sat quietly while Julia struggled for the right words.

"I didn't think I could ever be happy again. Everything around me dulled, like the world lost its detail. I struggled like anyone else who loses someone, but eventually felt like I was finally pulling myself out of the quicksand."

She took a breath before continuing. "A little over seven months ago, I found out my husband's death wasn't an accident. He was murdered. His murderers were just tried and convicted."

Dr. Jennings' eyes flared slightly, but she composed her expression.

"I have spent the past seven months working toward one goal. To see those men pay for what they did. And I told myself that once they did, I could move on. But..."

"But what?"

"But I don't feel any better. I should be happy, but I don't feel anything."

"Nothing?"

Julia hesitated. "You're right. That's not true. I'm angry. All the time."

Dr. Jennings sat quietly. She hadn't moved from her spot. Her pad of paper and pen lay on the top of her desk, untouched. Shouldn't she be taking notes? Maybe she thought Julia was a lost cause.

"What do you think? Am I crazy?" Julia blurted.

"No. I think you're mourning. And as far as being angry? I think you have every right to be angry." Dr. Jennings picked up her pen. "Now tell me about yourself."

Forty-five minutes later, Dr. Jennings set down her pen and folded her hands over her pad of paper. "I think that's enough for today."

Julia frowned. "But you didn't tell me what's wrong or how to fix it."

"Julia, I can't fix you after one session. This was supposed to be an exploratory meeting, to find out if we can work with each other. In truth, I can't fix you. There is no magic pill or exercise that will make things better. Therapy is a process. I would like to work with you. Do you think you can give us some more time to find a way to alleviate some of this anger?"

"You said that I was justified in my anger."

"I did, and you are. But anger should not be your only emotion."

Julia shook her head. "I don't want other emotions."

Dr. Jennings nodded. "Anger is safer, isn't it? But there's a reason you're here. Something told you enough is enough, right?"

"Yes."

"Okay. Then let's schedule another session, if you're game."

"I'm game."

She strode into the waiting room and made another appointment before walking to her car and collapsing in the driver's seat. She was exhausted, which was silly, since they hadn't talked about much of anything.

What in the world would it be like once they really delved into things? And would she be able to handle it?

Jack stood in Godfrey's office with his arms crossed while Connor and Devin sat in the guest chairs. It was hard to believe it had only been a couple of hours since the crazy witch wedding. Julia's comments about the supremacists attacking again and them being ready for it worried him. He couldn't let them go, so he started to think about what avenues they hadn't gone down.

Godfrey closed a file on his desk and sat back. "All right, gentlemen, fill me in on what's on your minds. But I'm warning you, I have to leave on time today. It's my anniversary, and I'm taking my wife out to dinner." Godfrey's wife was a defense attorney, and reportedly even tougher in the courtroom than Julia. Rumor had it that Godfrey and Savannah met when they were opponents in court.

Devin started the conversation. "Jack wants us to push again about talking to Tobin's defense attorney."

Godfrey's lips formed a straight line. "I already talked to him about meeting with us. He's pulling the client confidentiality card right now."

Jack decided to take a page out of Julia's handbook. "What if we play to his ego? Lawyers can be egotistical." He held up a hand. "No offense."

Godfrey's eyebrow went up. "None taken."

Jack moved closer to the desk. "Let's tell him how this is going to impact his business. He just lost a high-profile case, and now he's not playing nice with the Tribunal, who have very long memories."

"I like how you think, Jack. You could have been a lawyer."

"I'll stick to my current job, thanks."

Godfrey's phone rang, and he smiled. "Give me one second. I have to get this."

"Hello."

Godfrey listened for a moment before confusion flashed across his face.

"Sweets, I'm not sure what you're thanking me for."

Godfrey jumped up, all humor disappearing from his face. "Savannah. I didn't send you any flowers. Get away from them! Savannah! Savannah, answer me!"

Devin and Connor jumped up as well.

"Where is she?" Devin demanded. "Godfrey! Is she at home or her office?"

"Her office in the Carter building."

Jack's heart stuttered. Julia's office was in the same building.

Godfrey growled, his eyes flashing as he rushed

toward the door. Jack grabbed his shoulders and Godfrey bared his teeth.

"Pull it together. You have to get through the building without people seeing your wolf."

Godfrey nodded and his eyes lost their glow. They rushed out the door and down the hall, people clearing the way. The four of them burst out the front door, and Godfrey took off at a dead run. Connor hollered something about getting the SUV and ran toward the parking lot. The office building was on the same street as the courthouse, two blocks down.

While Devin and Jack ran after Godfrey, Devin pulled out his phone and called Giz to alert the healing center — which luckily was only a few miles away — that they might be bringing in Godfrey's wife.

Godfrey ran through the front door, and Devin and Jack followed him inside moments later. Godfrey was already slamming through a door down the hall to the right. Before they could reach the door, Godfrey's howl filled the hall.

Shit!

Devin slammed open the door and they both ran into an empty waiting room and then through the door to Savannah's office. A white florist box sat on its side on the desk and flowers lay scattered on the floor. Godfrey had an unconscious Savannah gathered in his arms.

Devin squatted down in front of them. "Godfrey, let me check to see if she's breathing."

Godfrey's eyes glowed orange and he backed up with her in his arms.

"Please, let me help her." Devin reached out slowly and placed his fingers on her neck, as he watched her chest. "She's still alive. Connor should be out front with the SUV in a minute, so let's get her to the healing center."

Godfrey stood up and cradled her closer in his arms as he headed out the office door.

Jack grabbed the small garbage bag out of the waste can next to the desk and picked up the flowers without touching them directly. He placed them back in the box, closed the lid, and put the box in the garbage bag, tying it shut. "Take these with you to the center so they can figure out what's wrong with them."

Devin handed him his car keys. "I'll go with Godfrey and Connor. Go check on Julia, and bring her to the healing center. I don't want her here alone right now."

Devin ran out the door after Godfrey.

Jack's heart pounded as loudly as his feet on the stairs while he ran to the third floor. He steadied his breathing as he opened the door. Tina looked up and smiled. "Hi, Jack."

He nodded. "Hi." He looked at Julia's closed door. "Does Julia have a client with her?"

"Julia isn't here right now."

"Where is she?" She said she was going back to work. But had she actually said that? Or had he simply assumed that was where she'd go after the wedding?

"She had a personal appointment."

"Where?" he demanded.

Tina frowned at his tone. "I don't know. She marked it on her calendar as personal. I don't pry in her personal business."

"Why are you harassing my assistant?" a voice demanded from behind him.

Jack spun around to make sure she wasn't a figment of her imagination. He let out the breath that had been lodged in his chest ever since he'd stepped into her office. "Where the hell have you been?" he barked.

Tina gasped behind him, and he told himself he needed to dial things back, but when he thought back to Godfrey clutching Savannah to his chest, all he saw was red.

Julia opened her mouth to more than likely argue and then she tilted her head and looked at him. She motioned to him to go into her office and she followed him in, shutting the door on a gaping Tina. Jack snorted. She doesn't pry into Julia's business, *my ass.*

"What happened?" Julia asked.

"Someone hurt Godfrey's wife."

Julia backed up, bumping into her door as her face drained of color. "Is she dead?"

Jack shook his head. "They're on the way to the healing center now. We'll follow them there in a few minutes."

"Savannah is human. Why wouldn't they take her to the hospital?"

Jack shook his head. "They won't know how to treat her, Julia. The attack was probably magical." He quickly relayed the events to her. As Julia listened, her color came back a bit, and she stopped leaning against the door.

"What about Savannah's assistant, Margaret? Is she okay?" Julia asked.

"There was no one in the office when we were there earlier."

"Let's make sure she's gone for the day. Tina and Margaret are friends, so she might know." She opened her door and walked over to Tina's desk. "Do you know if Margaret was leaving early today?"

"Yep. Savannah told her to take off since she was heading out for her anniversary dinner with Godfrey. Is something wrong?" Tina added, glaring at Jack.

"No."

Jack met her glare with what he hoped was a calming look. "Julia is leaving with me. Will you please change any appointments she has for the rest of the day?"

Tina's eyes widened as she checked Julia's reaction.

"I don't have any appointments you need to change. Why don't you shut down and take the rest of the day off as well?"

"Julia, what's going on?" Tina asked.

"I'll explain everything to you tomorrow. In the meantime, I would feel better if you shut down and took the rest of the day off."

Tina looked like she wanted to argue, but seemed to think better of it. She shut down her computer and straightened her desk quickly before reaching into her desk drawer for her purse. "I'll see you tomorrow."

When the door shut behind Tina, Julia turned to Jack. "The supremacists have finally shown themselves."

"Yes. Which means we'll need to up your security."

"You already checked my office and home. What else is there left to do?"

He already knew what Devin would say when he saw him again, so he didn't think it hurt to be honest with her. "You just acquired two bodyguards."

Outside the courtroom,
bad news can't be mitigated.

CHAPTER 15

Julia stood inside the healing center and took deep breaths to calm her racing heart. Jack had told her to wait for him while he tried to find Devin to get an update. She looked down the hall and closed her eyes to the memories. It wasn't as if she had spent time here when Thomas died, but that didn't help with the panic that swelled up whenever she was reminded of the fragility of life.

Godfrey stumbled out of a room and leaned up against the wall with his head down. Julia hesitated for a moment before giving herself a mental kick and heading down the hall.

He didn't look up, so she placed her hand on Godfrey's arm, and he flinched. She jerked her hand back when he spun to face her, his eyes glowing bright orange in the dimly lit hall.

"I...I'm sorry," Julia stuttered.

He blinked at her. "I can't talk right now."

"Of course. I understand."

He scowled. "There's nothing to understand or be sorry for. She's not dead."

She backed up at his tone.

He strode back into the room and shut the door. Julia blinked back tears.

A hand landed on her shoulder, and it was her turn to jump out of her skin.

Jack grimaced slightly. "Sorry to startle you. Don't take his attitude to heart. He's upset, and his wolf isn't making it any easier on him. His only thought right now is to protect Savannah. He's trying to maintain his human form, but his wolf is fighting him."

"How do you control it?" she asked.

Jack's eyes tightened before he responded. "Sometimes you don't. The wolf can overpower you, especially when something happens to people you love."

"Like when you were shot and Connor turned into his wolf?"

Jack frowned.

Julia continued. "When he testified during the trial, I didn't understand exactly what happened to him."

"His wolf went into protection mode, and Devin and Charlie had a hell of a time convincing him to let them help me."

Jack crossed his arms as if to end the conversation, so Julia changed the topic.

"Have they figured out what happened to Savannah?"

"Yeah. Come with me and we'll talk to Devin."

Jack led the way down the hall to a room with a long table in the center. Giz and Devin were staring at a large, see-through box that glowed slightly. Inside were a white box and a bunch of wildflowers.

Devin nodded. "Giz figured it out. It's a magical poison. Absorbed into the body by inhaling it. It's designed for humans."

Julia backed up.

"It's okay. The flowers are in a containment field."

"Is Savannah going to be okay?" Julia asked.

Devin walked over to the door and shut it. "Truthfully? I'm surprised she's still alive. The only thing I can think is that she was just starting to sniff the flowers when Godfrey warned her away from them. She's in a coma right now."

Julia choked back a sob.

Devin placed his hand on her arm. "Are you okay?"

She waved a hand and shook her head, swallowing hard. "I'll be fine. Have we checked on everyone?"

"Alex and Peggy are with Charlie and Sheila right now at the team house. The wedding planner office is closed for the night, and the staff has been instructed not to accept any unexpected packages."

Julia would have to tell Tina the same thing. Connor joined them in the room.

Jack spoke up. "Godfrey's on the edge, Connor."

"I know. I called his brother, and he just arrived to watch over him."

Julia set her briefcase down and pulled out a pad of paper and her pen. "Let's get started."

"On what?" Jack asked.

"On the investigation. We need to make a list of next steps." Julia wrote a number one with the word "florist" next to it. "Is the name of the flower shop on the box?"

"Yes," Giz said, peering into the containment box. "It's San Diego Blooms."

Devin sat down across from her. "I already called, and they're closed. We'll go there first thing tomorrow to find out who ordered the flowers, and if the florist delivered them to Savannah."

"We should talk to Savannah's assistant to see if she was there when the flowers arrived."

"We'll need to be creative about that. We don't want her asking questions."

Julia wrote a note on her pad. "We're going to need to think of something to explain why Savannah isn't at work tomorrow."

When someone knocked, Devin called out for them to enter. Darcinda walked in.

Devin's eyebrows shot up. "How did you get called in?"

"Alex called me earlier and asked me to help if I can."

"How is Savannah?" Julia asked.

"She's a strong woman. Still in a coma, but I just examined her. Her life force is stronger than before, and the healers are still working to rid her body of the toxins. Humans are a bit trickier for us to work with, since your bodies aren't as resilient, but Savannah is a fighter."

Julia nodded. "Yes, she is. She's a barracuda in the courtroom."

Darcinda smiled. "I'm going back, but I thought you'd like an update."

"How is Godfrey doing?" Jack asked.

"Better since I told him she seems stronger. He's not letting his wolf take over, and his brother's presence is helping now he's here channeling for him."

Julia let her breath out slowly while Darcinda left the room. She looked up to find Jack studying her a little too closely. He had a way of getting past her defenses and that made her…well, defensive.

"We should get back to our plan," she reminded them, a little too sharply.

An hour later, Devin got to his feet and stretched. "That's enough for tonight."

Julia ran her pen through her fingers. "Already?"

"Yep. I'm going to the house to check on Alex and get some sleep before going to the flower shop in the morning."

"What about protection for Savannah and Godfrey?" Julia asked.

"The pack has arranged for guards to be stationed here," Connor said, checking his watch. "They should be arriving any minute."

Jack went to stand next to her chair. "Let's get you home."

She opened her mouth, but Jack interrupted her. "There's nothing further we can do here tonight."

Julia packed her briefcase and followed Jack to the car while Connor went to confirm the pack members had arrived.

Jack held the door for her as she climbed into the back seat, and he followed her inside.

She turned to him. "What did Darcinda mean earlier when she said Godfrey's brother is channeling for him?"

Jack hesitated for a moment. "Werewolves have the ability to channel some emotion away from others pack members. If they engage their wolf, they can soothe another wolf who is agitated."

"Wow. That's amazing." She leaned back against the seat. She would close her eyes for just a moment to get her second wind, and then she would be ready to get to work once she got home.

"Are you okay?" Jack asked.

"Yeah. I'm just tired. I'll be good in a few minutes." She blew out a slow breath and closed her eyes.

The car jerked and she sat up and looked out the window. "We're almost to my house?"

"Yep," Jack answered. "You've been sleeping for a while now."

"And snoring," Connor chimed in from the driver's seat.

She shook her head. "I wasn't snoring."

Connor looked at her in the rearview mirror. "How would you know?"

"Very funny. Thanks for driving me home. Oh...shoot."

"What's wrong?" Jack asked.

"I left my car at the office. Sorry to ask you to do this, Connor, but can you take me over there to pick it up so I can get to work in the morning?"

"No need," Connor said. "We'll just drive you in the morning."

"You don't need to keep doing that. I'm sure you're both ready to go back to the house and get some rest."

Jack frowned. "I told you earlier that we would be your bodyguards."

"Right. You've checked everything for me, and I appreciate it."

Jack crossed his arms. "Julia, you're a smart woman. Bodyguards means that one of us will be with you twenty-four/seven until we stop these guys."

She took a deep breath and leaned toward him.

"No arguments, Julia. I wouldn't tell you how to try a court case, so please don't tell us how to protect you. Connor and I will check your house when we get you home. Then Connor will go to your office and make sure everything is okay before running to our house and grabbing some things for us."

"And some food," Connor chimed in. "We already know what your kitchen looks like."

She wanted to scream at both of them. It was one thing for them to protect her, but it was another for them to take over her life. "I'm going to talk to Devin."

Jack shrugged. "After what happened to Savannah, I don't think you're going to win any arguments this time."

Julia was angry. Pissed, really. She had never liked that word, but right now it fit. They pulled into her driveway, and before Julia could launch a counterattack, Jack tensed next to her.

"What?"

"I can tell by the look in your eyes that you want to let me have it, but before you do, you might want to take a look at your front porch."

Julia turned slowly while her heart picked up speed at his ominous words. The porch light shone like a spotlight on a white florist box leaning against the door.

Law is constant.
The only constant in love is that it varies.

CHAPTER 16

Julia sat on the couch while the team worked around her. She had lost the ability to concentrate on what they were saying. Now their voices sounded like the adults in the Charlie Brown cartoons. Wah, wah, waaah.

She had also lost track of the time. Connor and Jack made her stay in the SUV until the team arrived and had checked her house. According to Giz's security and magical detectors, no one had gotten inside. Which was a good thing. Otherwise, they would have been bunking at the team house, and Julia couldn't handle staying there. Her fraternity/sorority days were far behind her. She wanted the sanctity of her home.

Although that sanctity had been disturbed. Did everything in her life have to be tainted?

And now she would be living with the twins for the foreseeable future. She didn't bother broaching the subject with Devin. If he had his way, she would be placed in witness protection. Was there a paranormal witness protection program? She wasn't sure if she wanted to know the answer.

The wah-wahs subsided, and Julia blinked, taking in her surroundings. Connor and Jack stood in the hall watching the rest of the team leave for the night.

Julia got up and collected her briefcase, which she had dropped next to the couch when she took up her perch earlier.

"Were the flowers poisoned by magic?" she asked.

Jack and Connor turned to her and nodded simultaneously, in that eerie twin way they did sometimes.

"Are you going to the team house to get your things?" Julia asked.

"No need," Connor said. "Giz brought our go-bags. But I'm going to run out and buy some food. I checked the kitchen, and it's still a wasteland."

Julia gripped her briefcase more tightly. Could she swing it around and take them both out in one pass? Instead she escaped toward the back of the house to get away from the two of them before she was arrested for assault.

Connor headed out the front door and Jack followed her down the hall.

"Go-bags?"

"That's what Charlie and Giz call them," Jack said. "It's a military term. We have duffels ready to go in case we get pulled into a mission and there's no time to pack."

"Right. And that's what I am, a mission?"

He stared at her for a moment. "I'm not going to fight with you, Julia."

"Really? So it's okay for you to order me around, but I can't question anything?"

"I didn't say that. Why don't we talk through the plans? Gizmo will be back to set up some more security gadgets tonight."

"I don't want to live in a fortress. I won't be

intimidated by these guys. If I let them spook me into not living my life, then they win." Julia bit her lip to stop her whining. She hated whiners.

"They aren't going to win."

She walked to her bedroom door and reached for the knob before stopping. "Was there a card with the flowers?"

Jack didn't answer, and Julia turned to face him. She almost stepped back when she looked up into his eyes. Rage had taken up residence there, and didn't look to be leaving any time soon.

"What did it say? Just tell me."

He cleared his throat. "It said, 'I'll see you soon. Love, Thomas.'"

The fight left her like a deflating balloon. Her body felt wobbly, and she sucked in some shallow breaths. "I'm going to go change out of this suit. Then I'll be in my office."

He opened his mouth, as if to say something, then simply nodded. Julia rushed into the master bedroom and shut the door.

She looked down and realized she was still gripping her briefcase like a lifeline. She dumped it on the end of the bed, unbuttoned her suit jacket, and pulled it off. Then she took off her pants and hung the suit up in her closet. She pulled on a pair of yoga pants and slipped a cardigan over the camisole top she'd been wearing under the jacket.

She looked at the clock next to her bed. It was seven. She could still get some work done. She reached for her briefcase, but her hand shook so badly she couldn't pick it up.

Damn it!

Not now. She was *not* going to lose it now. She went to that crazy wedding, had her first shrink appointment, and her home was almost invaded by poison petunias. It had been a taxing day.

A few words on a note card were not going to intimidate her.

Since they had left the healing center, anger had been sustaining her, which was what she wanted. It was much more productive than sorrow. She dropped onto the bed when her legs would no longer hold her up. She was exhausted — from the tips of her toes to the top of her head…exhausted.

She flopped onto her side on the bed and curled into the fetal position. She tried to bottle her emotions, but her eyes refused to obey as tears streaked across her face and onto the mattress. She covered her mouth with her hands to muffle the gut-wrenching sobs. The last thing she wanted was for Jack to hear.

She hadn't cried for months, not since she learned Thomas was murdered. She cried for days then. But she had dried her tears and tucked them away with the rest of her emotions.

Until the cemetery and today. Her anger had escaped again, but it couldn't compete with the grief eviscerating her now.

Jack rechecked the windows and doors to confirm the house was secured.

As he went down the hall toward Julia's bedroom and the back office, he wondered if he should give her space. But he needed to make sure she was okay. He hadn't wanted to tell her what the note said, but she had a right to know. If he hadn't told her now, she would have gotten the truth from someone.

Jack stopped in front of the open office door and peeked inside. Empty. But it had been a while since Julia went to her bedroom to change.

He crossed the hall to her closed bedroom door and raised his hand to knock. A muffled noise stopped him.

He didn't need his wolf senses to hear her crying. Her sobs flayed his insides. He reached for the door, but then clenched his hand into a fist before he could grab the knob.

He wanted to hold her and let her sob it out in his arms, but she wouldn't welcome it. Jack knew Julia didn't want anyone to see her vulnerable. She wore a suit of armor that blocked the people around her from seeing her emotions. In that way, she actually reminded him of a man. Showing emotions would be a sign of weakness in her eyes.

The doorbell rang, and Jack headed to the front of the house and looked through the peephole to find Connor waiting on the stoop. He unlocked the door.

Connor handed him several grocery bags. "I'll be back with the rest."

Jack shut the door and watched his twin shuttle back and forth. He hadn't been kidding when he said one of them would be literally in the house with Julia at all times. This time, Connor had the chore of lugging everything in while Jack stood guard.

Once Connor brought in the final grocery bags, they carried them to the kitchen and started to put everything away.

"Shouldn't we ask Julia where she wants this stuff?" Connor asked.

"Julia's lying down in her bedroom."

Connor looked toward the door. "How is she doing?"

Jack shrugged. "She's been in there since you left. I told her about the note."

"Shit. Do you think that was a good idea?" Connor asked as he pulled items out of the bags and set them on the counter.

"She asked me point-blank if there was a note. It would have been worse if I had lied to her."

Connor scowled. "I want to wring the SOBs' necks."

"I'm with you," Jack growled.

"Maybe I should go check on her."

Jack opened up the pantry. "Don't. She needs some time to herself."

"I hate what this is doing to her."

"Once we get these bastards, maybe she can finally start moving on." Jack set cans on the pantry shelf along with a couple boxes of pasta.

Connor opened the refrigerator and started loading milk, cheese and meats inside. "I bought a lot of food so we don't have to worry about going back to the store anytime soon."

"Good thinking. What if we make something quick and easy for dinner? I know it's late, but none of us have eaten."

"Comfort food," Connor said. "Are you thinking what I'm thinking?"

Jack nodded, even though Connor's question tore at him. He couldn't hear his brother's thoughts anymore. But now was not the time to worry about his own problems. His priority was taking care of—no, *protecting*—Julia.

Sometimes the best strategy is to ignore the legalese and prepare a new defense.

CHAPTER 17

Julia opened her eyes when someone knocked on her bedroom door.

She must have fallen asleep. Her head throbbed, expanding as if someone filled it like a too-full balloon. She had been dreaming about something that made her stomach twist, something full of gray shadows and whispers she couldn't understand now she was awake.

Jack spoke through the door. "Julia? Connor's back, and we've made some food. Do you want one of us to bring you something?"

They didn't need to wait on her. "I'll be out in a couple of minutes."

Julia sat up and swung her legs off the bed, then went into the bathroom to get a good look at herself. She cringed at what she saw in the mirror.

Grabbing a brush, she fixed her ratty hair, then opened her medicine cabinet and shook out a couple extra-strength pain relievers that she swallowed with a gulp of water.

It would have to do for now. Julia left her bedroom and headed toward the sound of male voices. On the way, she noticed the smell of something yummy. Her stomach growled.

When she walked in, the twins stopped talking, and both gestured to a stool at the kitchen counter. Julia sat down as they turned back to their tasks. It was strange to be sitting there while they cooked in her kitchen.

Connor ladled soup into bowls and Jack flipped sandwiches from a griddle onto plates. They brought the dishes to the counter and set a bowl and plate in front of Julia.

"Grilled cheese and tomato soup," Connor said. "This was our favorite meal as pups."

"It was one of my childhood favorites, too."

Connor grinned as he sat across from her. "Good."

Julia glanced over at Jack, who was also taking his seat. He smiled slightly at her as well. Wow, she must look pretty bad if Jack was smiling at her.

"Thanks for making the food."

Jack nodded. "Did you have a good nap?"

"Yep. Although taking a nap before I go to bed probably wasn't too smart."

Connor cut his sandwich on the diagonal, picked up one side, and then dipped it into the soup. "I bet you'll be able to go back to sleep after this meal. That's what carbs are all about."

"I'll keep that in mind." She cut her sandwich and pulled the sides apart, cheese oozing out. She picked up half the sandwich and dipped it in her soup as well, taking a bite of it and groaning at the crisp bread and cheesy goodness.

Connor winked at her. "Now that's the way to enjoy food."

Julia's cheeks heated. "I didn't realize how hungry I was."

They ate in silence for a few minutes, finishing off

their food. Jack stood and turned the griddle back on again.

"Are you guys still hungry?" Julia asked.

"I'm making a couple for Giz. He's supposed to be stopping by in a few minutes to set up some sensors and exterior cameras."

Julia set down the last bite of sandwich, no longer hungry. "God."

Connor grabbed her hand and gave it a squeeze. "It's a safeguard for all of us."

Jack turned back to the griddle and didn't respond.

She picked up her plate, but Connor took it from her and went to the sink. "I'll clean up after Giz eats."

Julia opened her mouth to protest, but the doorbell interrupted her. She turned toward the front just as Connor jogged past her. "Nope. Stay back with Jack while I answer it. You won't be answering the door for the foreseeable future."

She gritted her teeth. She knew they were just trying to protect her, but she didn't like losing control of her own home. It was bad enough getting used to not one, but two, overbearing men invading her space.

Jack placed a couple sandwiches on a plate and set it next to the bowl of soup on the counter just as Connor led Gizmo into the kitchen.

"Hey, Julia."

"Giz."

"Please tell me those sandwiches and soup are for me," Giz asked.

"Yep," Jack replied.

"How'd you know I was starving?"

The twins answered simultaneously. "You're always starving."

She tried to keep a straight face. Giz was tall and lean and, from what she had heard, could eat the rest of the guys under the table. "I understand you're going to turn my house into Fort Knox."

Giz had already taken a bite of sandwich, so he shook his head at her question. After he swallowed he said, "Not that bad. We'll remove the extra equipment once we catch the supremacists."

"What are you doing with Peggy's place?"

Giz grimaced. "Actually, Peggy is moving into the team house with Devin, Alex, and me."

"What's that face about?" Julia asked.

"Because I've been assigned to watch her." Giz sighed.

Connor laughed. "Oh, boy. How did that go over?"

Giz glanced over at Julia. "I know she's your sister-in-law, so I don't want to say anything negative."

"That's okay," Julia said. "Let me hear it."

"She's so damn stubborn! I was in the Navy, and she still taught me new swear words today when Devin insisted she move into the team house."

Julia smiled. "I'm not surprised at all. With Thomas and Devin as brothers, Peggy was destined to be headstrong." She cleared her throat. "When you finish, would you please show me everything you set up?"

"Sure," Giz said. "I'll go through it with all three of you. That way you know how everything works."

Giz finished up his sandwiches, and Connor went with him to work on the alarm system. Julia closed her eyes for a second and took a deep breath. Would things ever get back to normal again? But then she didn't know what the definition of normal was anymore.

When she opened her eyes, she caught Jack staring at her.

"I know you would rather be alone, Julia. Hopefully we'll catch these guys quickly, so we won't be here too long."

She nodded. He actually could be perceptive when he wanted to be. And while she didn't like losing control, she wouldn't necessarily say she wanted to be alone. But alone was her future.

It was safer that way—both for her sanity and her heart.

During an argument with your lover, you can't yell "objection" and hope the judge rules in your favor.

CHAPTER 18

Julia was not a morning person. She understood it about herself, and adjusted accordingly. But what she had not anticipated was living with someone again. Two someones, actually, who were both up at a time of day that should be illegal. Maybe she could work on passing a law against early morning cheerfulness. Connor was the poster child. He was up making a racket before she could pry her eyes open to take in the day.

She might have beaten him to death with the griddle he was banging around in her kitchen if he hadn't made her amazing pancakes with real maple syrup. Connor would live for another day because of them. But she would need to lay down some ground rules with him later.

Now they were on the way to her office. Jack pulled out his cell and called Devin, putting him on speaker. "Hey Dev, we're checking in. On our way to Julia's office right now."

"Got it. I've got some good news. I called the healing center this morning. Savannah is doing better. She came out of her coma a couple hours ago.

Still extremely weak, but she's stable."

"Thank God," Julia said.

"I'm going to go to the florist when it opens at nine. I...hold on a second." A muffled conversation came through the phone and after a few moments, Devin came back on the line. "Sorry, Alex wants to participate, so I'm on speaker now."

"Hello!" Alex piped in. "I've decided to go with Devin to the flower shop. He could use my help."

Connor snorted.

"I heard that, Connor!" Alex said.

"How the hell did you know it was me?"

"Because Jack is considerate."

"And lacks a sense of humor," Connor muttered.

"Heard that, too!"

"You have ears like a bat."

Devin sighed loud enough to be heard through the phone. "Can we get back on point here? We'll let you know what we find out when Julia comes to For Better or For Worse for the staff meeting at eleven."

"Why isn't Giz going with you?" Jack asked.

Now it was Alex's turn to chuckle. "Peggy had an early meeting scheduled this morning with a potential wedding client, so Giz took her to work. I think he's going to need hazardous duty pay after dealing with her."

"Peggy's a walk in the park compared to..." Devin stopped talking.

"Compared to who, husband dearest?"

Jack grimaced while Julia covered her mouth to stifle her laughter.

"You're breaking up," Jack said. "We'll talk to you later." He disconnected.

"Oh, maaannnn, is he in trouble," Connor crowed from the front seat. "He's going to have to buy her something to make up for that slipup."

Julia laughed. "They're going to a florist. I'm sure Alex will come up with some suggestions."

Connor parked the SUV, and they climbed out and headed into the building.

"Before we get into the office," Julia said, once they were in the elevator, "I want to talk about making me breakfast this morning. It was nice of you to do it, Connor, but I don't want you to think I expect you to make me breakfast every day."

Connor shrugged. "Jack and I take turns. It's no big deal."

The elevator door opened and they continued down the hall.

"I guess I don't want you to feel like you need to wait on me." *Or wake up at the crack of dawn.* "I don't eat much in the morning."

Connor opened the door to her office. "You don't eat because you don't have any food in your house. Who doesn't want breakfast? You loved my pancakes this morning. No more complaining, or I won't make you my western omelet tomorrow."

Tina sat at her desk gaping at Connor's proclamation. "He spent the night at your house?"

Oh, no. "Yes…but let me explain."

"There's no need to explain. Look at him."

Connor chuckled.

"Enough from the peanut gallery," Julia scolded. "Besides, it wasn't just Connor. Jack was there too."

Tina's grin grew by the second. "*Both* of them stayed with you last night?"

God, she was not handling this well *at all*. Where had all her eloquence gone? Out the door when the wolfsey-twins moved in.

Tina stood and pointed to Julia's office. "Your office, now."

It was Julia's turn to stare in shock. She followed her paralegal in and shut the door.

Tina crossed her arms. "You're in some kind of trouble, aren't you? I wish they were staying with you for some fun, debauched reason, but since they've been watching over you, I know it's not that."

Julia set her briefcase on her desk. "The people threatening me left something deadly at my house yesterday. Connor and Jack got rid of it, but they're now my bodyguards until they catch the people who are responsible."

Tina grabbed her hand. "I'm sorry. Is there anything I can do?"

"I want you to be extra careful. Don't accept any packages that we aren't expecting. If there is anything that doesn't seem right to you, let Connor or Jack know. And I'm also going to have one of them walk you to your car at the end of each day."

"Okay. Are you safe?"

Julia motioned to the door with her thumb like she was hitching a ride. "With those two around me all the time? I'm definitely safe."

Tina let out a breath. "And they're definitely fine to look at as well."

Julia laughed. "You have a one-track mind."

"I just want you to be happy again."

"I'm hap—" Julia paused at the serious look on Tina's face. "I'm doing better. You don't need to worry about me."

"It's what friends do, Julia. I know you're my boss, but it doesn't mean I don't think of you as my friend, too."

Julia cleared her throat. "Thank you. I think of you as a friend as well."

"Great. Now, I'm going out to my desk to tell those two hunks they are not taking over my space. I need to lay down some ground rules."

"Good luck with that. I was just trying to lay down some ground rules, and you heard the results when we came into the office. They have the ability of convincing you their way is the best way."

"I've dealt with lawyers for years, I think I can handle them." Tina walked toward the door and opened it before spinning back around. "I almost forgot to tell you about Savannah."

"What about her?" Julia asked before holding her breath.

"Margaret got a call from Godfrey this morning. Savannah has come down with a bad case of the flu, poor thing, and he doesn't expect her back to work for several days. It's bad enough that he's taking time off to take care of her."

"I'm so sorry to hear that. Next time you talk to Margaret, please tell her I hope Savannah gets better soon. Can you give me a couple minutes to get settled before we go through my calendar?"

"Absolutely. Let me go herd the cats out of my office space."

Julia shook her head at the cat reference. If Tina only knew.

Instead of feeling important, Julia's bodyguards made her claustrophobic as they herded her down the hall and came to a stop at the outside door. Then Jack and Connor both scanned the exterior before allowing Julia to exit the office building. They escorted her to the SUV, and Julia slid into the back seat with Jack. Connor climbed into the driver's seat and drove out of the parking lot.

"I hope Devin and Alex got a lead at the flower shop," Julia said.

"We'll find out soon enough."

She joked with Connor for a few minutes before they arrived at the wedding planner building. Jack and Connor bracketed her as she entered the building and left her in the conference room.

Julia sat down at the table. Sheila and Peggy were already there.

"Is Alex back yet?"

Sheila shook her head. "Not yet. We heard about your poison flowers."

Julia shrugged to downplay her anxiety. "I never even got near them. Savannah was the unlucky one, but she's doing better now."

"That's great," Peggy said before exchanging a look with Sheila.

"What are you two up to?"

Peggy took a sip of coffee before answering her. "I hear there was quite a bit of excitement at the wedding yesterday morning. I can't believe I missed it."

Sheila insisted Julia start the story from the beginning, and she described the events with as straight a face as she could manage.

"So Jack saved you?" Peggy asked.

"I didn't need saving. He overreacted."

"I wish I had gorgeous twins guarding me," Sheila said.

Julia shook her head. "I don't think your Navy SEAL sea nymph husband would approve."

Sheila laughed. "I love Charlie, but I can still dream, right?"

"Greedy, greedy girl," Peggy chided.

Julia tsked at them.

"Seriously, Julia, how are things going with them both?" Sheila asked.

"They're fine. How are things going with Giz?" she asked Peggy.

Peggy sighed dramatically. "He's hovering, and driving me nuts. I had to tell him to find an empty office so I could get some work done. I don't need a bodyguard. And the last thing I want to do is live in the same house with my brother again."

Julia shook her head. "Cut poor Giz some slack, Peggy. He's probably not happy to be a bodyguard."

Peggy sat up straighter. "What's that supposed to mean?"

"Nothing." Julia smiled at her. "Just let him do his job."

"Like you've been letting the twins do theirs?" Peggy asked with a smirk.

Julia opened her mouth and then closed it again. If she was going to talk the talk, she needed to walk the walk. "Yes, good point, dear sister-in-law. I will let them protect me."

Lorinda, the indomitable owner of For Better or For Worse, swept into the room, bringing their conversation to a halt.

"Sorry I'm late. I was just finishing up with a client. Let's get started, and Alex can join us when she's back from the flower shop. Who wants to go first?"

Julia sat back as Peggy talked about the new clients the business just signed. A pair of werewolves were planning a large, tropical-themed wedding, and a set of nymphs were newly engaged and already retaining For Better or For Worse to plan their wedding. The business was in high demand, thanks to the full array of services provided by the team.

Sheila had just begun her update when Alex bustled into the room, sat down at the empty chair, and gestured for Sheila to continue. Julia wanted to ask Alex what had happened, but the sooner they finished the staff meeting, the sooner they could meet with the guys to discuss everything.

Sheila wrapped up her report on the exercise and spa services she provided for the wedding parties. "I'll be meeting with the werewolf couple to discuss diet and exercise plans for them. They both want to look their best for their wedding."

Lorinda beamed. "Wonderful. Julia, do you have anything to report concerning wedding contracts?"

"The Henderson-Foley contract is in final deliberations with the bride and groom. Hopefully we are close to finalizing. I didn't realize how particular gargoyles can be."

"They can be pretty set in their ways," Alex said.

Peggy smirked. "Kind of stating the obvious, since they do turn to stone."

Alex's face turned pink. "I didn't mean it that way. You guys are bad."

Lorinda patted her hands on the table. "Excellent. Sheila, do you need any last-minute help with the wedding this weekend?"

Julia frowned. "I thought Alex was overseeing that."

"I was, but Devin doesn't want me to be exposed to a wedding this weekend. After yesterday, he's a little bit worked up. I can't wait to get through this so things can hopefully go back to normal."

Julia picked up her gold pen and rolled it in her fingers. She looked up when the room went silent. Alex watched her with sad eyes.

"I'm sorry, Julia."

"For what?"

"For speaking so callously about things going back to normal."

Julia shook her head. "Don't, Alex. It's fine. We do need to move forward. You didn't say anything wrong."

Lorinda made shooing motions. "Meeting is

adjourned. Go talk about the investigation with the guys. Everything else can wait."

Jack drummed his fingers on the file cabinet while he and Connor waited for Devin and Charlie. Giz was already there, busy tearing apart some sort of mechanical device that spilled wires like spaghetti across the desk.

He wanted to hide Julia away from the craziness. Yesterday's wedding should have been a nonevent, but instead they ended up dodging glowing hands and screaming witches. Then those bastards tried to poison her.

It wasn't like Julia was going to sit back meekly and accept things, either. Why was he not surprised she jumped right into the fray? Even after he and Connor told her to hang back if anything happened. The woman was too stubborn for her own good. When she faced off with that witch, his instincts took over, and he wrapped himself around her before his brain kicked in, shouting for him not to touch her. And from the fire that shot from her eyes, she seconded the sentiment.

"How's it going with Peggy?" Connor asked Giz, interrupting Jack's thoughts.

Giz's eyes widened. "If you have to ask, for God's sake, whisper! She knows and sees all."

Connor laughed. "Holy Fates, are you scared of her?"

"Not scared. I just don't want to face her wrath. She's not happy about having me as her bodyguard."

"What is it with these stubborn women?" Connor demanded.

"Sounds like we're late to the party." Charlie spoke up from the doorway as he and Devin entered. "We already bashing the womenfolk?"

"No bashing," Connor said. "More like commiserating."

Devin crossed his arms. "Please tell me Julia is not going to complain about you guys again."

Connor held up his hands. "What's this *us* business? It was Jack who set her off before."

"We're getting along fine," Jack said.

"Good to hear." Devin sat at the table.

Jack moved away from the cabinet to join them. "What did you find out at the flower shop?"

"Alex will be here in a couple minutes with the others. If we don't wait, we'll have to go through everything twice."

Charlie and Connor burst out laughing.

"What's so damn funny?" Devin barked.

"You're not fooling us," Charlie said. "Alex told you to wait."

"I'm the team lead. I make the decisions."

Giz looked up from his wires. "When it comes to your wife, you only think you're in charge."

The laughter got louder.

"What's so funny?" Julia asked as she, Alex, Peggy, and Sheila filed into the room.

Connor offered his chair and held it for Julia. "Devin was just regaling us with stories of his leadership skills."

Devin scowled as he stood and gestured for Alex to take his seat. "Let's get this meeting started. Alex and I interviewed the manager at San Diego Blooms. Before we could get any real questions out, she asked if we were investigators from the insurance company. Apparently, her van was broken into yesterday. Her driver had loaded the deliveries into the van, and then went back into the shop to finish the paperwork. When he went back outside, he discovered the van's door had been jimmied."

"So they stole the flowers?" Julia asked.

"Yes, along with the driver's baseball cap and jacket. Both had the shop's logo on them."

Charlie leaned forward. "That was smart. It would make the deliveries look legitimate. Did anyone see anything?"

Alex jumped in. "The cops interviewed the other shop owners, but no one saw the robbery."

Giz pushed his gadgets to the side, and flipped open his laptop. "Does the store have surveillance cameras?"

"One. Inside," Devin replied. "So it's not going to help us. But I saw a camera in the back parking lot. The owner said it belongs to the company that owns the lot. They rent out the parking spots when there are events in the evenings."

Giz smiled. "I'll start digging around. See if I can find out who the company is, and if I can hack into the security feeds."

Peggy's eyes widened. "You can do that?"

Giz grinned like a damn school kid. "Yep."

Jack shifted in his seat. Maybe they could get to this a different way. "Are there cameras in your office building, Julia?"

"Yes! Darn, I should have thought of them sooner."

Jack cringed. They all should have thought of it sooner. "Let's see if we can find a video of the delivery to Savannah's office."

"Why do you think they delivered the flowers to Julia's home instead of dropping it off at her office when they delivered Savannah's?" Alex asked.

"That's a good question," Devin said. "Maybe they didn't want two incidents occurring in the same office building? It would have raised suspicion with the human police."

"They wanted to cause the most emotional damage,"

Julia spoke softly. "They knew it was Godfrey and Savannah's anniversary. So they attacked on a day that is important to both of them, and they sent it to Savannah's office so Godfrey would find her. They sent the flowers to my house since that is where Thomas and I lived."

Giz scowled. "I've got work to do to find these bastards."

"I'll help," Charlie said, "since we'll both be here at the office watching over Peggy and Sheila."

Devin placed his hands on Alex's shoulders. "I've got to go see the Tribunal. They are asking for a report from me, since Savannah was injured, and right now Godfrey can't go. Hopefully when Savannah is stronger, he can help with the case again."

"What was Godfrey going to do?" Julia asked.

Jack swore under his breath. *Don't say it, Devin. Don't say –*

"Before Savannah was injured, he was going to try to convince Attorney Barr to meet with us."

Don't say it, Julia. Don't –

"I can meet with Barr." She looked at Jack. "With the help of Jack and Connor, of course."

Devin frowned. "I don't think it's a good idea."

Julia crossed her arms. "I don't think we can play nice anymore, Devin. Not now. The supremacists have crawled out of their holes and are coming for us. It's time to stop asking nicely."

Devin opened his mouth, but Julia kept talking.

"Look at it this way. I'm going to be much more cordial to Barr than Godfrey would be. Once Savannah is feeling better, Godfrey is going to come out swinging. If I explain it properly, I'm sure Barr will agree that it would be better to talk to us before that happens."

Now is when Devin will tell her no. Better him than me.

Devin nodded. "Agreed, but Jack and Connor are with you at all times."

What the hell?

Julia smiled. "Deal."

Holy Fates, if Jack didn't know better, he would swear that woman was a witch casting a spell with her lawyer-speak. He agreed that Godfrey was going to be a loose cannon, but he didn't buy Julia's cordial act, not for a second.

Jack knew the truth. Julia was a force of nature, one he and Connor could barely rein in. And now Devin was letting her face down Barr. Their protection detail just ramped up to DEFCON one.

The reason we defend someone
is as much about our beliefs as their innocence.

CHAPTER 19

Julia stared at the fancy, gold-engraved plaque next to Attorney Barr's office door. *Meetings by Appointment Only.*

"You guys ready?"

"I'm thinking we should have made an appointment," Connor quipped.

Appointment-schmointment. "He wouldn't have seen us," Julia replied.

"He might not see us now," Jack said.

Julia shrugged. "I can be pretty persuasive. Connor, can you get close enough to his assistant to tell if she is supernatural or not?"

"Sure."

"Just nod if she is, okay?"

Jack opened the door and strode in first, followed by Julia and Connor. Barr's assistant, who was sitting behind the desk, stared at the three of them like they were fugitives from a most-wanted poster.

"Can I help you?" she asked, even though her body language was far from welcoming.

"Yes. I need to see Attorney Barr." Julia looked at Connor, who nodded.

The woman's mouth flattened into a tight line. "I'm sorry, but he doesn't see anyone without an appointment."

"He'll want to see me."

"I don't think—"

"He'll see me."

She reached for the phone. "Please don't make me call the police."

Julia stepped up to the desk. "You really aren't going to involve the human authorities, are you? Attorney Barr doesn't want or need that type of attention."

Her eyes narrowed. "Who are you?"

"Julia Cole."

The woman paled.

"Apparently my name precedes me. I'm sure Attorney Barr had a little to say about me after the last trial."

The back-office door opened and Barr entered the reception area. "What's going on out here?"

His assistant scrambled to her feet. "I'm sorry, sir. They just showed up and won't leave."

Barr crossed his arms. "I don't have anything to talk to you about."

"I think you'll want to hear what I have to say."

Barr pushed open his office door. "You have one minute."

Julia marched into his office, and Jack crowded in behind her.

Barr glared at Jack. "Why don't you wait outside?"

"She doesn't go anywhere alone," Jack growled.

Barr scowled at Julia. "I already told Godfrey that I can't talk to you about Tobin. I'm concerned about attorney-client privilege."

Julia pulled out her pad and pen and sat down at the small conference table in his office, making herself at home. "That might be true. If we were here to talk about your client. But we're actually here to talk about you."

"Me? What does that mean?"

"It means Tobin has already been tried and convicted. Now we've moved on to finding and convicting those responsible for the attempt to free him."

"And you're going to accuse me of being involved? Do you have any proof?"

Interesting. He jumped to asking for proof before declaring his innocence. "You spent time alone with your client before entering the courtroom. You had opportunity."

"Weak logic."

"Just means we have to dig deeper into your meetings and your background. Maybe you're a Vipera gang sympathizer."

"Is Godfrey sending you to do his dirty work instead of handling it himself?"

"You haven't heard? Godfrey is tied up right now. His wife almost died yesterday. This is no longer a case of tampering with handcuffs. It's graduated to attempted murder. Trust me, Godfrey will be involved with solving this case. I wouldn't want to be on the receiving end when he comes after the people who hurt his wife."

Barr glared at Julia, but not before she saw a flash of fear in his eyes. "I wasn't involved in any attack on his wife."

"Fine. If you're not involved, then tell me who could be. You pointing out potential suspects in a new case is not going to affect Tobin's guilty verdict."

Barr shook his head. "I have an obligation to my client."

Julia set her paper and pen down. "Let's not play games, counselor. Unless you're in with the Vipera gang, you don't owe them anything. As a matter of fact, I would get as far away from them as possible. I wouldn't be surprised if they come after you next. History shows that they hold a grudge."

When Barr's eyes narrowed, Julia knew she had pushed him too hard.

"We're done talking. I'm not involved directly or indirectly with what is occurring now."

Julia stuffed her pad of paper into her purse and stood. "I had hoped you would be cooperative. I should have known that was too much to ask."

"Don't condescend to me. You're a defense attorney like me."

"The difference between us is, I work for clients I know are innocent, and I can sleep at night. Can you?"

Julia walked out of Barr's office with Jack close on her heels.

Connor waited in the reception area. "Ready?"

"More than," Jack snapped.

"Ms. Cole."

She turned.

Has he actually grown a spine, or maybe a conscience?

He held her pen out to her. "I believe this is yours."

"Yes." She wrapped her fingers around the cool metal. But for once it didn't soothe her.

Jack could practically hear the wheels turning in Julia's head as they drove away from Barr's office and filled Connor in on the conversation.

"Do you think Barr is involved?" Connor asked.

Julia leaned forward. "I don't think he's clean, but I'm not convinced he knew anything about Savannah.

When I told him about her, I purposely left out the way she was injured. He said something about not knowing about the attack on her, which is a weird word choice if he knew about the poisoning."

"Or maybe he did and he was playing dumb." Connor turned the corner. "I think we should have someone follow Barr. If we made him nervous, and he is working for the Vipera gang, he might lead us to them."

Jack nodded. "It wouldn't hurt to have him followed, but we don't have enough evidence to arrest anyone yet."

"So should we follow him?" Julia asked, her knee bouncing.

Jack stopped himself from placing his hand on her knee to halt the bouncing. "We should either go back to your office so you can wrap up some things, or head home."

Her head whipped around to look at him. "What?"

"The three of us are not following Barr."

She frowned slightly. "How about we go to see how Giz is doing?"

"Us looking over Giz and Charlie's shoulders is not going to help speed things up. I know you don't like it, but investigations take time. We can't wrap it up quickly the way you see on TV shows. You have to dig through leads, and most are dead ends."

She sighed. "Okay. Work it is. I want to close out a couple of items and check on Tina."

Twenty minutes later, they pulled into Julia's office building parking lot and trotted after a determined lawyer-on-a-mission into her office.

Something had sent her into hyperdrive. Jack wasn't sure if Barr was the trigger, or if it was because Julia was a results-oriented woman, and right now? Well, right now they didn't have much to show for the investigation. Hell, he was frustrated too, but he needed to curb it since it seemed like her nerves were close to detonating.

Tina took one look at Julia, stood with notebook in hand, and followed her boss into her office without being asked. Jack glanced at Connor, who shrugged and sat in the waiting room looking through his contacts on his phone.

Jack sat down and glanced into Julia's office. Julia was rattling off a list of items that had Tina scribbling furiously on her notepad.

"I'm going to call in a couple favors and see if I can get someone to watch Barr for us," Connor said as he left the office.

Jack watched Julia bent over her desk, staring intently at her computer screen. She was absolutely gorgeous, and intelligent, and intense, and… Jack had been denying his attraction to her for so long, that the declaration, even though it was in his thoughts and not spoken aloud, still made his gut clench.

"She's a taskmaster." Connor spoke next to him, causing him to jump. When had his brother come back into the room?

"Yes, she is. But she's feeling useless right now, so she's trying to make up for it by working herself to death."

Connor's eyebrows went up. "Really, Dr. Phil? Do tell."

Jack punched his arm. "Shut up."

Connor grinned at him like a fool.

"Why are you grinning at me like that?"

"Because you're actually talking to me and not biting my head off. It's good."

Jack looked away from his brother's intense expression to school his own. "Don't get sappy on me, bro. Did you get someone to follow Barr?"

"Yep. Donnelly. He's a good private investigator, and is keyed in to our world, so he won't be surprised if he sees glowing eyes and furry things that shouldn't be furry."

Jack snickered. "You sure have a way with words."

"So the ladies tell me."

Jack laughed, and Julia looked up from her computer in surprise. His gut clenched again when she gave him a quick grin before returning to her discussion with Tina.

Jack turned to his brother and found Connor studying him like he was a lab experiment. Which made him nervous. His brother was trying to figure something out, and that never boded well for Jack. Time for a distraction. "I can't believe we shared a womb."

Connor nodded. "We shocked everyone, didn't we?"

That was the understatement of the century. He and Connor were considered an aberration in the pack. Multiple births did occur, but they were fraternal. Identical twins didn't happen. Until Jack and Connor were born. And they were identical except for their eye color. A little fact which their mother used as her proof every time she argued with anyone who said they were identical.

Even though werewolves were pack animals, they were independent vessels of power, and as such, they couldn't be split apart and formed into separate beings. But it's what happened in their case.

Jack and Connor didn't fit in the pack's neat little box, especially once they realized their twin-speak was not something everyone else could do. Jack still remembered the look of horror on their parents' faces when they told them they could sense each other.

The more they were told not to use their twin-speak, the more the power grew. How do you stop your brains from connecting? Hell, as children they didn't have any idea how it worked. As adults, they learned how to block each other at times, but there had always been the connection. Until the last few weeks, that is. Jack wondered if the connection they had was through their wolves. Since his wolf abandoned him around the same time his connection with Connor was severed, his supposition was probably correct.

Crap. This was the last thing he wanted to think about right now.

Connor's smile faded as he looked at his brother. "You went somewhere dark just now."

Jack shook his head and leaned forward, running his fingers through his hair.

He couldn't afford to let his guard down, for both his brother's and Julia's sakes. Until he figured out what happened to his wolf, he was a liability to both of them. But that didn't diminish his protective instincts. If anything, he was even more motivated to make sure neither Connor nor Julia got caught in his mess.

You can't cross out your regrets and create a revision,
they stay with you.

CHAPTER 20

Julia was practically quivering in anticipation of the team meeting. Ever since her meeting with Barr, she'd been dying to *do* something, fix something, save something. Her patience was not just gone. It had left the continent with no forwarding address.

It was as if the emotions she'd locked down were breaking out, and becoming their own, separate beings on a mission, and sometimes at war with each other. After her meeting with Barr yesterday, she worked poor Tina to death before heading home and falling, exhausted, into bed early. But sleep eluded her, and now she was even more wound up than yesterday.

Devin, Giz, and Charlie were already sitting around the conference table, waiting for her and the twins to arrive. Sheila and Alex walked into the room right after Julia and the twins did, and Alex sat down at the head of the table.

Why wasn't Julia surprised to find Alex smack dab in the middle of things?

"So what have you learned?" Julia blurted before Devin could start the meeting.

Devin gave her a smirk before nodding to Giz.

"Charlie and I examined the surveillance video behind the flower shop, and we saw the van break-in."

"That's great!" Julia said.

Giz shrugged. "Not too great. We couldn't get a clean shot of the guy's face to ID him. But we did get the license plate of the car he was driving. We ran it and found out it was stolen."

Julia groaned. Another dead end.

Charlie spoke up. "Cops found it abandoned yesterday, so it's in the impound lot."

"Didn't the owner report it missing?" Jack asked.

"She didn't know," Giz answered. "The sedan belongs to an elderly lady who goes out for groceries on Tuesdays, the hairdresser on Thursdays, and church on Sunday. Didn't need the car until today."

"Guess her perm will have to wait," Charlie muttered.

Sheila smacked Charlie in the arm. "Charles Tucker, behave!"

"Sorry. It's either laugh or punch something."

Julia agreed with him. "What about the cameras at my office?"

"Still working on those," Giz said. "They weren't as easy to hack into."

Julia drummed her fingers on the table. "I'll call the building owner and ask him to release the footage. I pay rent, so I should be able to ask for the tapes if I tell him I've been threatened." She turned toward Devin. "So did you call the meeting to tell us we're at a dead end?"

"No. I called the team together because I heard from Sutter."

Julia sat up straighter. "And?"

"And he's received clearance for you to visit McHenry."

"Hell, no," Jack growled. "What do you mean Julia's going to see him?"

"According to Sutter, McHenry was a little bit miffed that Julia questioned his work ethic. He wants to speak to the, and I quote, *besmircher of my name*, end quote."

Julia smiled. "The word besmircher hasn't been used in centuries, has it?"

"To McHenry it's still relevant," Devin said. "Jack and Connor will accompany you into the Burrows."

Julia stared at him in shock. She had assumed Devin would go with them. Her heartbeat rat-a-tat-tatted in her chest. "You're not going?"

"I can't. Elves aren't allowed in the Burrows without permission, so I'll be staying out of the forest tomorrow. But I told them you'll have two escorts, and that without them, there will be no meeting with McHenry."

Julia's heartbeat slowed down a little.

"The instructions from Sutter say to meet your escort at the Burrow entrance tomorrow at first light."

"This feels a little cloak-and-dagger to me," Julia said as she made a mental note to call Tina and tell her she wouldn't be at work tomorrow.

Devin sighed. "It's the way of the forest. Most supernaturals have acclimated themselves to living with humans. But others? They've decided to remain in their own supernatural bunker."

"And that's what the Burrows are?"

"Yes. Unlike the demons you have met before, the demons who live there don't understand about the world we live in."

"How can they not?" Julia asked.

"You'll find out what he means tomorrow," Connor said.

Julia frowned.

Jack touched her arm, and she looked up into his worried blue eyes.

"We'll be with you every minute."

She nodded. Was it good for her to rely on him? Because, independent woman that she thought she was, she liked having someone to lean on.

And that was not good at all.

Alex left the room while they finished up the meeting. When Julia and the twins were heading out, Alex pulled her aside.

"What's wrong, Alex?" Julia asked.

"I should be asking you that question. You are wound so tight, I'm worried about you. I was supposed to have an appointment with Dr. Jennings this afternoon at two. I just called and let her office know you'll be taking my place today."

"Alex—"

"Don't argue, Julia. You said you liked her when you saw her. So go see her again."

"I—"

"Your work will always be there. Tina can handle you not coming in for the rest of the day. You're going to have to call her to reschedule whatever you have on your calendar tomorrow anyway."

Julia stared at her.

Alex put her hands on her hips. "Well?"

"I didn't know if it was okay for me to talk now, or if you're going to keep interrupting me before I can finish a sentence."

Alex's eyes danced. "You're not the only stubborn woman in this family."

"I'm well aware of that."

Alex ignored the jibe. "I wish I was going with you tomorrow. I tried to tell Devin that I needed to go with you to the Burrows."

Julia cringed. "How did that go?"

"You know those veins on his temples that stick out when he's upset? Well, I thought they were going to burst."

"I'm not surprised. He's protective of you."

"Overprotective, but he's not the only one. I thought Jack was going to have a fit earlier about you going."

Julia shook her head. "That's his normal personality. He's bossy."

Alex pursed her lips. "Whatever you say. I better let you go before they think we're plotting something. I'm not sure why they jump to that conclusion all the time."

Julia chuckled. "Because you *are* always plotting something."

Alex laughed. "You're exaggerating."

The two of them walked arm-in-arm out to the parking lot, where the twins and Devin stood waiting for them. Devin wrapped his arm around Alex. "What are you two up to?"

Alex rolled her eyes. "Nothing."

The team said their goodbyes, and Julia was once again in the back seat of the twins' SUV.

"Do you want to stop for lunch somewhere before going to the office?" Jack asked.

"That's fine, but we're not going to the office after we eat. I have another appointment."

"Where?" Connor asked.

Julia recited the address and turned to Jack. "Before you get surly, I'm going to a doctor's appointment. It's not a place I frequent, so no one will expect me to be there. I need you both to wait in the car."

Jack opened his mouth, but Julia cut him off. "Please don't fight me on this."

He shook his head. "I'm not going to fight you. I just want..." He paused, as if choosing his next words carefully. "Are you okay?"

Julia blew out a breath. "I'm okay. Nothing to worry about."

He didn't say anything else, although his tight expression made it clear he didn't believe it. But she didn't want to bare her soul to the twins and tell them about seeing a psychiatrist. She wasn't embarrassed about it, but it was personal. With them both living in her house, she was already sharing more of herself than she had in years. They didn't need to know everything about her.

Dr. Jennings pushed her glasses up onto her nose before picking up her pen and notepad. Apparently today they were jumping right into the session.

"Alex asked me to let you take her spot. Why did she feel the need to send you here today, before your next scheduled appointment?"

Julia nodded. "I've been very stressed-out lately. I told you during our last session that the men who killed my husband were recently convicted. What I didn't mention is that not all the men responsible were captured. Right now I'm working with a team of investigators to find the rest of the men and arrest them."

"Are you in danger from these men?"

"Yes," Julia answered truthfully, "but I have two men serving as bodyguards for me."

Dr. Jennings made a quick note. "These men are cops?"

"More like private investigators."

"You hired them to protect you?"

"Thomas's brother Devin insisted I have protection until we catch the rest of the gang."

Dr. Jennings stared at her for a moment in silence.

"You don't like having these men watch over you."

Julia hesitated. "I prefer to take care of myself. It's hard to have someone living in my home."

"That's understandable." She stared some more. "What else is going on with you?"

"What I told you isn't enough?"

"You obviously felt a need to come here today," Dr. Jennings pushed. "Are you eating and sleeping?"

"I'm eating more than I have in a while. The men watching over me insist on feeding me."

She made another note on her pad. "That's not a bad thing."

"No, unless I stop fitting into my clothes."

"What about sleeping?"

"I haven't been able to sleep the last couple days. Every time I start to fall asleep, I keep having these dreams, but when I jerk awake, I can't remember what they were about."

She jotted another note. What the heck was she writing, anyway?

"Do you remember what you felt after you woke up?"

"Scared..." She thought for a moment. "Helpless."

"Helpless for yourself or for others?"

Julia thought for another moment. "Both, I think."

"It's hard to be unable to help others."

"I can't worry about taking care of others," Julia blurted, then was instantly sorry for the selfish statement.

Dr. Jennings cocked her head. "That's a funny statement, coming from a defense attorney. You work hard to help people every day. It's in your job description, right?"

Julia shook her head. "That's different. It's my job. I put together a defense and follow the rules in the courtroom."

"And in your personal life, there are no easy rules to fall back on, so you avoid personal relationships."

Julia frowned. "I have friends."

"What about dating? Is there a new man in your life?"

"No." She shook her head a bit too hard as blue eyes flashed in her mind.

"That was quite a forceful response."

"I'm married." Tears rushed to the surface, and she blinked them back. "I was married."

"Julia. You are not cheating on your husband if you start dating again." Dr. Jennings set down her paper and pen. "I know your brain understands this, but I also know that until your heart agrees, what I just said is meaningless."

Julia closed her eyes for a moment to collect herself. When she opened them again, she found Dr. Jennings waiting patiently for her.

"What do you want, Julia?"

"I want to stop feeling like my skin doesn't fit me anymore. I want to find a way to move forward, because living in the past is sucking the life out of me."

"Okay. We can definitely work on that. But therapy isn't a short-term fix. It's a long-term goal. Let's talk about your anxiety."

"I don't want medication."

Dr. Jennings shook her head. "I wasn't going to suggest it at this point. We're going to start with some exercises that might help you. And I want to reiterate that you have a very legitimate reason to be anxious right now. Your life has been threatened. Cut yourself some slack."

Julia nodded, even though her stomach churned. What if she never felt safe again?

You can't ask for a continuance
when it comes to choosing love.

CHAPTER 21

Jack rolled over for what felt like the hundredth time. He hadn't been getting much sleep lately, which was how he knew Julia wasn't sleeping at night either. Julia's routine for the past few nights consisted of tossing and turning, followed by endless pacing.

Was she not sleeping because of the case? The threats on her life? Or was it related to her doctor visit? He couldn't stand the idea that something might be wrong with her. How many problems could be piled on her shoulders before she crumpled?

He turned onto his back and laid his arm over his eyes to block out the moon shining through the window. Connor went out earlier in the evening to let his wolf out. When he returned, he told Jack to take a run, and of course he refused. His brother had looked at him strangely for a moment before nodding and walking away.

He couldn't keep the secret from him for very much longer.

A cry had him bolting to his feet and running toward Julia's room. Connor met him in the hall just as

Jack wrenched open her bedroom door. Julia sat in the middle of her bed, light from the moon shining like a spotlight around her.

"Are you all right?" Jack asked, rushing toward the bed while Connor checked the room.

"I'm...fine," she said. "Sorry to wake you guys up."

Connor looked in the closet and bathroom. "Everything looks okay."

Jack sat down slowly on the bed and held out his hands in front of him like he would to calm a wounded animal. "Did you have a nightmare?"

She rubbed her hand down her throat, as if to pull her earlier scream back inside. "Yeah. I haven't screamed like that from a dream since I was a child."

"You're allowed to scream all you want. It's your house."

She smiled slightly. "You both took over this house the moment you moved in. I must have scared you into saying that to me."

He smiled in return. "Sorry if we're a little bossy, but it's for your own protection."

"Domineering, overbearing, and overprotective is more like it, but I understand."

Connor chuckled as he walked toward the door. "I'm going to make you some tea."

"You don't have to do that."

Connor kept going and called back over his shoulder, "Not listening to you."

She huffed. "That is a perfect example of what I mean."

"He can't help himself." Jack shrugged. "He's overbearing, like you said."

"And you?"

"I'm the more laid-back one."

Julia barked out a laugh. "Now *that* was funny."

After a moment her smile faded, and he wanted to

pull her into his arms and absorb her pain. "Do you want to talk about it?"

She shook her head. "Even if I did, I can't remember the dream. It's fuzzy in my head, like an out-of-focus picture."

"Do you think you're anxious about meeting McHenry tomorrow? We don't have to go if you don't want to."

"Nice try. I'm going to meet McHenry tomorrow. He's our only lead right now, the only one who can help us figure out who helped Tobin break free."

"You were able to get the surveillance footage from your office for Giz to review. Maybe he'll find something to help us."

Julia leaned closer and took Jack's hand. "I'm okay, Jack. And besides, if I don't go, then McHenry won't meet with you guys."

Connor walked into the room with a mug in his hands, his glance landing on their clasped hands. Julia let go and sat back.

"Here you go." Connor smiled. "Chamomile and mint tea. It always knocks me out when I drink it."

Julia reached for the mug and took a whiff of the fragrant tea. "It smells wonderful. I didn't know I had this."

Connor's grin widened. "You didn't. I bought a box when I went food shopping. Promise me you'll drink some before you lie back down."

"I promise."

Connor nodded and left the room, shutting the door behind him.

Julia took a sip and let out a sigh. "He's right, this is good stuff. I'm sure it will put me right to sleep."

"Drink it while it's hot." He picked up the paper and pen on her bed and set it on the nightstand. "I noticed you tend to keep these on hand always."

Julia nodded. "I know that it's old school, but I write everything down on notepads, then I translate them into something that makes sense when I type them into my laptop. The pen was a gift from Thomas when I left the law firm and opened my own business. He said I needed to look professional, and the plastic click pens I used weren't cutting it. So I am very attached to that pen. Thank God it's refillable, or I don't know what I would have done." She paused. "You probably think it's silly."

Jack shook his head. "Not at all. The gifts that matter aren't necessarily expensive. It's the meaning behind them that makes them special."

"Exactly." She took another sip and then stared at Jack for a moment. "I'm okay now."

Jack didn't buy it for a second. "I think I'll stay for a little bit."

"Jack, you don't have to stay in my room. I'm a grown woman, and I don't need anyone to chase away the boogeyman for me."

"You might be an independent woman, but did you ever think that maybe I need to be needed?" *Hell, where had that come from?*

She opened her mouth and closed it again, so he rushed on before she argued with him.

"Let me stay in here until you fall asleep, Julia. I need to know you're safe. Please."

"Okay. But only until I fall asleep. You need to get your rest as well."

He gestured for her to keep drinking. "Deal."

They talked for a few more minutes, until she finished the tea. When she settled down on her side, Jack moved over to the chair in the corner of her room so she wouldn't feel like he was crowding her. Twenty minutes later, her breathing had regulated, and she was sleeping soundly.

He gazed at her face, peaceful in sleep, and his damn heart tightened in his chest. He wanted her, but that was not going to happen right now. But he could keep her safe.

He stopped himself from brushing back the hair that had fallen on her cheek before he slipped out of the room and closed the door, turning to find his brother leaning against the wall with his arms crossed.

"We need to talk," Connor whispered.

Jack motioned for him to follow as he headed down the hall into the kitchen. Connor shut the door behind them and crossed to the stove. "Do you want some tea, or something stronger? I found a bottle of vodka in her cupboard."

"I'd better stick to the tea."

Connor nodded and pulled out two mugs before turning the burner on under the teakettle. "The water should still be warm, so it won't take long to heat back up." He leaned against the counter. "Is Julia okay?"

"She's asleep. The tea did the trick."

"Did she tell you what the dream was about?" Connor asked as he dropped tea bags into the mugs.

"No, she doesn't remember." Jack cleared his throat, choking on the words he was going to say. "I think you should take Charlie with you to the forest tomorrow."

"Do you want to tell me why I would do that?" Connor asked, crossing his arms.

"I just think it would be better."

Connor frowned. "I already know, Jack. You don't have to keep lying to me."

Shit! Jack swallowed, hard. "You know what exactly?"

"Don't play dumb with me, Jack. You care about Julia. Hell, you might even be in love with her."

Oh, Fates, this was not a conversation he wanted to have. "You're crazy," he hissed in a low voice.

"I've been trying to figure out what's going on with you. You've locked me out of your life, but there are still strong emotions that pop through the wall you've built around yourself. And I finally figured it out when I saw your face in the hall after she screamed, and then when you looked at her in the bedroom. Why haven't you told her how you feel?"

Jack shook his head. "Not gonna happen."

"Give me a good reason."

"Because she's still not over Thomas. She might not be able to remember her dream, but odds are this one was about her dead husband. I'm not able to compete with that, nor should I."

"Why not?"

"I'm screwed up."

Connor stared at him for a moment in silence, the teapot's hiss the only sound in the room. Connor jerked it off the stove before it could whistle and set it on a different burner.

"Bull. You're as screwed up as you let yourself be, Jack. Man up and face whatever the hell is going on in your life. I'm here for you. Devin and the guys are here for you."

He had been avoiding this conversation, but it was time. Connor needed to understand what was at stake.

"I can't shift," Jack blurted.

Connor froze. "What?"

"I can't shift to my wolf."

Connor's eyebrows dropped into a straight line. "Since when?"

"Since I was shot."

"That was over six months ago! Why the hell haven't you said anything?" Connor demanded.

Jack couldn't get the words out.

"Have you talked to the pack healer?"

"No! You know what would happen if the pack

found out." He couldn't face being shunned. It was one thing to be a disappointment to his father, it was another to be a pariah to the entire pack. They would probably shun Connor as well just for spite.

"Fine. I understand why you didn't tell the others. Have you thought about going to see Darcinda? She's not going to out you to the pack."

"I don't know what good it would do."

"You won't know until you try. What about your wolf? Has he told you what's going on?"

Jack struggled to swallow. "My wolf isn't talking to me."

Connor's face turned white. "Jack," he whispered. "How long?"

"For a few weeks."

"Since you were tortured?"

"Yeah. I think that's when my wolf went away."

"Damn it, Jack!"

"You don't need my baggage weighing you down. I'm supposed to protect you."

Connor laughed harshly. "I don't need you to protect me. This older brother shit has got to stop. Father has totally screwed you up! Hell, he's screwed us both up. I was born twenty minutes after you were. How does that make me less of a man in this family?"

"It doesn't."

"Then why didn't you come to me for help? Hell, you've been blocking every time I try to reach out to you through our connection."

"No! I haven't been purposely blocking you. Did you ever think that our connection might be through our wolves?"

"So you can't connect with me either?"

"No."

"That's it. I'm calling Darcinda."

"It's the middle of the night. I'll talk to her soon. But

our first priority is keeping Julia safe. That's why you should take Charlie with you tomorrow."

Connor grabbed his shoulders. "Wolf or not, I trust you more than anyone, Jack. Plus, you care for Julia, so I know you won't let anything happen to her."

"Connor—"

"No, listen. We'll work through a plan for tomorrow. Everything will be okay. Besides, with the way you feel about her, would you really be able to stand aside and not follow her into that forest?"

Jack blew out a harsh breath. His brother was right. He couldn't stay behind. Not now. He might not be able to tell her how he truly felt about her, but that didn't mean he wouldn't protect her with his life. She deserved a life free of nightmares. A life where she could find happiness again.

Even if happiness wasn't in his future, and his wolf was gone for good, he would make sure Julia's future was free of fear.

Law means following the Rules.
Love mean breaking them.

CHAPTER 22

When is a forest just a forest? Julia stared at the trees in front of her. She wasn't sure what she was expecting, but this looked like your standard bunch of trees. Jack joined her while Connor pulled something out of the back of the SUV.

"What's Connor getting?"

"A backpack for his clothes."

"Why—"

A flash interrupted her sentence, and she looked toward the car again. Standard and everyday had officially just left the forest. A large gray wolf padded toward them with a backpack hanging from his mouth. She flinched before she could tell her brain it was okay. Would she ever get used to this? The wolf dropped the backpack in front of Jack, who picked it up and strapped it on his own back.

"Why has Connor gone wolfy?" Julia asked.

"Extra safety precaution. We thought it made sense for one of us to be in wolf form so we could sense any dangers in the forest."

Connor lowered his head and bumped it against her

hand. She reached up and awkwardly petted him on the head. His fur was much softer than she had anticipated.

Jack shook his head. "Quit flirting with her, Connor."

"Flirting?" Julia lifted her hand.

"Yep. He always says women can't resist animals."

"*Connor...*" Julia frowned at him.

The wolf dropped his head and looked up at her with sad, puppy eyes.

Julia huffed out a laugh. "Oh, you are shameless."

Connor sat up and smiled—a wolfy grin full of mischief.

Jack interrupted. "Let's get to the checkpoint. Our guide should be waiting for us by now."

Connor trotted ahead to take the lead.

"Stay by me, Julia. Connor will let us know if he senses anything."

She hiked alongside him. "This is the second time I've seen Connor in his wolf form, and it still shocks me."

"I can understand why it would."

They walked a few minutes in silence until Julia's curiosity got the better of her. "I've never seen you change before. Is your wolf an identical twin to Connor's?"

Jack stiffened.

"I'm sorry, did I ask something wrong?"

"No." Jack hesitated before continuing. "My wolf is identical to Connor's except for the eyes."

"That is amazing."

"Not according to my pack."

"What do you mean?" Julia asked as she dodged a low branch.

"Nothing. Never mind."

"Oh, no, Jack. You can't say something like that and then let it drop. You've known me long enough to know I will cross-examine you until you tell me the truth."

He watched Connor walking in front of them for a few moments before responding. "As far as I know, we're the first identical twins ever to be born in our pack. Our birth was not met with joy. I was born, and then Connor came shortly afterward. When they saw we were identical, the healer called in a mystic to determine whether we were cursed."

"You're kidding me."

Jack helped her step over a fallen tree. "I couldn't make up the train wreck of our birth if I wanted to. My mother was hysterical for days after we were born."

"How do you even know about what happened?"

"One of the elders in the pack told us about it. It was supposed to be a lesson in humility. He wanted us to feel grateful that we hadn't been exiled from the pack. Or, actually, that Connor wasn't exiled."

Julia watched Connor sniff the air in front of her before lowering her voice. "Why was Connor singled out?"

"Connor was the second born. The assumption was that I was the dominant wolf and should be acknowledged."

Julia gritted her teeth. "That is ridiculous!"

"Our pack leader thought so as well. So when the rumblings started in the pack, he overrode them."

"And your parents?" Julia asked, holding her breath.

"They acknowledged me and didn't care much what Connor did, as long as he stayed out of trouble and didn't embarrass them. Needless to say, Connor had a tendency to go out of his way to cause trouble. And I wouldn't abandon him. The reason we ran loose in the forest was because we could do it without any supervision."

A lightbulb went off. "Which is how you met Devin."

Jack nodded. "Yes. Devin's father took us under his wing and taught us how to be soldiers. Our father couldn't very well speak out against him. It would have negatively impacted elf-wolf relations."

"So that's why you didn't stay with the pack."

"I would never choose the pack over my brother."

Julia blinked back tears. "Of course not. You were born with a big heart."

Jack smiled. "You just gave me a compliment."

"So I did. I'll be sure not to make it a habit." She smiled back, her heart speeding up at his easy, open expression. And dear Lord, he had dimples like his brother. He really needed to smile more often.

In front of them, Connor froze and growled. Jack immediately switched into protection mode and pulled her behind him. She peeked around his back to see the air in front of them start to move like a waterfall, a shimmering square backlit with opal sparks. Beyond the wavy air stood a large, burly man with brown hair and beard. Standing with the trees as backdrop, he looked like a lumberjack.

"I'm here to take you to the McHenry," he announced with a deep voice that had a hint of Scottish accent.

Connor scrambled toward the wavy air and then pushed his snout through it. He pulled back and shook his head.

"In or out, wolf. It stings only if you linger."

Connor trotted through and turned back to nod his furry head at Julia and Jack.

"What is that?" Julia whispered.

"It's the portal. It blocks humans and other uninvited supernaturals from entering the Elven Forest and, by extension, the Demon Burrows. Haven't you visited Thomas's family?"

She shook her head. She had traveled to the sacred grounds for his funeral, but other than the ceremony, all the other events surrounding it were a blur to her.

"Are you comin'?" the lumberjack bellowed.

Much to Julia's annoyance, Jack kept her behind him until they stopped next to the barrier. Then he held her hand and let her go first. She entered the light, her skin tingling as if she touched a live wire.

Jack waited on the other side of the barrier until he saw that she had made it through safely, his hand still in the light as he held onto her arm.

"Are you okay?" he asked.

"Yes. Come through so it doesn't hurt you."

He walked through quickly, and they faced the big man. Now that they were on the other side of the barrier, Julia was able to get a better look at their guide. He looked to be in his early forties. His hair and beard had hints of red sprinkled throughout, and he would have been a handsome man if not for the perpetual scowl.

He looked her up and down, his eyebrows almost touching his hairline. "I was told wolves would be bringing the besmircher. Are you the one the McHenry sent for?"

"Yes."

"For such a wee thing, you have caused a lot of trouble."

She stood taller. "I didn't mean to cause trouble." *Okay, that was a little white lie.* "If McHenry would have come to meet with us, we could have resolved this much earlier."

The man shook his head as he turned and ambled away. "The McHenry doesn't leave the forest."

Julia bit back a retort, and she hurried in an attempt to keep up with the infuriating guide, only to realize she hadn't let go of Jack's hand. He released it as she walked forward, and she stopped herself from wishing he was still connected to her somehow. This forest was affecting her common sense.

Connor bounded ahead of them, and Jack strode alongside her, not seeming to be irritated in the least by this man's rudeness. Julia, however, did not feel the same.

She raised her voice, aiming at their guide's back. "I'm Julia, this is Jack, and the wolf is Connor."

The man didn't say anything.

"And you are?" she pushed.

"Late. You were supposed to be here at first light."

Oh, she needed to calm down. She started to count to ten in her head. *One — take a deep breath. Two — everything will be all right. Three — do not tackle the big oaf even though he deserves it. Four —*

The man jerked to a stop and looked at her. "I'm a demon, not an oaf."

Julia gaped at him. "How... Are you reading my mind?"

"No, you just said it out loud."

Julia's stomach bottomed out as she glanced over at Jack, and he nodded, his eyes sparkling. Connor made a huffing sound that could have been a laugh. But then he was still a wolf, so she had no idea if that was the case. Connor made another noise. This time it sounded like a snort. Yep, the hairy beast was laughing at her.

The rude lumberjack continued. "And before you ask, yes, I'm a demon. Our people do not look like the myths humans spew about us."

Julia had had enough. Stick a fork in it, because her patience was D.O.N.E. "I was married to an elf, and he didn't have pointy ears *or* work in Santa's workshop. So I get it. You shouldn't assume that just because I'm human I'm ignorant of the world around me." She continued walking before he could retort. After a moment, she called over her shoulder. "Aren't you coming? We're late. We don't want to keep the high and mighty McHenry waiting."

They continued through the forest, and the lumberjack skirted her. "I'm thinkin' I should be leading, since you don't know where you're goin'." A few moments later he spoke again. "Why are you questioning the McHenry's work?"

"I think that's something I should talk to McHenry about. And why do you keep calling him 'the McHenry'? Is he a Scottish laird or something?"

The big man looked at her and laughed. "It's a sign of respect, is all."

After a few minutes, the trees thinned out, and they were soon standing in a small meadow. Up ahead was a cobblestone courtyard that led to a large house and even larger workshop.

They walked toward the house and Julia stared at it in awe. Constructed of cut logs, the house had pieces of dark metal adorning the shutters and entry. A heavy metal knocker in the shape of a dragon hung at eye level on the door.

But their guide stopped and turned to face them before they reached it.

Julia frowned. "Aren't you going to knock on the door?"

"There's no need."

"What do you mean?" Julia asked.

He folded his large frame forward slightly, as if bowing. "The high and mighty McHenry at your service."

Oh, no, he didn't.

Holy shit. Jack held his breath waiting for the drama to unfold. Even Connor sat frozen, his wolf head cocked to the side. Red creeped up Julia's face and stained her cheeks.

"Are you gonna start countin' again?" McHenry asked.

Dear Fates, the man just lit the fuse. Should Jack step back and let Julia explode?

Julia's eyes sparked in fury. "No, I'm way past counting. There's no hope for my anger to go away now. What was the point of this exercise? Why would you lie to us?"

"I didn't lie to you. I never said I wasn't McHenry."

"I'm a lawyer, and even I think that's a weak attempt at owning up to the truth."

McHenry's eyes narrowed on her. "I was told that you questioned my work, implying it was below standard. I wanted to hear what you had to say before you knew who I was. I find that people tend not to be truthful with me."

"Maybe it's your sparkling personality."

"Excuse me?"

"I'm surprised the forest is big enough for you and your ego. You talk about yourself in third person? Who does that?"

Jack rubbed his hand over his mouth to hide his smile. She was a gorgeous Fury in all her glory. McHenry didn't stand a chance. Hell, Jack never stood a chance resisting her charms. He was in this, hook, line, and sinker. Even if he could never be with her, his heart was already hers.

She stared up at McHenry wide-eyed, as if shocked by what she just said. This was the Julia who had been missing. The Julia the world needed. Jack was just happy to be a witness to her rebirth.

McHenry stared at her for a moment, and Jack prepared to eviscerate the man if he made one move toward her in anger. Instead, he dropped his head back and laughed.

"You are a refreshin' change of pace, wee one. Tell me why you questioned my magic."

"Sutter didn't tell you?"

"Not the specifics, no."

Julia's eyes lit up. "By now you must have heard about Tobin, the leader of the supernatural supremacists, and his sentencing and attempt to break out of the courtroom."

"I've heard rumors about it throughout the forest. Some sort of brouhaha taking place. What does it have to do with me?"

"He was wearing your cuffs when he attacked the courtroom with his magic."

McHenry froze. "That's not possible. My cuffs would have suppressed his powers."

"We were all in the courtroom when Tobin lifted his arms and the cuffs fell away in a flash of light," Jack said. "Then all hell broke loose."

McHenry crossed his arms. "I want to examine them. Did you bring the cuffs with you?"

"We brought a link from the cuff." Jack reached into his pocket and pulled out a small bag with the link inside.

McHenry frowned. "I need to see the whole thing."

"We couldn't bring the cuffs," Jack responded. "They're evidence."

"And you didn't want to give them to me in case I was guilty?" McHenry held out his hand and Jack dropped the bag into his palm.

"Precisely," Julia chimed in, showing no fear.

McHenry strode toward his workshop without another word. Jack nodded to Connor, who took up guard duty in the courtyard. As Jack watched Julia hurry after McHenry, he wasn't sure which one of them was the more obstinate. If he had to lay odds, he'd pick the wee one. But then, he'd pick her every time.

Love is not about prosecuting those closest to us,
it's about defending them.

CHAPTER 23

Julia came to an abrupt halt after she followed McHenry into the building. The space was a cross between a blacksmith's forge and a wizard's workshop.

McHenry placed the bag with the link on a table with vials of liquid. He shook the metal link out on a glass dish and picked up one of the vials. Milky liquid swirled around as if it was alive. McHenry uncorked the vial and let one drop land on the metal link. A sizzling sound accompanied a chant from McHenry. Julia didn't understand what he was saying, but the link began whirling, picking up speed until it became a circular blur.

Afraid to say anything for fear she would disturb whatever test he was running, Julia looked over at Jack beside her. Before she could ask him what McHenry was doing, Jack winked at her. *Winked!* She would expect that from Connor, but not Jack.

Was there something about the forest that made them behave differently? First she lost her filter and said anything and everything that entered her agitated mind, and now Jack was all relaxed and flirty? He gestured for her to turn back and watch the McHenry show.

The link slowed its spin until it came to a halt. Julia waited for McHenry to speak. Instead the giant man cursed. Once again, it wasn't in a language Julia understood, but most swearing didn't need translation. It was all in the delivery.

"Well?" she asked when she couldn't stand it anymore.

"Nothing."

"What does that mean?" Julia pushed.

McHenry picked up the dish and walked to the side of the room where a fire pit burned brightly. He grabbed a small clamp with a long handle, picked up the link, and then immersed it in the hot coals. She gasped at the proximity of his hand to the coals. Even with the long handle, the fire had to be hot enough to burn him.

After a few more moments, he pulled the link from the fire and set the metal, now red from the heat, onto an anvil.

"Did you burn yourself?" Julia asked, taking a step toward him until Jack stopped her with his hand on her arm.

McHenry picked up another set of pincers and pried the link apart, flattening it into a line. "My tools are bespelled so when I use them, my hands are protected from heat and injury."

"Wow, that's amazing. What are you doing now?"

"I'm heatin' the metal to transform it back to its primal element. I can then examine it to see if my magic has been tampered with."

"Your magic is imbued in the metal?" Jack asked.

"Yes, when I forge it. Which is why I don't know how Tobin broke the cuffs."

"What does your magic do?" Julia asked.

"For the cuffs, I place a dampening spell within the metal. It absorbs the powers of the supernatural. The more power they use, the more the cuffs absorb. The same goes with strength. A werewolf or demon with super strength should not be able to break the cuffs."

"Can you tell if your magic is faulty?" Julia asked.

A muscle in McHenry's jaw rippled for a moment before he replied. "That is what I'm doin' now." He pushed the metal back into the coals. After a minute, he pulled the metal out and set it on top of an anvil. He held the molten piece still with the clamp and recited a spell over it.

He stood and shook his head. "The magic is sound. It should have worked."

"Then if the magic is sound, the problem must be the metal," Julia said.

McHenry shook his head. "That's what my earlier test was. I tested to see if there was a defect in the metal composition."

Julia tapped her finger on her chin. "What if it isn't a defect?"

"Where is that mind of yours going, Julia?" Jack asked.

She looked around the room at the supplies and numerous pieces of metal in various stages of creation, all separated and placed in different bins. "Why do you keep your metals separated?"

"So they aren't contaminated. I use separate anvils as well, depending on what materials I am using."

"You have different spells depending on the composition of the metal?"

"Yes. Metals have different molecular makeups, so the spell has to be specific to the metal."

Julia's eyes lit up. "So maybe your metals have been cross-contaminated?"

"I would notice if the metal was contaminated."

"What if it was a trace amount of metal? Would you notice it then?"

McHenry opened his mouth and then hesitated. "I don't know if I would."

"Can you test to see what types of metal were used for those cuffs?"

McHenry set the hot thread into water and pulled the darkened metal back out of again. "This should be iron. I'm going to test to see if another metal has been added." He walked back over to the table with the vials. "This is going to take some time. You might want to take a break."

Jack let out a whistle and Connor trotted into the building. Jack pulled his backpack off and set it on the floor. "Thought you might want to change back so you can watch McHenry's testing to see what the metal content is."

Connor nodded, and a glow surrounded him. Jack placed his hands over Julia's eyes just when things were about to get interesting.

"Connor! You couldn't wait until Julia was out of the room?"

"Nope. I don't think Julia is a prude...are you?"

Jack spun Julia toward the door and marched her outside. She hollered back over her shoulder. "I'm not a prude, wolf-boy."

Jack led her over to a bench on the front porch of the house and sat down.

She sat next to him and blew out a long breath. "I'm sorry."

He turned to her. "For what?"

"I kind of lost it with McHenry. I don't know what came over me."

Jack grinned. "I think the real Julia is breaking free."

Julia shook her head. "I was never that over the top in the past."

"Then maybe a new Julia is coming out. You've always fought for your clients and the people you love. Maybe now you're fighting for yourself."

She sat back at his words. "I...never thought of it that way before."

"Don't look so shocked. You've never had trouble putting me in my place."

"You're so obstinate, it's not hard to find the words."

Jack looked out over the courtyard. "Funny you should call me obstinate. I was just thinking the same thing about you and McHenry, wondering who would be the winner in the obstinate contest."

"And which one of us would come out on top?"

He turned back and started at her for a moment, his eyes blue as the clear sky above them. "I'll always bet on you, Julia."

Um. Ah. Oh...hell. She didn't know what to say. Her stomach fluttered.

Dear Lord, was it nerves or food poisoning? More like guilt. She could not feel anything for him right now. The new Julia he claimed was emerging needed to get the hell back into her cocoon. She might be peeking out of the chrysalis, but her wings were not ready to carry her away. She was not ready to get carried away.

"Guys!" Connor called from the door. "McHenry found something."

Thank God, or the Fates, or whatever intervened just now by having Connor interrupt their conversation, because she still had no idea what to say to Jack.

She stood and walked quickly toward the workshop, Jack's footsteps signaled he was close behind her.

"What did you find?" Julia asked before she came to a stop next to McHenry's workbench.

"There are minute bits of silver in the link. Even though the spell I cast is intact, it's designed for iron. Silver would undermine the effectiveness." McHenry growled and stared at the metal as if it was his enemy.

He backed away from the table and ran his fingers through his hair. "It would be better if I had more of the cuffs to examine to confirm the silver was truly the cause."

Jack pulled another small plastic bag out of his pocket with a couple more links inside. "Will this work?"

McHenry scowled. "Why didn't you give me this before?"

"Didn't trust you," Jack said.

"And now?"

"Not sure if I trust you completely, but you look pretty upset about someone tampering with your cuffs."

"Damn straight I am!" McHenry bellowed.

Connor marched into McHenry's face at the same time Jack moved closer to Julia, ready to push her behind him.

She sidestepped Jack and put her hands on her hips. "Are you finished with your outburst?"

McHenry scowled at her. "This is my work, my reputation!"

"Yes, it is. And, as a lawyer, I understand what it's like to rely on your reputation. But this is about more than you and me. It's about a group declaring war against others because they dare to love someone from another species. If someone has tampered with these cuffs, we need to find them. If we can find the loose thread, we can pull on it, finally unravel what's left of the supremacists, and stop them."

McHenry stared at her for a moment. "You're the lass who spoke in court that day."

Julia nodded.

"I've heard the stories about a warrior woman facing off with Tobin. At first, I thought it was blown out of proportion, as most stories are. Now I think the stories didn't do you justice."

Heat traveled up Julia's neck and spread over her face. What was it today with all these males giving her compliments?

She motioned to the bag Jack had placed on the table. "Why don't you confirm your suspicions?"

McHenry got to work while Connor stood next to him, overseeing the process. Julia took a breath and backed away from the table into Jack's hard chest. She turned her head and looked up at him, flinching at the scowl he was throwing McHenry's way. What had McHenry said to set him off?

What the hell kind of game was McHenry playing at? Julia had blushed like a schoolgirl moments ago when he went on about her being a warrior woman.

Hell, he agreed with McHenry's assessment of her, but that didn't mean Jack wanted McHenry waxing poetic over her. The demon needed to watch what the hell he said.

Jack should be the one to tell her how amazing she is. He tried to share his thoughts with her a few minutes ago on the porch, but she backed away from him like a spooked doe.

In the past, when he ran in wolf form, he came across deer in the forest. Most would run scared from him, but some would stop and stare, as if sensing his *other*, and not understanding how man and wolf could be one.

That look of total confusion was similar to Julia's

earlier, when he blurted out that he would pick her. He knew better than to reveal his feelings to her. She wasn't ready, and he wasn't normal. Or normal for a werewolf, that is.

He needed to figure out what was going on with his wolf before he ever ventured into a relationship with anyone, let alone Julia, who needed some stability in her life after what she'd been through. He shouldn't have allowed this closeness, and it was time to call a halt to it.

But she was gazing up at him with wide eyes, her back to his chest, and all he could think about was wrapping his arms around her and holding her tight. Instead, he schooled his features and backed away.

"Damnation!" McHenry growled, yanking Julia's attention away from him.

"What is it?" she asked.

"These links have silver in them as well. The cuffs were contaminated on purpose."

"Could they have been altered after you sent them to the holding facility?" Jack asked.

McHenry shook his head grimly. "No."

"Which means they were contaminated here," Connor interjected. "Who else has access to the metal?"

McHenry closed his eyes for a moment. "My strikers, but they wouldn't do it."

"What are strikers?" Julia asked.

"Blacksmith assistants. But I canna believe it."

Jack had noticed McHenry's burr slipped out when he was upset, but they didn't have time to cater to his moods. They needed to understand what was going on. "Why don't you believe it?" he pushed.

"Because they're my nephews."

Shit. "We need to talk to them."

"I sent them both to buy supplies. They won't be back until tomorrow."

"You can't call them?" Julia asked.

"The forest doesn't allow for cell phones, wee one. Even if there were towers, the magic here interferes with them."

"Well, that's not helpful."

"You are more than welcome to stay here overnight."

Connor and Jack exchanged looks before Julia spoke up. "If we don't let our team leader, Devin, know what's going on, he'll come in here looking for us. We don't need an elf-demon war on our hands."

Connor said, "I'll go to the edge of the forest and call Devin to let him know we're staying."

"No!" Jack barked, instantly regretting his tone when Julia eyes widened.

"What's wrong?"

"Nothing. Let me talk to Connor for a second." Jack headed out of the building with Connor following behind him.

"What's the problem, brother?" Connor asked.

"I'll walk to the forest edge. You stay here and protect Julia."

Connor frowned. "I'm surprised you're willing to leave her."

"I shouldn't be anywhere near her. You're stronger than I am right now."

"Jack, you're a soldier."

"Don't. It's the right call. I'll be back as soon as I can." Jack walked away.

Connor called after him. "You're not going to tell Julia you're leaving?"

It was best to distance himself from her, in more ways than one. "You tell her."

Love isn't proofread, signed in triplicate, and notarized, but it is perfect in its imperfection.

Chapter 24

Julia stumbled back into the building. *What was that about?* She rushed over to the table where McHenry was tinkering.

Connor came into the workshop moments later. "Jack volunteered to go call Devin instead of me."

Julia nodded, biting her lip to hold back her questions.

"Since you stayed behind, why don't you make yourself useful and cook dinner for us while I'm finishing up out here?" McHenry said. "Unless you can't cook?"

Connor grinned. "I know how to cook."

"You'll find everything you need in the house."

"Are you coming, Julia?" Connor asked.

"I'll be in to help in a minute."

McHenry leaned closer to her and whispered, "Did you learn anythin' interesting while you were eavesdropping?"

Julia's face heated. "More than I wanted to, you egotistical man."

He smiled at her. "Hearing part of the story is a recipe for misinterpretation."

"What are you, the Dalai Lama?"

"No. Just an observer. Why don't you go ask him why Jack insisted on leavin'?"

"It's none of my business," Julia rushed to say, her breathing speeding up at the lie.

"Go on, before he comes looking for you. They're both very protective of you. Not that I blame them."

Julia walked toward the house, thoughts bombarding her.

Alex was right. Something was really wrong with Jack. He'd seemed to be doing better, but just now he reverted to his troubled self.

The realization was enough to force her to set aside her own selfish thoughts. Pain was not solely hers to own. But when you were immersed in pain, it was hard to move beyond your tunnel vision to notice others were hurting too. Maybe it was time for her to do just that.

She opened the front door and took in the huge great room with rustic furniture. She headed down the hall toward the sounds of pans clanking and found Connor peeling potatoes at the sink.

"Connor?"

He looked up at her, and for once there wasn't a smirk on his face.

"Are you okay?"

His eyebrows rose at her question.

"I heard your argument with Jack earlier. What's going on?"

His shoulders slumped. "It's not my story to tell."

"You're worried about him."

"Hell yeah, I am. He's been keeping me at arm's length recently."

"Alex said you have some sort of twin-speak."

Connor nodded. "We can feel each other's emotions. Sometimes we can talk to each other through our minds as well."

"That's amazing. Do other werewolves have this gift?"

"Normally not siblings. In rare instances, mates will have some connection."

"So you're unique."

Connor smirked. "That's not the word our family would use, but yes, we're unique."

Connor peeled the potatoes so hard he was turning them into hash browns.

"Let me do that."

He looked down at the mess he was making and handed her the peeler.

"Why did Jack say you were stronger?"

Connor turned toward her, pain in his gaze. "I can't…"

Julia swallowed down the lump that threatened to form in her throat. "Sorry, I won't ask you to betray his confidence. It's been a hard time for all of us these past months. We've all been hurt by the supremacists. Jack almost died."

Connor grimaced. "That was a scary day. When Jack was shot, I turned into my wolf to protect him, and had a hard time turning back."

"You talked about that at the trial. What do you mean exactly?" Julia asked, rinsing off the potato Connor had mangled and dropping it in the pot of water.

"Under extreme stress, our wolves can become unpredictable. Mine was all about protecting Jack. I almost attacked Devin and Charlie when they found us."

"So you're normally in control when you're in wolf form?"

"Yes, we're cognizant of what's going on most of the time, but that day my wolf overrode me."

"Does it hurt when you change?"

He shrugged. "The first couple times, until you get the hang of it."

She started peeling another potato. "Were you planning to make mashed potatoes?"

"Yeah. He's got chicken. I'm going to oven-cook fried chicken with a cornmeal batter."

Julia tilted her head. "You can make more than breakfast, huh?"

Connor finally grinned. "Yep. Living in a house full of guys either means learning to cook or eating pizza and burgers all the time. Pizza and burgers can get real boring, real fast. Of course, with our team, we took it a step further. Cooking has become a competition."

"Who is the best cook on the team?"

Connor propped his hip against the counter. "I'm pretty good, and so is Giz. But we both cook from recipes we find online or on food shows. Charlie just throws things together, and it always tastes fantastic. He's annoyingly good at it."

Julia chuckled. "And I'm sure he doesn't let you forget it, either."

Connor opened a few cupboards and finally pulled a couple of bowls out of the cabinet. "He absolutely loves rubbing it in. Charlie's ego is a little over the top."

Julia threw the last peeled potato in the pot and washed her hands. "Um, I think what we have here is a case of the pot and the kettle."

Connor snorted. "Whatever could you mean?"

Julia smacked Connor with the dish towel. He laughed as he poured flour into a flat dish and then mixed the cornmeal in with the flour.

"Can I help?" she asked.

Connor's mouth gaped in what she hoped was mock horror. "Do you know how to cook?"

She shook her head at him, smiling. "You can watch over me so I don't poison us."

They worked together in silence for a while, interspersed with Connor's occasional instructions. He really did know his way around the kitchen.

Connor pulled the last of the chicken out of the pan just when McHenry entered the kitchen and took in the food sitting on the table.

"Well, it looks like you can cook, wolfman, but the proof is in the eatin'."

"Wash up and then sit down and try it yourself," Connor said.

"I washed up in the workshop."

"Should we wait for Jack?" Julia asked.

Connor shook his head. "No, he might be a while."

They sat down and dug in. The chicken was crunchy, and the mashed potatoes creamy, but Julia couldn't fully enjoy the meal. She was too busy worrying about Jack. Wondering what was wrong with him. It had to be bad if Connor wouldn't tell her.

Julia took her plate to the sink when Jack walked into the room. "Did you talk to Devin?"

Jack nodded. "Yes. He's agreed not to storm the forest tonight to rescue us. Everything all right here?"

Connor placed two pieces of chicken on a plate and handed it to Jack. "Everything's fine. Eat while it's warm."

Julia rinsed her plate. They had already cleaned the prep dishes prior to sitting down for dinner, so once the plates and serving bowls were washed, the kitchen would be clean.

McHenry stood. "Leave the dishes, Julia. We can attend to them later. I thought you would like to see more of my workshop. I can show you some of my other metalwork."

"Sure, I'd like that."

McHenry turned to the twins. "Do I have your permission, or will one of you need to accompany us?"

Jack opened his mouth to say something, but Connor spoke first. "Go ahead. I'll finish the cleanup while Jack eats."

Jack frowned and then looked down, concentrating a little too hard on his food.

McHenry winked at her as they walked out of the house.

"What was the wink for?"

"No reason."

She stopped in her tracks and stared at him. "You don't strike me as someone who does things for no reason."

McHenry let out an exaggerated sigh. "I have never met anyone like you before, Julia. People don't talk to me the way you do."

"And what way is that?"

"The unvarnished truth. Most people are afraid to be honest with me. It could be my reputation for being a bit of a hothead."

Julia laughed. "A *bit* of a hothead? I would say there is a *bit* of truth in that. As far as being afraid of you." She looked up at him and cocked her head. "I've decided that I'm not going to let fear stop me anymore. Besides, you are more bark than bite."

He grinned at her. "Can the same be said of the wolf twins?"

"Connor, Jack, and I are working together to stop the supremacists."

He gestured for her to continue walking, and when they entered the workshop, McHenry guided her to a workbench in the far corner that had small tools made for intricate work. "Yes, you are. But it's more than that. I asked you out here to show you my work, but I think it will also serve to make your man a little jealous."

"Jack's not my man."

McHenry reached for a flat box on a shelf and set it on the bench. "I didn't say who I meant. It's interesting that you jumped to the conclusion that I meant Jack."

Heat flooded her face. She had been blushing a lot lately.

"I did mean Jack, of course. He wants to be your man, but something is holding him back. We'll see how long it takes him to come check on you. My bet is less than five minutes."

"You're awfully sure of yourself."

"I am an observer of people. I can read them most of the time. I'm never wrong." He frowned. "But then our conversation with my nephews tomorrow might prove the opposite to be true."

McHenry opened the box. Several necklaces sat in square compartments.

Julia leaned closer to look at them. "These are amazing. You made them?"

He nodded while he pulled one out of the box. A silver cross hung from the chain. "These are the smallest items I make, and they are the most challenging. I find the irony refreshing." McHenry set the cross necklace down and held up another necklace with an intricate knot woven in a circle. "This one is perfect for you."

Julia shook her head. "I couldn't accept that."

"Of course you can. It's a caim, which is the symbol of sanctuary. It was made for you."

He gestured for her to turn around, and he hung the necklace around her neck, clasping it. Julia ran her fingers over the metal. "Thank you."

"You're more than welcome, wee one."

"Julia."

She gasped in surprise and turned. Jack stood behind them scowling.

Before Julia could ask what the heck his problem

was, Jack spoke up. "It's been a long day, Julia. We should probably turn in."

McHenry reached for the box and placed the lid back on top of it. "He's right. I'll be in a moment to show you the guest rooms."

"Thank you again for the necklace." She followed Jack toward the door. When she peeked back at McHenry, the big showoff leaned against the bench with his arms crossed and a wicked grin on his face.

Before she could turn away, he winked at her.

Rivals in law and love
can cause complications and heartbreak.

CHAPTER 25

Jack walked out on the porch and stared into the dark courtyard. It was what he called deep night, since the trees blocked most of the stars. Julia was settled in her room, and he took a slow breath in an attempt to relax. Since he continued to pace around the large house, his previous attempts to relax clearly weren't working.

"Thought you were turnin' in?" McHenry interrupted his thoughts.

He turned to find the demon sitting in a rocking chair in the far corner of the porch. Jack hadn't realized he was there. *Damn.* Another example of his weakness without his wolf.

"Couldn't sleep."

McHenry leaned forward so Jack could see him in what little light shone through the window. He held a glass in his hand. "Got some whiskey, here. Grab a glass if you'd like some."

"No thanks."

"Where's your twin?" McHenry asked, gesturing to the bench.

Jack sat down. "He's close by. His wolf was restless."

Mc Henry took a sip. "You don't feel like running tonight? I know how much the forest can be a lure, especially for your wolf."

"My wolf is fine." Jack almost choked on the words. He'd never been much of a liar.

"I don't see you going far. Your first instinct is to protect Julia. I get that."

Jack bristled at his words. "What exactly do you get?"

McHenry didn't answer at first. Instead he poured some more whiskey into his glass and took another sip. "She's an amazing woman. She would bring out the protective instinct in any male. Although she wouldn't be happy to hear that. She thinks she can take care of herself."

"She can," Jack blurted. "You called her a warrior woman."

"I did, and she is. But that doesn't mean she shouldn't have someone looking out for her. And I think you've filled that spot for her now her husband is gone."

Jack sat back in shock. "Did she talk to you about Thomas?"

"No. But when she confirmed she was the woman who spoke at Tobin's trial, I realized she had been married to Thomas Cole. Those are intimidatin' shoes to fill."

Jack got up and grabbed the porch railing. "I'm not trying to fill Thomas Cole's shoes. No one can do that."

"True. I chose the wrong words. You could be a new beginning for her."

Jack turned back to him and crossed his arms. "Are you playing matchmaker?"

McHenry shrugged. "I don't think that's the title I'm going for. I'm hoping she finds peace. She's on a mission now, but once all the bad guys are put away, she's going to need to move on."

"I thought you—" Jack bit off his words. *What the hell was he doing?*

McHenry set the bottle down on the porch railing. "I won't lie to you. She's a temptation, and I haven't been tempted in a long time."

Jack gritted his teeth.

"Hold onto your wolf, Jack. I'm not going to try anything with Julia. But then I'm not one to go after a woman who's already spoken for."

Jack opened his mouth, but McHenry held up his hand to stop him. "I'm a noble bastard at times, much to my chagrin. And I can tell that you feel something for each other. If I were you, I'd step up and let her know how you feel before someone who isn't so noble decides to go after her."

Jack swallowed. "She deserves better than me."

"That's the case for most women when it comes to us men." McHenry stood. "But from what I've seen over the years, in the right relationships, men become better because of their love for their mate." McHenry held out his glass to Jack. "Here. It looks like you could use this."

Jack held the glass in his hand and swirled the liquid around for a moment before swallowing it in one shot. Heat burned a trail down his throat into his stomach, and he concentrated on it, blocking out everything else for that single moment in time.

But the burn subsided, and his thoughts returned. He couldn't deny his feelings for Julia. Hell, if McHenry saw it in less than a day, he wasn't hiding it well at all. But only after they got these supremacist bastards—and they would—would he let Julia know his feelings, wolf or no wolf.

He set the glass down on the railing and took a deep

breath to calm himself, until Julia screamed. Jack tore up the stairs with McHenry close behind. He pushed open the bedroom door and ran inside.

Julia lay thrashing on the bed. Was she having a nightmare again? But when the necklace around her neck started to glow, Jack didn't think it was as simple as that.

He reached for the necklace to yank it off.

McHenry grabbed his arm. "Don't!"

"What the hell did you do to her? The necklace is glowing."

"It's not hurting her. I cast a protection spell on it to signal if someone tried to attack Julia magically."

Jack looked around the room. "No one is here."

"It doesn't have to be a person, it can be a thing."

"Shit." Jack pulled the blanket back and scooped her up. Walking out of the room, he watched the necklace and the light faded.

McHenry walked out into the hallway with him. "It must be in her bedroom. Maybe I can sense it," he said as he reentered the room.

Julia snuggled her face into Jack's neck. "Thomas, don't leave me."

Her words tore at his insides.

"Julia, baby. Wake up."

She stiffened in his arms and then blinked up at him. "Jack?"

"You're okay."

"What happened?"

"You were having another nightmare. Do you remember what it was about?"

Julia nodded, her eyes filling. "Thomas. He was talking to me. I could hear his voice like he was with me. I have wanted to talk to him so badly, but he said horrible things. What's wrong with me?"

"I don't think it's you. McHenry thinks someone just attacked you magically."

She jerked in his arms. "What! How?"

"I don't know how. McHenry's looking around the bedroom."

Jack set Julia down on her feet even though he wanted to keep holding her in his arms. A few minutes later, McHenry strode out with a hand towel bunched together.

"What is it?" Julia asked.

McHenry opened the towel and Julia's gold pen lay in the center. "Someone cursed this."

"No!" Julia cried out, reaching for the pen.

Jack tucked her closer to him. "No, Julia, you can't touch it. We need to get it away from you."

Julia closed her eyes. "They're trying to take everything away from me."

"And we won't let them."

McHenry wrapped the towel around the pen again and headed down the hall. "I'm going to try and figure out what type of spell this is."

Jack took one of Julia's hands in his and tilted her chin up with his other hand. "You are going to be okay. I won't let them near you again."

She blinked as if his words confused her. "Can you give me a couple minutes alone?"

He wanted to scream no, but he kept his voice calm. "I don't think that's a good idea."

"I'll come downstairs soon, I promise. I just need a few minutes," she whispered before turning and heading into the bathroom.

Jack went downstairs and met Connor in the doorway.

"I met McHenry on the way to his shop. He just told me someone tried to curse Julia. Is she all right?"

"Physically she's fine. Emotionally, I don't know for sure. She needs a couple of minutes to collect herself." Jack paced in the living room. "I don't understand how this could have happened. We're supposed to be protecting her, and someone got close enough to curse her."

"Then we up our game."

"How? We're crowding her now. Do we not let her out of our sight? I don't think that's going to go over well."

Connor held up his hands. "Jack. Calm down. We'll figure it out."

Jack stepped around him and continued to pace until McHenry joined them.

"What did you find out?" Jack asked.

McHenry frowned. "It's definitely been altered magically."

Connor crossed his arms. "Can you tell what type of curse it is?"

"Not specifically, but if I had my guess, I would say it attacked her emotions. It can ramp up her fear and anxiety, and make sure she can't escape the pain."

"Shit." Connor hissed.

"Have you noticed a change in her?" McHenry asked.

Jack nodded. "She hasn't been sleeping much at all the past few days, and she had a nightmare a couple of nights ago. Are you saying it's been attacking her all this time?"

"Yes. The more she's exposed to it, the higher her anxiety levels. I'm running some tests on the pen in my workshop."

"How were you able to detect the magic?" Jack asked.

"It's infused in the metal, and that's my world of expertise."

Jack marched up to McHenry. "How do we know you didn't curse it?"

McHenry clenched his fists. "That wouldn't be smart,

now would it? Why would I curse her while she's here and can point a finger at me?"

Jack tightened his own fists. "You put some sort of spell on the damn necklace you gave her."

"Yes, but it's a protection spell. The symbol is a caim, which I told Julia meant sanctuary. But it is also a circle of protection."

"And why did you feel the need to protect her?"

McHenry's face turned red. "Because if these supremacists are as bad as you say they are, they're going to go after her. I was planning to tell her about the spell just before you left. I didn't think I needed to tell her the moment I gave it to her. I thought you two were protecting her."

Jack growled and Connor jumped between the two men.

"Enough," Connor barked. "Let's get back on the subject. What does it take to curse an object?"

"Not much," McHenry answered. "If the supernatural is powerful enough, they can place a quick curse on the object. Touchin' it would have transferred the curse to the metal."

"Who in the hell would have cursed her pen? She has it with her all the time," Jack said.

"Attorney Barr," Julia said from the doorway. "You're right, that pen is never far away from me. But I accidentally left it in his office when we spoke to him the other day, and then he gave it back to me."

"I'm going to kill him," Jack growled.

Julia shook her head. "No. We have no proof."

"We can't let him get away with this!"

"We won't. Since he cursed my pen, we now know he's part of the supremacists, and we'll bring him down with the rest of the group."

"How can you be so calm about this?" Connor asked.

Julia cleared her throat. "Because I've decided I'm done with these supremacists having power over me. I've let them control me for months. Upstairs was the last time. Not again. So we find out who besides Barr is behind this, and we make them all pay."

Jack's heart thumped. Here was his warrior woman, standing fearless in front of them. The look in her narrowed eyes said she was through being the victim. And even though her strength made him proud, it terrified him at the same time. Because not only would they need to protect her from the supremacists, but they would also need to protect Julia from herself.

Opponents can derail the most convincing arguments.

CHAPTER 26

Julia sat in the kitchen rubbing her eyes, a large mug of coffee gripped in one hand. It was early, but after the revelation about the curse last night, she hadn't gotten much sleep. From the looks of the tired faces sitting around the table, no one else got much sleep either. Connor had yet to stand up and make any attempt at breakfast.

McHenry looked especially drawn. Even after the excitement last night, he clearly hadn't forgotten that they needed to confront his nephews today. Now, more than ever, they had to find out the truth.

Bells sounded, and McHenry set down his mug and got to his feet. "That'd be the boys with the supplies." His shoulders bowed slightly, he hurried toward the front, and Julia followed him with the twins close behind.

"I thought we talked about you staying back last night," Jack said.

Julia shook her head. "You talked *at* me while you escorted me to bed. I won't get close to them, but I want to hear what they say to McHenry. Plus, if it becomes necessary, I'm probably the best interrogator of the group."

Jack's jaw muscle worked hard, as if he was biting back words. Julia turned away and kept walking. When they emerged onto the porch, they saw a cart with bells attached to the side sitting next to the workshop. It contained stacks of various metals, as well as several wooden boxes.

Next to the cart stood two young men who looked to be in their early twenties. One was tall like his uncle, but hadn't filled out yet. The other was shorter, with the beginnings of a scrawny beard. Both looked like McHenry, especially around the eyes. Eyes that were confused when they noticed the visitors in the courtyard.

McHenry gestured to the taller nephew and then the second. "Andrew and Jamie, meet Julia, Jack, and Connor. They came to talk to me about the cuffs I've been supplyin' the holding center."

Jamie perked up. "Are they going to increase the order?"

"No. There was a problem with the last set."

Andrew frowned. "What sort of problem?"

"The prisoner was able to break out of them," McHenry replied.

"That's not possible." Jamie's eyes widened.

"It's a lie," Andrew growled. "They're lying to you."

"I thought they were mistaken as well," McHenry said, "until I discovered the cuffs had been tampered with."

Andrew threw up his hands. "You know better than to trust an outsider, Uncle. This could be a trick to lure you out of the forest."

"Enough!" McHenry bellowed, going to stand in front of his nephew. "Andrew. You were the one who helped me with the cuffs for Tobin."

Jamie backed away. "What did you do, Andrew?"

"Nothing!" he seethed. "I did nothing. Why would I destroy our business?" He marched up, toe to toe with McHenry. "Do you think I would betray my own family?"

"No. But I'm trying to understand how the iron was contaminated with another metal."

"Right. Why am I not surprised that you would accuse me first? What about Jamie?"

"Me!" Jamie blurted, his voice rising an octave as he stumbled back a few more steps, away from the group and toward the house. "I'm not the one who worked on the cuffs. Besides, I wouldn't know how to add silver to the iron."

McHenry turned toward him. "I never said it was silver."

Jamie's face changed in a flash from innocent confusion to anger. Growling, he raced across the yard and up onto the porch, grabbing Julia in the blink of an eye.

Julia gasped as his fingers dug into her upper arms. He spun her around, pressing her back to his chest. *God.* Julia had never been a hostage or a human shield before. It was something she could have lived without, especially after she announced last night she was through being a victim.

Connor's clothes tore away as he flashed into his wolf. Jack lunged toward the porch, only stopping when McHenry latched arms around Jack's torso.

"Wait!"

"Let her go, or I will eviscerate you," Jack said. His voice dropping so low that it made Connor's wolf whine and the hairs on Julia's neck stand on end.

McHenry whispered something in his ear, and Jack stopped struggling. McHenry released him, and Jack stayed where he was, even though he looked like he was ready to pounce.

"Let her go, Jamie," McHenry said. "It's not too late. Help me understand why you did this, and I'll stand beside you with the magistrate. Did the supremacists threaten you? Are they blackmailing you? Tell me, and I can help. But first you need to let Julia go."

Jamie's hands tightened around Julia. He breathed heavily behind her. "Not the plan. What to do?" he whispered. *Was he talking to her?*

"Jamie, please." McHenry held out his hand. "Let me help you, son."

Jaime trembled against Julia's back, mumbling. "Wrong. Stop. No, it hurts..." He spun her around, and his eyes glistened. Just as quickly his face changed to a scowl. Julia slammed her boot into his instep, and he let her go.

"Bitch," he hissed.

He reached for her again. *No more!* She slammed the heel of her palm into his nose, and he bent over and howled in pain.

Seconds later, the wolf tackled the groaning man to the ground.

Julia stopped herself from rolling her eyes. Overkill. She'd already taken care of her would-be captor. But the thoughts drained out of her when she saw Jack stalking toward her, fury on his face and in his every move.

He scooped her up in his arms.

"Jack! Put me down." But he ignored her pleas. She grabbed on to him as he spun toward the house.

Jack stormed up on the porch, through the door, and up the stairs to the guest bedroom Julia used the night before. He was having trouble catching his breath, but it had nothing to do with exertion.

He slammed the door with Julia still in his arms and stood in the center of the room. Julia's arms were around his neck, and his muscles were so tight, he didn't want to bend over and set her down. She didn't say a word for several moments, which was a blessing, since Jack was in no shape to have a conversation. Tremors ran along his body — small jerks to remind him of what could have happened to her.

After a few more moments, Julia spoke softly. "Jack, it's okay. You can put me down now. Carrying me around is becoming a habit with you."

He set her down and stumbled back before turning and slamming his hand against the wall. Pain shot up his arm and told him to calm the hell down.

"What's wrong?" Julia asked.

He spun to face her. "What's wrong? He attacked you, and I couldn't protect you."

She frowned. "I'm a defense attorney, Jack. The minute I decided to work in a courtroom, I took self-defense classes. I followed that up with kickboxing for years. Thomas encouraged it, so I could feel safe when he wasn't around to protect me."

"I didn't protect you last night, either."

"It was a curse, Jack. There was no way you could protect me."

He reached for her, but she jerked away.

Fates, now she was scared of him. "Sorry, I was just going to help you to the sink so we can wash your hand and get a better look at it."

She looked down at her bloody hand.

"I think the blood is his. I might have broken his nose."

"Good."

She looked up at him. "Good that the blood isn't mine, or good that I broke his nose?"

"Both. Let's get you cleaned up."

He walked with her to the bathroom, careful not to crowd her again. He turned on the water and reached for her hand slowly. She nodded, and he ran it under the warm water, washing away the blood, the sight of it swirling down the drain making his own blood run cold.

He examined her palm and, other than some redness which would probably turn into a bruise, she was fine. Until he felt a slight tremble.

Looking into her face, his heart sped up. She was trying so hard to be tough, but her pupils were dilated. As if she knew she was giving herself away, she dropped her gaze. Julia had never dropped her gaze from him, ever. Even when she was royally pissed, she maintained eye contact. It was part of her arsenal.

"Julia…"

"We should check your hand. Did you break it when you slammed it into the wall?"

"No. It's fine."

She huffed at him. "It was a stupid move, Jack, and over the top, just like your brother. I busted a guy's nose, and Connor got all wolfy and tackled him after I had already taken care of him."

"Exactly. I should have been the one."

"Exactly, what? What's the big deal? Connor changed into his wolf. It made sense for one of you to stay human."

Jack closed his eyes.

"Damn it, Jack. Tell me what's wrong. It's more than me having to defend myself."

"It wasn't that I chose to stay human." He cleared his throat so he could force the words out. "I can't shift anymore." There. He said it. Now she would understand why she should stay far away from him.

She took a step closer. "What do you mean you can't shift?"

"My wolf is gone."

She flexed her hand. It was probably tender. He placed a hand towel in the sink and ran cold water over it so he could avoid looking into her shocked eyes. He didn't want to see her pity.

"How is your wolf gone?" she asked while he wrapped up her hand in the cold towel.

"I don't know."

She crouched down to force him to look her in the eyes. "Give me more than that to work with, Jack."

"I haven't been able to shift for months. Ever since I was shot."

Julia gestured for him to go on. "And..."

"And I haven't been able to communicate with my wolf for weeks."

"Since when, exactly?"

"Since around the time Sheila was attacked."

"Could it be a reaction to Dr. Williamson torturing you? He made you relive your shooting over and over again, I can't imagine what that must have been like."

"Yes, but I don't know why that matters."

Julia's eyes tightened on him. "It matters, because if we determine the cause, we can try to reverse it. Have you spoken to Darcinda?"

Jack frowned. "Now you sound like Connor."

"And based on your non-answer, I assume he did suggest it, and you haven't." She rested her uninjured hand on his arm. "Jack, if you're sick, you should go to a healer."

"What about you? You're seeing a doctor. Are you sick?" he blurted, holding his breath.

"No..." She hesitated. "I'm seeing a psychiatrist."

Shit. "I'm sorry. I shouldn't—"

"There's nothing to be sorry about. I don't know why I've been keeping it a secret. I'm not ashamed of it. Alex suggested it, actually. I need to stop dwelling in the past."

Fates, she was talking about Thomas. "Is it helping?"

"I think so. It's still early days. But I was scared to go see her. So, I get the fear, Jack. Fear of facing the unknown. Promise me you'll talk to Darcinda."

Jack nodded. He had to do something. Standing by helplessly while Connor tackled that bastard in wolf form slammed that reality home. Losing his wolf was more than losing a limb. It was half of his soul.

And if he couldn't protect Julia, then he couldn't expect her to take a risk on him.

Don't be afraid to throw the contract out and start fresh.

CHAPTER 27

Julia stood on the porch watching Jack and Connor guard Jamie in the courtyard. Connor's wolf paced around the young man where he huddled on the ground.

Blood spattered his shirt. His nose was swollen, and bruises were starting to show beneath each eye. Julia felt bad about it now, but she didn't know what he would have done to her, so she had to let it go. He had to be in pain, but he didn't show it. Simply sat there and stared into space, as if he was unaware of the world around him. Jack continued to ask him questions, but Jamie didn't utter a word or acknowledge Jack at all.

Once Andrew recovered from the shock, McHenry sent him for the forest magistrate and then went into his workshop. He still hadn't come back out.

After a few more minutes, Julia went over to the workshop and peeked in the door. McHenry worked at his forge, dipping something into the molten coals. After a minute, he pulled the strip of metal out and laid it on the anvil, shaping it on the side with the round edges. She watched in silence as he manipulated the metal into a circle. Then he immersed it in the water until steam boiled out. Next he set it on the workbench and attached it to links on a matching cuff.

"I never thought I would make a set of these for my own nephew," he said, keeping his eyes on his work.

"I'm sorry."

"There's nothin' for you to be sorry about. He attacked you." McHenry glanced up. "He didn't hurt you, did he?"

"No."

He filed one of the cuffs. "I'm glad, for both your sake and his. Jack would have killed him if he'd truly hurt you."

"Jack's still interrogating Jamie right now. He's not talking."

"He wouldn't answer any of my questions earlier, either," McHenry said as he held up the cuffs to inspect them.

"Tell me about Jamie."

McHenry sighed as he set down the metal with a resounding clink on the workbench. "What do you want me to say? That yesterday when you came to me with proof that the cuffs had been tampered with, I still didn't believe my nephews would do this. And Jamie? His heart takes up most of his chest. As a child, he used to bring home injured forest animals to care for them until they were strong enough to fend for themselves. Does that sound like a member of the supremacist gang to you?"

"No."

McHenry paced across the workshop floor, head down. "But then he attacked you."

Julia looked out into the courtyard. Jamie sat on the ground in the exact position he'd been in when she went into McHenry's workshop.

"I think something's wrong with him. Come look at him."

McHenry hesitated.

"Come here, please."

He stood next to her and studied his nephew.

"He hasn't moved at all. It's almost like he's in a fugue state."

"Or is he just bein' stubborn?" McHenry said.

"No. I've questioned a lot of people over the years, and he's not faking whatever is going on right now. When he was holding me hostage earlier, he was mumbling to himself, almost as if he was having an argument with someone."

McHenry strode out of the workshop and across the courtyard until he knelt in front of his nephew. Julia watched from several feet away.

"Jamie." He stared at him hard. "Jamie!" he bellowed.

Jack watched the exchange with his arms crossed. "It's no use. He's not conscious of what's going on around him."

McHenry closed his eyes and took some deep breaths. After a moment, he opened his eyes and got up from his crouched position. "I sense some sort of power around him, but I can't identify what it is."

Julia frowned. "Are you saying someone did this to him?"

"Possibly," McHenry answered. "But I'm not sure what set him off."

"Maybe because we questioned him, and he realized he slipped up?" Jack volunteered.

McHenry looked down at Jamie. "But why is he not talking now?"

"If it's magically induced, could they have set up a fail-safe spell or device to stop him from talking if he was caught?" Julia asked.

"Yes." McHenry turned to her. "Hopefully it's something that can be reversed."

"When we leave the forest, we'll take him to a healer."

"We have healers in the forest." McHenry's scowl deepened.

"He's coming with us," Jack said. "We'll take him to a healer, and then question him. We have to stop these supremacists, McHenry. It was bad enough in the past when their gang was made up of volunteers. If Jamie has truly been coerced by magic to work for the gang, then we have even bigger problems on our hands. We have to stop this."

"No offense, wolf, but I don't trust you with my nephew."

"Jack won't hurt him," Julia said.

"I can't promise that," Jack responded. "Not if he touches Julia again."

"You can come with us and watch over him," Julia offered, hoping to calm McHenry.

Color drained from McHenry's face, until it looked like it was carved in stone. "I don't leave the forest."

Before Julia could question him further, Andrew walked into the courtyard with another man. Introductions were made, and the events were relayed to the magistrate, who agreed that Jamie would be placed in the custody of Jack and Connor. Andrew volunteered to go as well, so he could look out for his brother.

Julia turned away when McHenry placed the cuffs on Jamie's wrists, the tortured look on McHenry's face more than she could bear.

As they got ready to leave, Julia went over to McHenry and laid her hand on his large arm. "We'll get to the bottom of this, I promise."

McHenry nodded and, without a word, turned and disappeared into his workshop.

The group left in a loose formation. Connor's wolf led, followed by Andrew and the magistrate, who escorted Jamie. Jamie stumbled along between them, but if one or the other wasn't touching him, he would stop. Andrew kept his hand on his brother's arm and guided him forward.

Jack and Julia brought up the rear.

"I hope Darcinda can help Jamie. I feel bad about punching him."

Jack shook his head. "Even if he isn't fully in control of what he's doing, he still could have hurt you. You did the right thing."

"Have you seen anything like this before?" Julia asked.

"No." Jack lifted a branch out of her way. "Not this severe. Vampires can thrall humans, and certain control spells can be used, but I've never seen one that incapacitates someone like this."

"Maybe Darcinda will know. She's an amazing healer."

Jack looked sideways at her. "Julia."

"What?" she asked, widening her eyes.

"You're not being very subtle right now. Until recently, I would have said you've been spending too much time with Alex, but I think you can stand on your own when it comes to manipulating people."

Julia shrugged. "It's the lawyer in me."

"It's the stubborn woman in you."

"That, too. I'm not going to spend the rest of my life sitting on the sidelines."

He stopped and turned to her. "I can't imagine you have ever been on the sidelines."

"Not with you," she realized with surprise. "But before that, I was spending quite a bit of time there."

His blue eyes studied her for a moment. "You're allowed to let others take over."

"I could say the same for you."

He blew out a hard breath. "I see why you make a good lawyer."

She smiled as they started to walk again. "I use whatever tools are handy."

"Okay. Point taken. I'll talk to Darcinda."

"Thank you." Julia's heartbeat slowed at his agreement. She had been trying to play it calm, but inside she was having a hard time not grabbing him by the arms and shaking him. He needed help, and she wasn't going to let him back away. It was too important.

He was too important...and that scared her more than she cared to admit.

Jack came to a stop by the magistrate, who held up his hand.

"This is as far as I'm going to go. Your team should be waiting for you. I had one of my deputies travel out of the forest earlier and contact them about picking up the prisoner. I wanted you to have backup. I didn't realize the state Jamie was in until I arrived at McHenry's."

"Thanks for your help," Jack said.

After they crossed through the shimmering wall of light, they found Devin and Giz standing on the other side.

The two were introduced to Andrew, and then everyone was brought up to speed about what happened with the curse and Jamie while they headed back to their vehicles. Giz secured Jamie in the team van and Andrew crawled in beside him.

Giz then opened the back door of the van and pulled out a duffel. "Charlie's watching over the ladies at the wedding planner office, but he sent this along. Figured one or the other of you would have wolfed out and lost your clothes, so he packed extra."

A flash of light came from Julia's right, followed by Connor's voice. "Thanks, man."

Devin and Jack both turned Julia in the other direction. She shook her head. "I'm an adult, guys. I can handle seeing a naked man."

"Yeah, she can handle seeing a naked man," Connor called out.

"Shut it, Connor," Jack growled. He was going to have to kill his brother one of these days.

Julia sighed. "I think we should contact Darcinda and see if she can examine Jamie right away."

"Agreed," Devin said. "We'll see where she can meet us. I'm not comfortable taking him to her house. He's still a prisoner, even if he doesn't appear to be cognizant of his surroundings."

An hour later they arrived at the healing center where Darcinda asked them to meet her. She joined them in what looked like a large living room.

"What happened to him?" Darcinda asked as she held her hands over his head for a moment.

"We were questioning him about tampering with the cuffs used on Tobin," Connor explained. "At first, he was totally convincing that he didn't know anything. Then, when he slipped up and we realized he was guilty, he grabbed Julia and threatened her."

Julia spoke up. "While he was holding me, it was as if he was arguing with himself about what he was doing. Like he had a split personality or something."

Darcinda nodded. "Okay. I'm going to take him into one of the healing rooms. Give me some time to examine him."

"Someone should go with you," Devin said.

"He won't hurt me," Darcinda said with a twinkle in her eyes.

"Even so," Devin insisted. "I would feel better if someone was in the room with you."

"I'll go with her," Andrew volunteered. "I want to hear what she has to say about my brother." He led Jamie down the hall to the healing room.

Devin motioned for the group to sit down. Julia, Jack, and Connor sat on the couch, with Giz taking a seat across from them.

Devin stood at the stone fireplace and kicked off the conversation. "Tell us about McHenry. Are we sure he's not involved in this?"

"He's not," Julia said. "He's just a bit egotistical."

"A bit," Jack mumbled under his breath.

"But he's not responsible for what happened. The man is a true craftsman, an artist."

Jack snorted. He couldn't help himself. Listening to Julia go on about McHenry made him want to punch something.

Devin looked between Jack and Julia with a smirk on his face. If he kept that up, Jack would end up punching something sooner rather than later.

Devin cleared his throat as if to get back to business, or maybe to stop a laugh from leaking out. Either way, Jack was glad he didn't have to hurt him.

Devin continued. "While you guys were in the forest, we were able to review the film from Julia's office building. We IDed the guy who delivered flowers to Savannah."

"Who is he?" Jack asked.

Giz held up a tablet and turned it around. A still photo of a man stared back at them. "Marcus Hamilton. A gargoyle. Unfortunately, that's about all we know about him. There is no current address on file. According to his tribe, he's a loner who doesn't participate in their group activities."

Devin continued. "Charlie and I interviewed his family, and several stated that he's become increasingly negative about the way things are now between the various races."

"And no one thought to bring it to the attention of the Tribunal?" Connor asked.

"They didn't think he was involved with the supremacists. They believed the Vipera had all been captured," Devin answered.

"So how do we find him?" Julia asked.

Giz set the tablet down. "I've been working on a locator spell. It's a long shot, since I need an object that belongs to Marcus. What I have is a jacket he hasn't worn in several years. One of his cousins gave it to me."

Julia straightened. "I don't want to go too far off topic, but how is Savannah doing?"

"She's home now," Devin said. "Godfrey's been watching her like a hawk. He's been hesitant to let us talk to her while she's recuperating."

Julia smiled. "Oh, Lord. Savannah is probably going crazy by now. She will throttle him if he keeps babying her. Maybe I should go for a visit to see how she's doing, and if we happen to talk about the incident, then all the better."

Devin nodded. "Diabolical, but worth it. Charlie and I have been keeping an eye on the holding center as well. We don't want another escape attempt from Tobin. We've also been working on a covert transfer to the Elven Prison. The fewer people who know what's going on, the better."

Darcinda entered the room, followed by Andrew. From their serious expressions, the news was not good.

"How is Jamie?" Julia asked.

"I've put him under a sleeping spell."

Before Devin could protest, she held up her hand. "I can pull him out at any time, but I thought maybe if we could get him to relax, it might help release him."

"Release him from what?" Jack asked.

"That's the problem. I don't know for sure. I can tell you that there is something—or someone—controlling him. He's not faking it. When I tried to touch his thoughts, I was shoved away quite violently."

"Are you okay?" Devin asked.

"I'll be fine," Darcinda answered. "I've been able to determine that he's not under a vampire's thrall. I also don't think a spell could exert this much control over him. It's something that is controlling him so completely even his speech and motor skills have been impacted. I'm going to keep working to figure out what it is." She paused. "I'm afraid that if I don't figure out something soon, the control will eventually be irreversible, or kill him."

Jack drummed his fingers on the couch arm. How were they ever going to be able to stop these bastards if they couldn't get a break in this case?

Devin doled out assignments to Giz before telling Julia, Connor, and Jack to get some rest for a couple of hours. The team disbanded, leaving Julia, Jack, and Connor in the room.

Jack started for the door.

"Where are you going?" Julia asked.

"You heard Devin, I'm not going to rest, but I am going to get cleaned up so we can go visit Savannah. I assumed you would be chafing at the bit to do the same thing."

"You agreed to have Darcinda examine you."

"You told her about your wolf?" Connor blurted.

"Yes, I told her. But you heard Darcinda. She needs to figure out what's going on with Jamie. I don't want to distract her from that."

"Jamie is sleeping right now. She has time to examine you."

"Julia—"

"She's right, bro," Connor interjected. "It's time to figure out what's going on."

Damn. When they tag-teamed him, he knew it was a lost cause. He had never met two more stubborn people in his life.

Darcinda stood in front of him with her eyes closed and her arms raised. Jack looked over at Connor, who sat to his right. The wait was killing him. Now that he had decided to talk to Darcinda, his patience had evaporated.

"What do you think?"

She opened her eyes and gave him a puzzled look.

"My wolf?" he pushed.

"The good news is that it's still there."

Beside him, Connor let out a gust of air. "That's a very good thing."

Darcinda nodded.

"But..." Jack asked.

"But, I don't know why your wolf is not responding to you. It doesn't feel magically driven, like it would if someone had attacked your wolf. Physically, your wolf feels fine."

"So you're telling me it's psychological? My wolf is having some sort of breakdown?"

"I'm telling you something is stopping your wolf from coming to the forefront. I'm not sure how to help you, but I'm going to keep working on a solution."

"Could it be PTSD?" Julia asked.

Jack shook his head. "Come on, Julia."

"What? You were shot and almost died, and then

you were forced to relive the trauma repeatedly. Why is PTSD beyond the realm of possibility?"

"It's possible," Darcinda said. "Your wolf is a sentient being. However, he might not understand what happened to him during your torture."

"So now my wolf has PTSD."

"Anything's possible, Jack. I'll do some research on PTSD as well, and let you know what I find. There are some spells that might let me speak to your wolf, but I will have to confer with some other healers first."

Jack shook his head. "Jamie is first priority right now."

"I agree," Darcinda said. "But that doesn't mean I can't multi-task. 'I am woman, hear me roar,' and all that."

Jack chuckled. "Why am I surrounded by headstrong women?"

"Just lucky, I guess," Julia chimed in.

Connor laughed out loud. "Give it up, Jack. There's no fighting it."

He stared into Julia's dancing eyes. "Isn't that the truth?"

Compromise is at the heart of every negotiation
and every happy couple.

CHAPTER 28

Julia walked up to the door, each step an attempt to keep her patience in check. It had been too late yesterday to visit Savannah, and it had practically taken an act of God for Godfrey to agree to Julia's visit today. She turned to look at the stubborn bookends behind her. Was it really too much to ask to go alone to see Savannah? Could they not wait in the car, for goodness' sake?

"Guys, Godfrey is going to flip out if you start interrogating Savannah."

"If he asks about why we're here, just make something up about us being too overprotective," Connor said.

"How exactly is that made up?"

Jack grabbed her arms and turned her around. "Knock."

"Brute."

Connor laughed behind her as she knocked on the door. After a few moments, Godfrey answered the door.

She stared at him in shock. She had never seen him

outside the courthouse and his designer suits. Today he had on a pair of jeans with a brown Henley shirt that brought out his eyes. Eyes that narrowed at the two men standing behind her.

He crossed his arms, and Julia saw his lawyer face slip on. "When I said you could come over, Julia, I didn't know you were bringing the team with you."

"I'm sorry. I didn't realize I would be bringing the twins, but they refuse to let me go places on my own right now. They are being ridiculous."

"They're protecting you," Godfrey said. "I understand that feeling firsthand. If only my wife would be more understanding."

Julia nodded. "You know Savannah. She's probably just going stir crazy. Let me go spend some time with her while you guys compare caveman notes."

Jack frowned. "You're not funny."

A voice spoke up from across the room. "Actually, she's hilarious," Savannah said from a doorway.

Godfrey headed toward her, but Savannah held up her hand. "I swear, G, if you come to help me back to the couch, I will never have sex with you again."

Godfrey froze in mid-step. *Smart man.*

Connor and Jack both choked back a laugh.

"Nothing is funny here, Frick and Frack. Spend some time with my husband while I have some girl bonding time with Julia."

The twins' mouths snapped shut, their eyes widening.

Savannah reached for Julia's hand and dragged her into the den, shutting the door with a decided thump. "Thank God you're here. I'm going to kill him, Julia. I love him, but that doesn't mean I won't take him out if he makes me one more cup of tea."

Julia laughed. "It's cute that you call him G."

"Well, I sure as hell am not shortening his name to God, even though he's egotistical enough."

Julia squeezed her hand. "I figured you were going crazy by now."

Savannah gestured for her to take a seat. "I knew when I married him that he would be protective. He can't help it with his wolf, but WOW. He is suffocating me, and that makes me want to smother him with a pillow. But maybe I don't have it as bad as you do."

Julia looked at her in confusion. "What do you mean?"

"I have one hovering wolf, it looks like you have two. And they're identical. Do they do everything together?" she asked, waggling her eyes.

Julia's mouth fell open. "Savannah!"

"What, a girl can't live vicariously through someone else? G has been treating me like I'm made of porcelain. He hasn't even kissed me in days."

"TMI. I have to face Godfrey in the courtroom, I don't need to think about your sex life when I'm trying to win a case."

"Why not? I'm thinking about your sex life right now."

"I don't have a sex life!"

"That's a crying shame, dear. The wonder twins look scrumptious."

Julia rubbed a hand over her face to hide the blush.

A knock at the door saved Julia from further mortification. Godfrey poked his head into the room. "Do you two need anything? I could make you a cup of—"

"Finish that sentence and your nookie days are over. Now go play with your wolf friends, sweetie, while we have some girl time."

The door shut promptly.

"We need to figure out how to keep you from murdering your husband. Pronto."

"Agreed. Which means getting these creeps arrested. How is the investigation going?"

Julia filled her in on what happened over the last few days, swallowing hard when Savannah pulled out a pen and pad of paper from the side table to take notes. The same thing Julia had done hundreds of times before, using the pen Thomas gave her. Savannah interrupted her downward spiral.

"Huh, not too promising right now. So you decided to come interview me."

"I wanted to check on you too, but I won't lie and tell you I didn't also want to find out what you know."

Savannah shrugged. "I don't blame you. The faster we get this case solved, the faster I can get my life back."

"On the day you received the flowers, what happened?"

"Nothing out of the ordinary. I had a light day scheduled since I was leaving early for our anniversary dinner. When the flowers arrived, I assumed they were from G. I called him and was opening the box and pulling out one of the flowers to smell it when he told me he didn't send the flowers. By then I started to feel dizzy, and I don't remember much of anything after that until I woke up in the healing center."

"Was there a card with the box?"

"Yeah, it said, 'Happy Anniversary.'"

"Then whoever planned this knew it was your anniversary. How?"

Savannah frowned. "The supremacists tried to sabotage our wedding two years ago."

"True, but do you honestly think they're keeping a calendar of all the wedding dates they sabotaged? It just seems like too big a coincidence that the flowers were sent on your anniversary. Who would have known?"

"Good question. We had a large wedding, but I don't remember anniversary dates years after I attend a wedding."

Julia leaned forward. "Me either."

"I understand they sent you flowers, too."

"Yeah. Set them on my front porch with a note from Thomas."

"Sickos." Savannah looked out the window. "Ok, so let's back up and start again. Maybe we've missed something."

"Did you meet the delivery man?" Julia asked.

"I saw him from behind as he left the office."

Julia pulled her phone out and showed Savannah the picture Giz sent her. "Do you recognize him? Name is Marcus Hamilton. He's a gargoyle."

Savannah looked at the picture for several seconds and pursed her lips. "He looks familiar to me, but I don't know where I've seen him before." She shook her head. "I can't place him, and the name isn't familiar, either."

"Don't force it. Look at him while we brainstorm some ideas about where you might have seen him."

Savannah smiled at her. "Are you lawyering me right now?"

"Damn straight." Julia smiled in return. "You know the drill, but I'm going to lead you through it anyway. Is he a former client? Or someone you've seen at the courthouse?"

"No."

"Is he someone you have seen in the grocery store?"

Savannah shrugged. "I have our groceries delivered. Somewhat snooty, I know, but with our two schedules, it's a life-saver."

"What about exercise class? Or any other groups you belong to?"

Savannah shook her head.

"Other businesses, like the car repair shop, or any businesses you frequent? Clothing stores, bookstores, the post office?"

Savannah ran her finger over the phone screen to look at the guy again. "Nope, nope, and nope. Damn."

"Okay, we can come back to him later. Let's go back to the flowers. Did Margaret give you the flowers?"

"No, they were sitting on the table outside my office."

"Is that where you would expect them to be?"

Savannah shook her head. "No. Normally Margaret brings things into my office."

"So instead of bringing them into your office, she called you to come get them. Why?"

"She was getting ready to leave. I told her she could leave early that day as well."

"Okay. What time did you receive the flowers?"

"I hung up at three-thirty from the call. I remember, because I made a note in my calendar so I could charge for the time. Margaret buzzed me a second later to tell me that flowers had just been delivered. I walked out into the reception area as the guy left. Margaret had shut down for the day and was also heading toward the door."

"She couldn't wait a few seconds to say goodbye or to see if you needed anything? And she didn't wait to see you open the flowers?"

"No, why?" Savannah asked.

"No offense, but based on the dealings I've had with Margaret, she's one of the nosiest people on the planet. It seems strange that she wouldn't have waited a few seconds to see the flowers." Julia tapped her hand on her leg. "Something is not adding up."

Julia held out her hand, and Savannah handed her the phone. Julia looked at the picture again. "What time did you say the flowers arrived?"

"Three-thirty, why?"

"Because this picture was taken in the hall outside your office, and it is timestamped at three-ten. Why did he go into your office and wait for twenty minutes before leaving again?"

Savannah frowned. "If he asked for me and Margaret told him I was busy, he might have been afraid she would open the flowers instead?"

"Okay, but that doesn't explain how he stayed in the room for twenty minutes. Was he chatting her up so he could stay until he made sure you got the flowers? And if she was getting ready to leave, I wouldn't think that she would spend twenty minutes talking to some random delivery guy."

"No, especially since she has a boyfriend." Savannah's eyes widened "Shit!"

"What is it?"

"I know where I've seen this guy before. Margaret showed me a picture of a recent boating trip. She was on a sailboat with some friends and her boyfriend." Savannah scowled as she reached for the phone and looked at the screen again. "Yep, that's him, but his name was not Marcus Hamilton. She said it was Todd something or other."

"Okay, so we have another lead. And Margaret knew it was your anniversary."

"If Margaret is involved in this, G isn't the only one who needs to worry about their health." Savannah stood and paced around the couch. "Let's figure out our next steps."

When Savannah calmed down enough to sit next to Julia, they put their plan together.

Now they had to convince the cavemen in the other room to help set the plan in motion.

"G!" Savannah yelled.

Godfrey flung open the door and tore inside with Connor and Jack right behind him. "What's wrong?"

Savannah smiled at him. "You came in even after I threatened you."

"Woman, your safety is my first priority. Always."

"And I love you for it. But now I need you to listen and keep an open mind about what I'm about to say."

Godfrey closed his eyes. "You're scaring me."

"*Now* she's scaring you?" Connor blurted. "She's scared me since the moment we walked into the house."

Savannah laughed out loud. "Smart wolf. Now let us get you up to speed on what we figured out about the case."

Julia and Savannah repeated their conversation to the three men. The more they talked, the more Godfrey's face turned ferocious, his wolf threatening to break through the surface.

"Are you telling me you think Margaret is part of this?" Godfrey asked, his voice a low rumble.

Savannah sighed. "I don't know. I hope not. I think at the very least she is being used by this Marcus Hamilton. If that's the case, then she could have told him about our anniversary. It makes sense that the supremacists would try to infiltrate your office to see what was going on with the trial. And if they couldn't get close to you, they might try to get information through me, right?"

Godfrey grabbed her and pulled her into an embrace. "I never meant for someone to use you to get to me."

Savannah rubbed her hands up and down his back. "I know. It's okay. At least we have a lead now and can go after him. I think the key is talking to Margaret. I don't want to call her on a Sunday, because it might spook her. Tomorrow morning, I'll go into the office."

Godfrey stiffened. "Hell, no, you're not."

Savannah backed up. "G. I need to do this. If Margaret is involved, and if you or the twin mountains behind you question her, it's going to backfire. If I talk to her, it won't seem too weird, right? I'll stop in the office and tell her I'm grabbing some of my things to catch up on work at home while I recuperate."

"I'm not letting you go alone," Godfrey growled.

Julia continued. "She won't be alone. I'm going to go with her as her designated driver. I'll tell Margaret I'm helping Savannah with her cases. We'll have a little girl talk with her, and see what she's willing to tell us. If she isn't cooperative, then you guys can interrogate her."

"Julia," Jack grumbled.

"You guys can wait in the hall while we talk to her. That way you can be there in a heartbeat if we need you."

When they all looked like they were going to argue, Julia held up her hands. "This is the first break we've had in this case so far. We have to play it through, or things will never get back to normal."

"You want things to go back to normal, don't you, G?" Savannah placed her palms on each side of Godfrey's face and stood on tiptoe to kiss him softly on the lips.

"Scary woman," Connor mumbled.

Jack gave Julia a hard look. "She's not the only one."

If a guy looks too good to be true, odds are he is.
Make sure to read the fine print.

CHAPTER 29

What's worse than two overprotective men? *Three.* Julia glanced at Savannah as they walked down the hall. They rolled their eyes at each other while testosterone saturated the air in a corridor much too narrow for five people.

When they reached the office door, Savannah turned, held her hands up, and spoke softly to the men. "We agreed that you would stay out here while Julia and I have girl bonding time with Margaret."

Godfrey opened his mouth, and Savannah shook her head. "We'll be fine, G. You're right outside the door. If we need you, I'll call out. You know I have no trouble raising my voice."

He grinned at her. "Yes ma'am."

Julia looked at the twins. "What she said."

Connor smirked. "You do know we'll be able to hear every word without you having to yell."

Savannah nodded. "I'm well aware of your wolfy hearing. I was just making a point to my nervous-Nellie husband."

Savannah opened the office door, and Julia followed

her into the reception area. Margaret was at her desk, and jumped to her feet when she caught sight of Savannah.

"Savannah! It's so good to see you. How are you feeling?"

"I'm doing much better. I'm just here to grab a few things. I'm lucky I was able to escape Godfrey's clutches long enough to come in today."

"He's just worried about you," Margaret said. "When he called and told me you were so sick, he sounded panicked."

"He's a good husband, just a little too bossy for his own good." Savannah gestured to Julia. "Julia is going to handle some time-sensitive things for me over the next couple of days."

Margaret's eyes widened. "So when do you think you'll be back to work full-time?"

"I'm going to be working from home for a few days, until I get my strength back. I'll be able to call and email you with assignments."

"Of course." Margaret grabbed a stack of messages. "I rescheduled your meetings this week, and also reviewed these messages and prioritized them into stacks for you."

"Thanks. I know it's been crazy for you. I'm sorry you had to spend extra time at work and missed out on anything with your friends or boyfriend."

Margaret shook her head. "Todd totally understands. He is so considerate. He keeps asking me how you're doing."

Julia gritted her teeth. She wanted to find this gargoyle and kick his stony butt.

"That was nice of him," Savannah commented in a calm voice.

Julia glanced at her. Savannah had slipped into lawyer mode. Julia recognized it, because she used it herself in the courtroom. Little emotion showed on Savannah's face, but Julia doubted the same could be said about what was going on inside.

Savannah started to look through her messages, which gave Julia an opportunity to pick up the conversation.

Julia smiled at Margaret. "I didn't know you have a boyfriend. How long have you been going out?"

"About two months now."

Convenient, since that was the same time as the start of the supremacist trial. "How did you meet?"

"I went to Murphy's Pub after work and Todd bought me a couple of drinks. We got to talking, and he asked me out. He's been so sweet. He's interested in me, you know? I mean, he asks me about work, and listens when I talk to him about it."

Of course he does. Julia glanced over at Savannah, who had crumpled a handful of messages in her fist.

Julia leaned up against the desk. "It's rare to find a man who will listen to you. How do you know he's listening and not faking it?"

"Because he asks me all sorts of questions. He didn't know what a paralegal does, so I had to explain everything to him. He's thinking about going back to school, and is interested in law, so he asks about what Savannah does as well." Margaret smiled at her boss. "I've told him you and Godfrey are super lawyers."

Savannah interrupted. "He's asked about Godfrey?"

"Yep. I mean the DA's offices are portrayed on TV all the time, and Todd is fascinated by it."

"I'm surprised you haven't brought him into the office to show him around," Savannah said.

Margaret's smile faltered slightly. "Um. Actually, he did come in here once."

"Really? I would have been glad to speak to him about a law career."

"I know you would have, but it happened to be the day you were leaving early for your anniversary. He actually delivered your flowers that day."

"What a small world," Savannah said. "I didn't know he works for a flower shop."

Margaret bit her lip. "I wasn't supposed to say anything about it. He was helping out a friend who got behind on his deliveries, and when Todd found out flowers needed to be delivered here, he volunteered."

"Why weren't you supposed to say anything?" Julia asked.

"Because he didn't want to get his friend fired from his job."

Damn. This guy was good in a very, *very* bad way.

"He sounds like a gem," Julia prompted. "When you see him again, can you ask him if he has a single brother?"

Margaret laughed. "I'm seeing him after work. I can ask him then."

Jackpot! Julia's nerves danced along her skin. Now, how to ask where they were meeting without sounding like a stalker?

Savannah spoke before Julia could formulate a plan. "Where are you two going? I would love to pay for your meal after all the hard work you've been doing here."

Margaret held up her hands. "That's not necessary."

"I insist," Savannah said a little more forcefully than necessary, but she pasted a sincere-looking smile on her face.

"We're just going to Murphy's for burgers and a beer right after work. Todd works nights, so we have to make an early meal of it."

Of course they had to make an early night of it. He couldn't exactly explain why his sorry ass turned into stone after the sun went down, now could he?

Savannah turned to Julia. "Why don't you head back to your office, and I'll join you in a few minutes. I'm going to grab my laptop and some files to take home."

Julia said her goodbyes and headed out the door. She found three anxious men in the hall. Who could have imagined werewolves tended to hover?

Godfrey remained by the door to listen to Savannah while Julia beckoned the twins down the hall so they could talk.

"Did you hear everything?"

Connor nodded and held up his phone. "I'm going to call the team and let them know to get ready for a stakeout."

Jack scowled at Connor's retreating back. She had forgotten about his wolf. He probably didn't hear a thing that happened in the office.

"I don't think Margaret's in on it. Her so-called boyfriend is using her to gather intel. The good news is that she's meeting him for dinner after work at Murphy's Pub, so we can grab him."

"There is no *we*," Jack said. "You will be far away from the pub."

"Fine."

Jack's eyes widened. "What did you say?"

"I said fine."

He crossed his arms. "That was too easy. What are you up to?"

"Nothing. You guys go grab him, and I won't get in your way."

"But?" he asked.

"I want to be at the interrogation," Julia answered.

"Fine."

She smiled. "But?"

"You can watch, but not interact with him."

"Are you sure you're not a lawyer underneath that scowling exterior?"

"Nope. I'm a man of few to no words. I'll leave the wordplay to you."

"Which is why you should let me interrogate him."

"Enough, woman. You're not getting more out of me."

It had been so long since she had bantered with anyone. Julia's smile widened. "We'll just see about that."

When they're not backed up by action,
words are meaningless in law and in love.

CHAPTER 30

Jack shoved his fists into his pockets so he wouldn't punch something. Grabbing Marcus in the pub was a nonevent, but now they were being paid back by the Fates. He turned back to the computer screens Giz had set up to watch and film the interrogation room. Julia sat beside him, huffing every time Marcus refused to answer questions. She was going to hyperventilate soon if she didn't watch it.

Devin and Charlie had spent the past thirty minutes talking to a brick wall, pun intended. Gargoyles were notoriously closemouthed, and Marcus was not straying from that perception, other than being a cocky bastard, which made Jack want to punch something again.

Since that wasn't productive, it was time to take action. Before they grabbed Marcus, Jack stopped at a store to buy a few items they might need if Marcus wasn't cooperative.

"Be right back. Need to get something out of the car."

Julia nodded, not taking her eyes off the computer screen while she took notes of the interrogation. Not that there was much to write down. But it was distracting her for the moment, which was a plus.

He went to the SUV and took a small duffel out of the back, yanking off the price tag. He had bought it to both carry and conceal his newest toys. He couldn't exactly parade around with them in front of the team. Maybe he wouldn't have to resort to using them if Marcus cooperated, but by the time he got back in, Marcus's attitude had ramped up to obnoxious times a thousand.

Marcus's lip curled up like a twisted Elvis impersonator as he glared at Devin and Charlie. "I'm not telling you shit."

"That's a mistake," Devin warned.

"Why, exactly? It's not like you're going to do anything to me."

Devin frowned. "You don't think prison for life is bad enough?"

"You won't be able to keep us in there. You couldn't keep Tobin in cuffs in a roomful of guards."

Devin stood and walked out, and Charlie followed. Jack watched Marcus on the screen. The cocky ass leaned back in the chair like he was watching his flat screen on game day.

Jack was done. Time to finish this. Words weren't working. And since words weren't his forte, action was required.

Julia tapped her pen on her notepad. The plastic click pen felt strange in her hand, but she wasn't going to let it get to her. Let *them* get to her. No more emotions wasted on the supremacists. Devin and Charlie joined them at the table strewn with Giz's tech toys and monitors.

Devin rubbed his hand over his face. "Shit. He's a tough one. I'm not sure what to try next."

"Maybe someone else should go in there and talk to him. Shake things up a bit. It couldn't hurt. What do you think, Jack?" Julia turned, only to find him gone. "Jack?"

The door closed to the interrogation room. Julia and the team turned back to the monitors. Jack strode to the table and stared down at Marcus.

Marcus sat farther back in his chair as if to demonstrate how relaxed he was. "You missed tea time. Your friends already tried. I'm not talking."

Jack set down a small duffel on the table. "I'm not here to talk." He looked at the clock on the wall. "The sun has been down for about an hour now. I understand that at some point tonight you'll need to turn into your other form, correct?"

Marcus shook his head. "I don't have to turn tonight."

Jack's right eyebrow rose. "That would be a feat, but even if you could hold off, I doubt you can do it again tomorrow night."

"So what?"

Jack pulled out a chisel and a mallet, dropping the bag on the floor.

Marcus jerked upright. "What the hell?"

"Like I said, I'm not here to talk. When you turn into stone, I'm going to try out my new tools."

Julia gaped at the monitors.

"Holy shit," Charlie mumbled.

"You're bluffing," Marcus said. "You guys don't hurt people."

Jack gripped the tools in his hands. "I want you to look me in the eye and see if I'm bluffing. You tried to kill two women this week. I don't do tea parties, and I am sick of you bastards, so it's time to take things into my own hands."

"Devin?" Giz whispered, although Julia wasn't sure what he was whispering for. "Do you think you should go in there?"

Devin crossed his arms. "I'm going to let Jack play this out some more." He grinned. "If I didn't know that Connor was watching over Alex, Sheila, and Peggy right now, I would think he was the one in that room. I would expect something like this from him or Charlie, not Jack."

"I'm right here," Charlie grumbled.

"You're just jealous because you didn't think of it first," Devin said.

"Maybe."

Julia held up her hand. "Shhh. I want to hear what's going on."

Except it was quiet in the interrogation room. Jack stared Marcus down until he looked away.

Jack rolled the chisel around in his hand. "I hear that the need to change for a gargoyle can turn into something almost painful."

"You don't scare me."

He shrugged. "Don't care if you're scared or not." Jack rapped the mallet on the table with a hard thunk, and Marcus jerked.

"I always wondered if you guys feel pain in your stone form."

"You're crazy."

"Takes one to know one." Jack gave Marcus a feral smile, and Julia's blood chilled.

Marcus's eyes darted to the door. "Where are your teammates?"

"They're going home. I'm guarding you tonight."

Marcus tried to stand, but his cuffs held him in the chair. "I want to talk to the others."

"No."

"Hey!" Marcus yelled. "Don't leave me with this guy! Hey!"

"Devin?" Julia asked. Now she was whispering.

Devin held up his hand. "Let's wait a little longer."

Jack scraped the chisel along the metal table with a sickening screech.

Marcus jerked his cuffs against the chair harder. "Hey! Don't leave me! I'll tell you what you want to know, don't leave me here!"

Giz and Charlie high-fived while Julia forced herself to take slow, deep breaths to keep from hyperventilating.

Devin grinned. "Gotcha." He went over and opened the interrogation room door. "What's all the yelling about?"

Julia sighed, and Charlie chuckled when she scrunched up her face at him.

"You guys should be actors."

"If it gets our gargoyle to sing, we're happy to put on an act."

Twenty minutes later, Julia had to agree with Charlie. Boy, could the gargoyle sing. It didn't hurt that Jack stayed in the room, periodically tapping the table with his mallet while Devin talked to Marcus.

Julia took notes, even though Giz recorded the conversation. Recording her impressions along with the facts would help her later.

Giz was already researching the five supremacists Marcus named. The best part was, the Vipera was scheduled to meet tomorrow night. If the team could grab them, it might mean the supremacists' reign of terror would soon be over, but Julia didn't want to get her hopes up.

After all, Marcus hadn't given them anything regarding Attorney Barr, or the person or persons responsible for brainwashing Jamie and tampering with Tobin's cuffs. Maybe one of the others would know who had that kind of power. Julia had a feeling whoever it was had become the new de facto leader now that Tobin was incarcerated. How appropriate that the Vipera gang's emblem was a two-headed snake. If they chopped off the second head, maybe it would finally die. Jack came out of the interrogation room and sat down next to her.

"That was an interesting interrogation technique."

Jack shrugged. "We needed a break. I took a risk, and it paid off."

"What would you have done if he called your bluff?"

Jack stared at her for a moment. "Who says I was bluffing?"

Julia nodded. Maybe she should follow Jack Dawson's playbook and make things happen instead of just talking about them. But the real question was, would Jack be okay with her pushing the issue? Especially if the issue involved helping him?

Withholding the truth is another form of lying,
in law and in love.

CHAPTER 31

Jack stopped just outside the door to the kitchen to watch Julia while she poured a cup of coffee and sat down at the counter. He was getting used to seeing her first thing in the morning…and that was a dangerous thought.

Connor stood at the stove, frying eggs and laughing. "I still can't believe he threatened to chisel him. And the worst thing is, I missed it!"

Julia poured milk into her coffee. "You should watch it on tape. It was quite impressive. I think Charlie was jealous."

"I'm jealous. I missed all the fun."

"You were watching over Alex, Peggy, and Sheila. I can't imagine you were bored."

Connor scooped eggs on a plate and handed it to her. "No, those three keep you hopping. They tried to convince me to take them to the warehouse so they could watch the interrogation."

Julia salted her eggs. "Devin would have loved that. Especially when it wasn't going well."

Connor plated some more eggs and set them on the

counter without turning. "You going to come in the room or eavesdrop some more from the doorway, Mr. Hammer and Chisel?"

"Fun-nyyy." Jack walked into the room, sat down, and sprinkled tabasco sauce liberally on his eggs.

Connor slapped a hard-fried egg between two pieces of toast and took a large bite, chewing quickly before heading toward the door. "Going to take a shower."

After Connor left the room, Julia set down her fork and cleared her throat. "I have an appointment with my psychiatrist this morning. Can I still go, or do you need to be with the guys planning the raid tonight?"

"You don't need to cancel. Plans are already happening, and we don't need to sit around all day talking things through."

Julia smiled at him. "I forgot, you're a man of action, not words."

Her smile punched him in the gut. "Yep. When I take you to your appointment, I want to sit in the waiting room instead of the car. I don't like being that far away from you."

"That's fine. I was actually thinking about having you come into the appointment with me. I want to talk about when Jamie grabbed me. I thought it might help if you were there."

He sat up straighter. "Is that still bothering you?"

She looked away. "Maybe. A little bit. But remember, I said I don't want to give them any more power, right? So I want to talk it through with Dr. Jennings."

The eggs turned in his stomach. "I'll come in with you."

She beamed at him. "Thanks."

An hour later, Jack took in the office and doctor in

front of him. Dr. Jennings was a serious woman. Expensive suit, glasses perched on her nose, and hair pulled into a tight bun, she looked like someone who took no prisoners. But then, as a psychiatrist, she probably heard some pretty awful things.

Her eyes widened slightly when Julia asked if Jack could attend the session, but then her unflappable expression reappeared.

Dr. Jennings invited them both to take a seat, and she settled in a chair across from them. "So let's jump right in. Tell me why Jack's here with you today."

"You know we've been working to bring the people who killed my husband to justice."

Dr. Jennings nodded.

"A couple of days ago, we confronted someone who grabbed me and threatened my life."

"Did he hurt you?" she asked, while scanning Julia.

"Not physically," Julia replied.

Dr. Jennings picked up the pen and pad of paper next to her desk. "Emotionally?"

"It was scary. I didn't know what was going to happen. Afterward, I thought I was fine, but I keep thinking about it. Reliving it. I want to just forget about it."

"That's perfectly understandable. When we face a traumatic experience, we can handle it in a number of ways. We can continue to relive it over and over and over, like you're doing. Others push it out of their minds, as though it never happened. But forgetting about it isn't healthy either. Not facing the problem can cause a number of other problems."

Julia's eyes darted in his direction.

What was that look about?

"So if I don't face the trauma, I could make it worse?" Julia asked.

"Yes," Dr. Jennings replied. "That's the crux of post-traumatic stress."

He sat straighter. *Oh, hell no.* Did she honestly think he was so dense he couldn't figure out what was going on?

"Why am I here, Julia?"

She looked at him, her eyes a bit too wide. "I wanted to talk through my attack, and since you were there, I thought it might help to have your input."

He crossed his arms. "The attack where you basically beat the crap out of the guy before any of us could step in?"

Her eyes darted away for a second before she looked him in the eye. *Busted!*

Julia opened her mouth, closed it, and then opened it again. "Fine. I thought it would be good for you to come here and listen to what Dr. Jennings had to say about trauma. You need to face what happened to you."

Jack scowled at the doctor. "And are you in on this too?"

Dr. Jennings shook her head. "No, I don't coerce patients into seeing me."

Julia sat forward. "Jack, you were shot and almost died, and then you were tortured. That would affect anyone. Maybe if you talked about it, it might help with what's going on with you."

Jack shot to his feet. "This is your session, Julia. Worry about your own problems. I'll wait for you outside."

He shut the door with a resounding click and marched out into the waiting room. He sat down and then popped back up again.

What the hell was she trying to pull? He wanted to get better more than anyone, but what exactly could he tell a human doctor? He couldn't tell her about his wolf. So how could she help him?

Julia leaned back against the couch. "Wow, did I royally screw that up."

"I would second that," Dr. Jennings said.

"I shouldn't have tricked him." She sat up and looked at Dr. Jennings. "And I'm sorry I pulled that. It was unfair and unprofessional of me. If you don't want to see me anymore, I'll understand."

Dr. Jennings set down her notepad. "We can still meet. But you did throw me for a bit of a loop just now. To be honest, my initial reaction was anger."

"Initial?"

"Yes, until I started thinking about what you just did. The woman who keeps telling me she doesn't get involved in other's emotional baggage just tricked a man into seeing a therapist. And I have to ask myself why."

"Because he's obviously having trouble."

"Yes, he is. But why do you care so much?"

Julia opened her mouth, and then closed it without responding.

Dr. Jennings smiled slightly. "Right. That's the question you need to answer, Julia. What is it about Jack that made you break your cardinal rule?"

Thirty minutes later, as Jack drove them back to her office, Julia obsessed over Dr. Jennings' question. The car was eerily quiet. After several minutes of awkward silence, she couldn't stand it anymore.

"I'm sorry for tricking you."

He kept driving in silence.

"It wasn't fair to do that. I know I caught you off guard, but I figured you wouldn't go see her on your own."

"So you made the decision for me."

"Right. But now you're saying it out loud, I know how wrong it was. If Alex had tried to trick me into seeing a therapist, I would have been furious."

Silence again.

"I'm not sure why I did it. I mean, I don't want to get involved in other people's problems."

Jack pulled over to the side of the road and parked.

"What are you doing?"

"You are spouting so much bull right now, I can't concentrate well enough to drive."

Julia sat up straighter. "I don't know what you're talking about."

"I think you're a fake, Julia Cole. You declare that you don't want to get involved with helping others, but it's part of your genetic makeup. From your clients, to the wedding planner business, you can't help yourself. You are a caretaker. Accept it."

She narrowed her eyes. "Since when did you become an expert in my behavior?"

"I've spent every waking moment with you for days, Julia. I think that qualifies me as an expert. Call it on-the-job training."

"And why are you telling me this?"

"Because you're fighting your natural tendencies, and it's guaranteed to come back and bite you on the ass. You block out everything you can't control."

Her temples started to throb. "Did you seriously just say that to me? You are the biggest control freak I've ever met!"

"So I know of what I speak."

"Wow. I think you should continue going to therapy with me. Maybe we can get a group discount with Dr. Jennings."

He chuckled. "You never give up."

"Okay, fine. If you won't talk to a therapist, then talk to me. Tell me what's bothering you, Jack."

He shook his head.

"Okay. Then tell me how I can help."

He smirked. "See? I told you. You can't help but help."

"Maybe so. If I admit to having an issue, will you do the same?"

He sighed. "I know something is wrong, but I haven't been able to communicate with my wolf in weeks. How can I get it to come out if it won't talk to me?"

"Maybe you should let Connor try to talk to him instead. If your wolf is mad at you, maybe he can be coaxed out by your brother. If anyone can get him to talk, it would be Connor. I've never met anyone as stubborn as he is."

Jack's eyes pierced hers. "I have."

Julia spent the next few hours catching up with Tina at work. She wasn't used to being away from the office this much, but hopefully after the raid tonight, they would be close to getting back to normal. Jack and Connor would move out of her house, and she would go back to being a workaholic. She frowned. On second thought, going back to the way things had been didn't sound very appealing.

"What's the look for?" Tina asked.

Julia stretched the truth. "Just thinking about the work I need to catch up on."

"Everything is fine right now. Your caseload is light, and we're keeping up with everything. I think it's good you're getting out of the office."

"Really?" Julia's eyebrows rose. "Am I that hard a boss to have around?"

Tina rolled her eyes. "That's not what I meant, and you know it. You need to have other things in your life besides work."

"I do."

Tina set her notepad down on Julia's desk and stared at her for a moment. "Julia, I know you're my boss, but I'm going to say this anyway. You're not happy."

Julia opened her mouth to speak, but Tina rushed on.

"You have a very legitimate reason for your unhappiness. Losing Thomas was like losing half your soul. The two of you together was something to see. And I've watched you bury yourself in your work. I can't tell you to stop grieving. I would never do that. But maybe if you would open yourself up to new experiences and new people..." Tina looked pointedly toward the reception area, where Jack stood guard. "You might find some happiness again."

"I don't know," Julia answered truthfully.

Tina reached across the desk and grasped her hand. "These past weeks, you have seemed more alive than I have seen you in years. You've always been a fighter for your clients, but now I see you fighting for yourself. Don't let that go."

"I'm trying not to." Julia squeezed Tina's hand. "I don't know what I would do without you."

Tina smiled. "I'll remind you of that when it comes time for my increase."

Julia laughed. "Get out of my office."

Tina opened the door, and Jack glanced up from his spot in the reception area while he talked on his cell. Julia checked the clock on her desk. It was time to get moving so the team could finalize their plans for tonight.

She shut down her laptop and tucked it into her

briefcase. By the time she walked out of her office, Jack was off his phone.

"I'm going to drop you at For Better or For Worse."

"No."

"Julia, you aren't coming tonight."

"I know, but I want to be in your final planning session, and then I want to be there for the interrogation."

Jack opened his mouth, but she rushed on.

"There's absolutely no way Alex and Sheila aren't going to attend the team meeting. They're going to want to make sure you all are safe."

He shook his head. "We've done this before, you know."

"I know, but they'll still want the reassurance. You might as well give in now, Jack."

Behind Jack, Tina was punching her fists like a boxer. Julia grinned. By the time Jack turned around to see what Julia was looking at, Tina was typing furiously at her computer.

Sometimes it takes more than one point of view to build a case.

CHAPTER 32

Jack escorted Julia into the team house toward the dining room, where the guys were meeting. He opened the door to discover that Devin, Charlie, Connor, and Giz were not alone. As Julia had predicted, Alex, Sheila, and even Peggy were in attendance. Connor got up to offer Julia his seat.

Devin sat at the head of the table looking over some schematics. "Okay, let's get this meeting started now that *everyone* is in attendance."

Giz tapped on his tablet, and a picture of a man appeared on the other tablets sitting on the table. The man was older, with salt and pepper hair.

"The first picture is a canine demon by the name of Harvey Donaldson. He owns a car dealership."

"So he has no problem doing business with humans and other supernaturals, but doesn't want them to be in relationships?" Julia asked.

"Apparently not," Giz said. "He has no record in either the human or supernatural courts."

Giz clicked on his screen and two pictures appeared. Both men had black hair and frowns.

"Keith and Karl Turner. Elf brothers."

Devin turned to his sister, Peggy. "Tobin must have recruited them. I can't believe elves from our clan are involved in this."

"We'll stop them," Peggy declared. "They won't get away with what they did to Thomas and the others."

Jack watched Julia out of the corner of his eye. She didn't flinch at the sound of Thomas's name, but she did swallow hard.

Giz continued. "Both faced magical mischief charges in the Tribunal court as youngsters."

"Magical mischief charges?" Julia asked.

"They're similar to vandalism," a voice answered from the doorway.

Jack turned to see Godfrey and Savannah walk into the room.

Devin sighed. "More meeting-crashers. How did you find out we were meeting tonight?"

Julia raised her hand slightly as if in school. "Ah, that would be my fault. I've been keeping Savannah up to speed with the investigation."

"Right." Devin sighed. "Okay, Giz, show us the last two."

Giz changed the picture. "Simon and Brock Franklin, wolf cousins."

Jack stared hard at the pictures. "Not from our clan."

"No." Giz clicked on his keyboard. "They're originally from the East Coast clan. Brock has a battery charge on his record in human court."

Devin pushed a tablet over to Godfrey and Savannah. "We talked through this earlier, but I want to make sure we all understand our assignments. Charlie will stay here tonight with Alex, Julia, Sheila, and Peggy."

"That's not necessary," Alex said.

Devin shook his head. "Alex, there's no way in hell you're coming on this raid with us tonight."

"I know that, silly elf. I just meant that the whole team needs to be part of the takedown. I called Julian and Fiona. They have invited the womenfolk over to their place. Julian's house is a fortress, and both he and Fiona are practically vampire ninjas, so we should be fine. Since he's one of your best friends, I figured you would be okay with him protecting us."

"That's a good idea." Devin's eyes widened.

Alex patted his arm. "I know, dear. I do come up with good ideas on occasion."

Julia snickered next to Jack.

"Okay," Devin continued. "That means that Charlie can join us for the raid."

"And me," Godfrey growled.

Devin dropped his head to the table with a thud. "Godfrey, you're a damn fine lawyer, but you're not trained as a soldier."

It was Jack's turn to snicker. He wasn't surprised when Connor and Godfrey joined in.

Godfrey smiled a bit, showing his canines. "Devin, you know better than that. All wolves are trained from the time they're pups to defend the clan. I can hold my own. I want in on this raid."

Savannah gaped at Godfrey. "You telling me you're a soldier, G?"

"Yes."

"Well, damn. I already knew you were sexy, but this—"

Julia interrupted. "TMI, Savannah. Table that discussion for later."

Devin interrupted. "Julia's right. Let's take a look at points of entry, and who will cover what now we've got some extra hands."

Jack listened to the new plans, and wasn't surprised

when Julia and the other women threw in some good suggestions. Giz noted everything down so he could print the plans out for review one more time.

Going after Vipera was a big deal, and everything had to run smoothly. Jack wanted nothing more than to put them away for good for Julia's sake...hell, for everyone's sake.

Three hours later, Jack was at the back entrance of the building with Connor, waiting for Devin to give them the go-ahead to enter.

Giz was overseeing the operation from the van, watching through the building's security cameras, which he'd hacked into.

Devin, Charlie, and Godfrey were out of sight around the front of the building, watching for the last of the men to arrive.

"Harvey Donaldson just pulled in, and he brought three friends, which means more to take down up front," Devin advised them through their earbuds. "When they're in the building, we'll give them a few minutes, and then I'll give the order to go in. Prep now."

Jack and Connor exchanged glances before Connor knelt and pulled out his lock-picking tools. There was no need to crash through the door and alert the supremacists to their presence ahead of time, especially now they had eight to deal with instead of five. After a slight click, Connor straightened with a nod, tucking his tools away. But still they waited, the minutes dragging by until their comms came to life again.

"Go!"

Jack and Connor stole quietly through the door and into the kitchen. The door ahead of them led to a hall off the main meeting room area, according to the schematics they had memorized.

"Freeze! You're under arrest!" Devin yelled, followed by shouts and thunks.

One of the elf brothers ran into the kitchen, but stopped when he caught sight of the twins. His eyes glowed. Power started to flow around him, and Jack slammed into him before he could fully charge himself, taking him to the ground. The elf roared, and it felt like pins piercing Jack's skin, but he didn't back off. He flipped him over and cuffed him, and the elf went limp. Since there wasn't time to have McHenry create cuffs, Darcinda infused several pairs of regular cuffs with dampening spells.

Jack jumped up to find Connor facing off with two wolves. The bigger one attacked, and they rolled around the kitchen, pots and pans banging while they slammed around. The smaller wolf turned and bared his teeth at Jack.

Jack pulled out his tranquilizer gun and shot, hitting the wolf in his front leg. The wolf howled and jerked his leg, the tranq flying out and rolling across the floor. Jack shot again, but he missed the wolf, who jumped behind a metal island.

Damn! Had the guy gotten enough of the tranquilizer?

The wolf growled, and Jack ran around the island, but the wolf plowed right over him, taking him to the ground before running out the back door.

Jack hauled air into his lungs. He turned to make sure Connor was okay, and found his brother sitting on top of an unconscious wolf. Jack slipped a collar around the wolf's neck, and the wolf turned back to his human form.

Light shimmered around Connor as he also turned back to human. "Where's the other wolf?"

"Ran out the back."

"I'll go outside and see if I can scent him. Maybe the tranq got him." Connor flashed back to his wolf and ran outside.

Jack looked at the two unconscious supremacists. Darcinda's spell would make sure they stayed out for a while. In the meantime, it was time to check on the rest of the team. He walked into a front room that looked like a bomb had gone off. Pieces of furniture lay scattered around the room. Charlie bent over one of the men, snapping cuffs on him. The other four lay on the floor, unconscious and cuffed as well.

Devin and Godfrey stood next to each other like bookends with their arms crossed. Neither looked too beat up. Devin had a bloody lip, and Godfrey a scratch next to his eye. He was also naked, which meant he changed into his wolf during the fight.

"You stopped the others?" Devin asked.

"The elf and one of the wolves. I got a tranq in the other one, but he bolted. Connor is hunting him in case he's close by."

"Let's get everyone packed up and back to the warehouse," Devin said as he turned to Jack. "Go tell Connor we're leaving. I'm glad we packed some extra clothes. I don't need you guys running around town naked. I'm not sure how you manage to keep your clothes on all the time while your brother consistently ends up naked, but I just want to thank you for it."

Jack cringed on the inside. He really needed to tell Devin and the rest of the team what was going on with him. Soon.

Julia practically growled as she sat with Devin and Giz, listening to the newest interview on the monitor. The interviews had gone on all night and into the morning. On the one hand, the men being questioned had no loyalty to each other. They were throwing each other under the bus, the train, anything with wheels.

And from what they revealed so far, the good news was this time they caught the majority of the remaining supremacists, with the exception of the missing werewolf, Brock Franklin, and the boss. And then there was Attorney Barr.

"Do we know where Barr is?"

Devin shook his head. "Barr gave the guy Connor had following him the slip yesterday. We don't know where he is, other than he hasn't been at his office or house today."

"I can't believe none of these guys know who their boss is either," Julia said.

Devin frowned. "It might be they've been told to forget. If this person has enough power to totally control Jamie, it stands to reason that he or she can also manipulate the other supremacists' memories, right?"

"True," Julia replied. "It has to be someone at the detention center. None of these people have connections there. It makes sense that Jamie met the boss when he dropped the cuffs off at the center."

"I agree. I think it makes sense to go to the center ASAP and interview the guards again before news gets out about the arrests. Hopefully Franklin has gone underground and hasn't blabbed anything to the boss, or it might be too late."

"I'll come with you."

"No. It would help if you stayed here to go over the interview tapes with Godfrey, so we can solidify this case and be done with it. I'll take Jack with me."

Devin and Jack left while Julia lost track of time reviewing the recordings with Godfrey. After a while, she stretched and then headed toward the back room the team had set up as an impromptu healing center.

Darcinda and Alex sat in the room poring over spell books. Darcinda had taken care of the minor injuries of the team, as well as the supremacists while they were unconscious. Alex insisted on coming to help Darcinda, but the truth was she couldn't stand not knowing what was going on. Julia couldn't blame her.

Julia sat down next to them. "I don't know what to do next. Every one of these interviews is the same when it comes to asking who the boss is. No one knows." She looked at Darcinda "You still have no idea who could have done this?"

"I'm amazed anyone could have sufficient power to control this many different species."

"Maybe the boss is a high-powered faery?" Alex asked.

Darcinda tapped her chin. "Let's approach this another way. What do the supremacists have in common?"

"Nothing," Julia replied. "They come from different species. They're different ages, and they didn't know each other until they joined the supremacist movement. They have different jobs, and live in different places."

"They're just closed-minded, stupid men," Alex said.

Darcinda dropped her hand from her chin. "Men! Is it possible?"

"Is what possible?" Julia and Alex asked simultaneously.

"I didn't consider this, since I thought they were extinct. What if we're dealing with a siren?"

"Sirens exist?" Alex gasped. "As in sing songs and lure fishermen to their deaths on the rocks, sirens?"

"Yes. Sirens have the ability to control men. Powerful sirens can order men to do almost anything. Are any of the guards at the center women, Julia? And when I say women, I mean drop-dead gorgeous women?"

Julia struggled for breath. "Not the guards. But Alina, the warden, is gorgeous."

"That might be it, but I won't know for sure until I get close to her."

Julia's stomach dropped. "Devin and Jack went to the center to question the guards."

Alex flinched. "We need to go to the center and protect them."

"Let's go," Julia agreed. "I'll drive, but we go alone."

"Is that smart?" Darcinda asked.

"We bring the other guys with us, and what if she tells one of them to kill us?"

"Good point."

Jack and Devin were on their way out of the detention center. Once again, the interviews with the guards had been a bust.

Warden Schuler smiled at them. "I'm sorry you were unable to find who you're looking for. I have interviewed the staff as well, and can find nothing suspect in their answers. I've decided to move Tobin and the other gang members to a more secure location."

"Not a good idea," a voice called out.

Alina's eyes widened, and Jack turned to see Julia, Alex, and Darcinda coming toward them.

"What isn't a good idea?" Devin asked.

"Moving Tobin," Julia replied.

"I thought you wanted him moved," Jack said.

"I do, but not while the new gang leader is still loose."

Devin nodded. "We didn't get any new information from interviewing the staff. Darcinda, do you think you would be able to sense something from one of them?"

"No need," Darcinda said.

"What do you mean?" Jack asked.

"I don't need to spend time with the guards, since I know who the boss is." Darcinda stared at Alina for a moment. "You're a siren. You do a good job of suppressing it, but I can sense it. You are the one who's controlling Jamie, and you've forced the others to forget who you are."

Devin stepped toward Alina.

"Don't," Alina warned in a singsong voice.

Devin frowned and looked down at his feet. It was as if they were stuck in muck while he struggled to move.

Jack reached for her.

"Stop."

His hands froze in the air. *Damn! What was happening?*

Julia stalked right up to Alina, hauled her arm back, and punched her in the mouth. Alina dropped to her knees and moaned while she clutched her face.

Holy shit! Julia *was* a warrior woman. *His* warrior woman, if he had anything to say about it.

Darcinda held up her hands and chanted. Bands of light wrapped around Alina's wrists and her mouth with some sort of magical gag. Then she turned to Julia. "We talked about this on the ride over here. If you had waited another second, I could have cloaked her voice."

"You weren't fast enough." Julia shrugged. "She could have turned one of the guys on us." She glanced at Devin and Jack. "Can you break them out of the spell, or do I have to persuade her to do it?"

"I want to persuade her too," Alex chimed in.

Darcinda's eyes widened. "You two have anger management issues."

Alex shrugged. "You don't mess with my man. Sheila would have taken her on as well if she were here. She teaches kickboxing. Can you break the hold?"

"Now that I know we're dealing with siren magic, I can break the hold," Darcinda assured her.

Julia looked up into Jack's eyes, and he gazed back into her beautiful face.

"Hurry," she said.

Damn. He needed to get his wolf back and convince this woman she belonged with him. But once this case was behind them, would she be ready to move forward?

Law does not always reap the truth.
The same could be said for marriage.

CHAPTER 33

Julia watched the prisoner on the monitor. Her heart beat in a frantic rhythm, the way it had the first time she interrogated a witness.

"Are you sure you want to do this?" Jack asked.

"No, but I'm not letting her anywhere near you guys again."

"Now who's being overprotective? Darcinda has blocked her powers until she can be brought before the Tribunal."

"I know, but I still need to do this."

Julia walked into the interrogation room and sat down across from Alina.

Jack opened the door a minute later, and Attorney Barr rushed into the room. "My client will not be answering any questions. This interrogation is uncalled for."

Hot damn, he showed up. Jack winked at her before closing the door and leaning up against it. Barr's arrogance would be his downfall. "I don't need to interrogate her, counselor. Interrogating means that I need to ask questions to determine what her crimes are." Julia set a stack of affidavits in front of her. "That's not necessary. After we released the other supernaturals from Alina's amnesia spell, they were very happy to tell us everything."

"I want to review these so-called affidavits."

Julia smiled. "You'll have plenty of time to read them. The added benefit was they told us about your involvement as well. Two birds with one stone and all that. You're both going to prison for life, if I have anything to say about it."

Attorney Barr jumped to his feet, and Jack pinned him facedown to the table while the rest of the team burst into the room. Connor slapped cuffs on Barr and hauled him out of the room while the attorney yelled about his rights.

Alina still sat in her chair, unfazed by the excitement. "What precisely was the purpose of this meeting? To gloat?"

"No," Julia said. "We needed to tempt Barr out from under his rock, and figured he would show up as your counsel. But I'm curious. I want to know why. Why did you do this?"

Alina leaned forward. "I am one of the last of my kind. Humans destroyed us over the millennia. It's what you do. You kill what you don't understand. And you expect me to feel anything for you? We should always stick with our own kind. Now supernaturals are polluting the gene pool with your human DNA, and we're losing who we are."

Julia stared at the once-gorgeous woman sitting in front of her. As the words spewed out of her, her true ugliness surfaced.

Alina scowled. "I don't want your pity."

Julia shook her head. "I thought you could read my thoughts. This isn't my pity face. It's my disgust face. You've let your anger and sorrow destroy your soul.

Maybe I would have pitied you if you hadn't hurt others, but murdering anyone for their willingness to love and accept others is sad and twisted." Julia stood. "And don't preach to me about how horrible humans are. You also kill what you don't understand, you hypocritical bitch."

Julia stalked out of the room and past Jack, who waited by the door. She kept on going toward the outside.

"Julia," Jack called after her.

She needed air. She couldn't talk until she could suck fresh air into her lungs. She pushed the door open and stumbled outside into clear, fresh air. But it didn't help. Nothing cleared the tightness in her chest.

"Julia."

She turned and Jack pulled her into his arms. One hand rested on her back, the other on the back of her head. He pulled her face lightly against his chest, and she took a breath of Jack. He smelled like a warm day and fresh coffee.

"Let me support you for a change."

She relaxed against him and took slow breaths.

"Let it go," he murmured.

His words couldn't have been more appropriate. She wouldn't let fear and pain rule her anymore. She had already said she would no longer give them power over her. She risked becoming just like Alina, twisting her own soul, if she didn't let go of the past.

After another minute, Jack loosened his grip on her. She looked up at him, and he reached out and ran his fingers over her cheek, pushing her hair behind her ear.

She leaned into his touch for a moment. Jack dropped his hand and took a step back. "Better?"

Julia nodded, trying to understand what his eyes were telling her. She wanted to ask him to wrap his arms around her again. "Yes. Thank you. I'm...going to see how Darcinda is doing with her spell to free Jamie."

Julia beat a hasty retreat to the back room to join Darcinda. So much for being strong.

Devin ambled up to join Jack while he watched her walk away. "Is Julia okay?"

"Yeah. It's just hard for her to face these people after everything they've done to her."

"I get that." Devin stared hard at him for a moment. "You have a thing for Julia."

Jack shook his head. "It's not a *thing*."

Devin held up his hands. "I'm not going to give you a hard time about it. I think she needs someone she can lean on again, and you would be good for her."

"Don't let her hear you say that."

Devin grinned. "I understand all too well. Alex has been bugging me nonstop about you two. I didn't see it at first, but now it makes sense. Just don't screw it up."

"I care for Julia a lot, and I can't stop the need to protect her, but I'm not the best person for her right now."

"Why the hell not?"

Jack hesitated, but he needed to tell him the truth. "I can't turn into my wolf."

Devin gaped while Jack filled him in. When Jack got further into the story, Devin's expression changed from astonishment to anger.

"I know you're mad. I shouldn't have continued to be part of Julia's protection detail with my wolf gone."

"I'm not mad about that, you idiot. I'm mad that you didn't think you could tell me sooner. I spent months without my powers, but that didn't stop me from going after the supremacists, did it? Your powers don't define you, Jack. I didn't pick you for this team because of your wolf. I picked you because of the man you are."

Now it was Jack's turn to gape at him.

"Plus, the team could have worked on helping you, too. Several heads are better than one, right?"

"Right."

"So the next order of business, after we deliver Alina to the Tribunal and free Jamie from his brainwashing, is finding your wolf."

He nodded at his team leader and, more importantly, friend.

Julia wasn't the only one still mired down in the past.

It was time to move forward.

Julia watched in silence while Darcinda referred to an old leather volume and then poured liquid into a bowl. After a few more moments, Julia couldn't stop herself from interrupting. "Is this for Jamie?"

"Yes. He's under a stronger spell then the rest were. I wanted to be sure I could break them out first before I tried anything with him, since I think he's in a more fragile state."

"Are you close?"

Darcinda reached for some powder, which she sprinkled into the mixture. "Very. I'm going to have Jamie drink this potion."

"When will you know if it worked?"

"I don't know. Siren powers are almost as ancient as faery. It may take a while for Jamie to fully regain his will."

"I'll let you get back to it, then."

An hour later, Julia paced outside the room while the team sat with Giz compiling their case notes. Julia couldn't concentrate, however, so instead she drove everyone else crazy.

"Jules," Devin sighed. "Sit down already."

She sat down next to him, and then popped up again when Darcinda emerged from the back room.

"How's Jamie?" Julia asked.

"He's out of the spell, but he's groggy, like he's just come out of a drugged sleep. Andrew is with him."

Julia clasped her hands together. "Thank God."

"Do you think he'll be okay?" Jack asked.

"Physically, I think he'll recover quickly, but emotionally it will take him longer. He's been traumatized. Someone stole his will, and forced him to do things against his true nature. That's a hard one to bounce back from."

Julia's heart ached at the sheer horror of what he'd been forced to suffer. "I want to help him, Darcinda. When can we take him home to the forest?"

"Not for a few days. I want to make sure he's recovering before you take him back."

Darcinda headed back to the room. Julia grinned at Connor, and looked around the room at the other smiling faces, until she reached Jack. He was not smiling. He walked out the door, and a few minutes later, Julia found him at the spot where he had comforted her hours ago.

"What's going on, Jack?"

He looked over her shoulder for a moment, as if to collect his thoughts.

"Jack?"

His eyes met hers. "Why do you want to go back to the forest?"

"I promised McHenry I would watch over Jamie."

"And you did. Andrew can take him home."

"I know, but I feel like I need to go back to the forest."

"So this is about McHenry."

She froze at his words. "What does that mean?"

"McHenry is attracted to you."

She shrugged. "Whether he is or not doesn't matter."

"How can you say that?"

"Because the last time I checked, I'm a woman in charge of my own life, and I decide who I want to be with."

"And who do you want to be with?"

Jack moved closer, and she moved backward before she could will her feet to stop.

"What are you doing, Jack?"

"Throwing my hat into the ring."

He cupped her face in his hands, bent down, and kissed her. Lips touching hers so softly, like a whisper. So light that Julia wondered if she had imagined the touch, until he pressed against her mouth harder this time. Tentativeness gone, his mouth descended for more.

Warmth spread throughout Julia's body as she leaned into him, drawn to his heat and his drugging kisses. God, it had been so long. Guilt splashed cold water down her spine, and she stiffened against him. She was kissing someone besides Thomas. "I can't."

He looked into her face, and whatever he saw made him jerk back. "I'm sorry, I shouldn't have pushed you."

"It's not that." *What was it?* "I...I'm not ready."

His face closed down, his tender expression leaching away. "I understand, Julia."

Julia watched him walk away.

She wanted to call to him, but her voice didn't work. How could he understand when she didn't understand anything right now?

Even lawyers need advice from outside counsel.

CHAPTER 34

How could she have moved a step forward, only to fall two steps back? Julia sat on the couch in Dr. Jennings' office, her right leg bouncing. After pleasantries were exchanged, Dr. Jennings got right down to business. "How are things going, Julia?"

"Fine."

Dr. Jennings looked down at Julia's manic knee. "Really?"

"With the exception of one person, we caught the rest of the gang."

"And that's a good thing, right?"

"Of course." Julia pressed her hand down on her knee to stop the bouncing.

"Are you worried about the person who got away?"

"No. We think he's gone underground. He no longer has a support system, so he shouldn't be a threat."

"Then you no longer have a need for bodyguards."

"No." And there went her knee again.

"Julia, these are all great things. So tell me why you're not celebrating right now. Is it Jack? Did he not forgive you for tricking him?"

"He forgave me for that. It's something else now." She hesitated. "I pushed him away."

"Because?"

"Things were getting too personal between us."

Dr. Jennings crossed her legs. "Would you care to elaborate on this a little more?"

Julia hesitated again.

"You obviously want to talk about it. Give your doctor *something* to work with."

"Jack kissed me."

"And?"

"*And?* That's what you say to me? *And?*"

"What would you like me say to you? I don't think you want me to spout the overused phrase, 'And how did that make you feel?'"

"Psychiatric humor?"

"Fine, he kissed you. How did you respond?"

"I panicked and pushed him away."

"Because you didn't want him to kiss you?"

"Because I did."

"Ahh."

Julia gritted her teeth. "I want you to be honest."

Dr. Jennings's eyes widened. "I didn't know I was being dishonest."

"I don't mean that you're lying to me. I just mean don't go soft on me. Tell me the hard truth."

Dr. Jennings tapped her pen against the ever-present notepad in her lap. "What hard truth would you like me to share with you?"

"That I'm screwed up. But I don't know how to move forward." Julia scrubbed her face with both hands. "I can't stop loving Thomas. It's not a switch I can turn on and off."

Dr. Jennings shook her head. "And there's the crux of the problem."

"What do you mean?" Julia asked. Did Dr. Jennings

honestly believe she could just forget about her husband?

"You believe loving Thomas is an either-or proposition. But it doesn't have to be the case. You will always love Thomas. No one can take that love away from you. However, it doesn't mean you can't love someone else as well."

"I don't know," Julia choked out.

Dr. Jennings set down her notepad. "Are you telling me you don't care for anyone else in your life? What about Alex? Do you love her? Or your other friends and family?"

Julia looked down at the notepad sitting on the table between them. "That's different."

"How? Your heart loves. Each love you experience is unique, because each relationship is unique. Your love for Thomas is part of your heart. You have room for infinite amounts of love, Julia." She smiled. "It's not your heart that's holding you back. It's your guilt, and fear, and pain."

Julia felt like she was sucking water instead of air into her lungs. She struggled for breath as tears ran down her cheeks and she angrily swiped them away. "I asked for the unvarnished truth, didn't I?"

Dr. Jennings handed her a box of tissues. "If you think about it, Julia, you already knew the truth."

She wiped her eyes. "I guess I did. Then how do I get past the guilt?"

"Let's consider another scenario. What if you had been the one to pass away, and Thomas was still living. Would you want him to spend the rest of his life without love?"

"Of course not."

Dr. Jennings held up her hands, palms up in a "go on" gesture.

Julia blew out a hard breath. "Okay, I get what you're saying."

"Why should you expect anything less for your own life? From what you've told me about Thomas, I believe he would be the last person to want you to close yourself to love."

"Well, duh," Julia mumbled.

Dr. Jennings laughed. "I like to call these epiphanies V-8 moments."

Julia smiled. "In other words, you just gave me a mental smack upside the head."

"Exactly."

"So how, oh wise one, do I get past the fear and pain?"

"The pain will fade over time. I'm not going to lie to you, it will never fully go away. But it will get to the point where you only have moments of pain versus days of pain. I think you were already heading down that path until you found out Thomas was murdered, which ripped your heart open again."

"And the fear?"

"That one is harder to conquer, especially fear of the unknown. You know better than most that there are no guarantees in life. And you may be sure someone else you love during your lifetime will die, whether it's a friend, or family member, or lover. But does that mean you don't want to be a part of that person's life? Would you go back in time and erase meeting Thomas if you could?"

"No. But if I meet someone I want to be with, is it fair to ask him to take on my emotional baggage?"

"Of course it is, if that someone is the right person. Did you not just bring Jack in here to talk to me? It seems like you're willing to be part of his life even though he's got his own emotional baggage."

Julia slid down and dropped her head on the back of the couch. "God, I'm an idiot."

Dr. Jennings shook her head. "No you're not. You're an extremely intelligent person whose job description includes determining different scenarios and potential outcomes in the courtroom. Is it any wonder you do the same thing with your emotions?"

Julia gaped at her. "You did it again—another V-8 moment. I'm going to have to ask you to limit yourself to one per session, because you're giving me a headache."

"I'll make a note in your file. I do think you've had enough for today. Think about your feelings for Jack between now and the next session, and I'll make sure to stock up on some aspirin."

Julia stood. "Are psychiatrists supposed to be closet comedians?"

Dr. Jennings walked Julia to the door. "I can't speak for others, but the old adage is true. Laughter is often the best medicine."

Jack frowned as he sat next to Giz going through paperwork. They were pulling the case notes together to turn over to the Tribunal, and he couldn't wait for this mess to be over with.

But there wasn't much to look forward to once they wrapped up this case. At least now busywork kept him from worrying about his wolf and Julia. Darcinda had assured him that she was ready to work on his problem now Jamie was cured.

Connor came over to join them. "You ready to take a break?"

"For what?"

"To go pick up our stuff from Julia's."

Jack couldn't look his brother in the face. "No. You pick it up. We don't both need to go."

Connor came to a stop across the table from Jack. "What's going on with you? If I didn't know any better, I'd say you were avoiding Julia."

"I'm not avoiding Julia," he barked. He was so avoiding her, and now he was lying to his brother.

The chair next to him scraped back as Giz got up and hurried away. "I'm going to take a quick break," he said.

Connor dropped down in his seat. "Way to go, Jack. You scared Giz away."

"Go away, Connor."

"No. I'm not letting you revert back to your previous cranky-ass ways. Tell me what's going on."

"I kissed Julia."

Connor leaned forward. "And?"

"And it was a disaster."

"You're exaggerating."

"No I'm not." Jack closed his eyes. "If you could have seen the look on her face." He opened his eyes and shook his head. "She's not ready for a relationship. Hell, I don't know if she'll ever be, and even when she is ready, who's to say she'll want to be with me?"

"I think you're wrong."

"And what makes you an expert?"

"Because I've seen you two together. She has feelings for you, Jack. She's just confused and needs to figure things out."

Jack opened another folder in front of him. "Which is why I'm giving her space."

"You're avoiding her. That isn't a good idea, especially now."

"What the hell does that mean?"

"Darcinda told Devin Jamie is healthy enough to go home. Julia is planning to travel back with him. Do you really want to let her go spend time with McHenry alone?"

"If McHenry makes her happy, then I'm not going to get in the way."

Connor didn't respond. Jack looked up and saw his brother gaping at him. "What?"

"You *are* in love with her."

"No—"

"I might not be able to get in your head right now, brother, but don't lie to me. You're willing to let her be with another man if he makes her happy. Which means you're in love with her."

"It doesn't matter. She's not in love with me."

Connor stood, shaking his head. "Don't blow this, Jack. Lately you've been a cranky bastard on a good day, and Julia's brought back the old, smiling Jack. Don't let her get away."

Jack watched Connor stomp out of the room. He wanted to be with Julia more than anything, but he couldn't force things. He never again wanted to see the look on her face after he kissed her.

He couldn't force her to let go of the past and love him. He needed to do what was best for her, and that meant being the bigger man and staying away from her.

Law works to free the innocent.
Love hopes to free the soul.

CHAPTER 35

Julia was living in a world of awkward. Jack and Connor had moved out. Well, more like Connor came by and picked up their things yesterday, making some excuse about Jack working on the case.

Maybe he was, but Julia was pretty sure he was avoiding her. On the one hand, it made her angry, but on the other, she understood why. She'd shoved him away like she was scared and angry at him.

But the reality was she was scared and angry with herself and her emotions.

Now she stood on the edge of the forest. It was time to take Jamie home. Jamie was another part of her awkward existence. He wouldn't look at her or speak to her. He waited next to her while Andrew and Connor pulled bags from the car.

Julia turned to him. "I'm glad you're feeling better, Jamie."

Jamie wouldn't look her in the eyes. "I can't believe you're being so nice to me."

"Why wouldn't I?"

He studied his feet. "Because I tried to hurt you. I'm sorry. I would never hurt a woman."

"Thank you for the apology, but there's no reason to be sorry. You weren't in control. I could hear you struggling with her demands. Don't let Alina continue to have power over you. She did those horrible things, you didn't."

Jamie glanced up at her. "Thank you."

"Your uncle is right, you're a good man. I'm glad we can take you back home."

Connor handed her a cell phone.

"What's this for?"

"One of Giz's gadgets. Devin didn't like us being cut off last time, so Giz came up with something. You can make calls out of the forest with this. He said it's like a magical cell tower that will transmit phone calls."

"Cool."

"You ready to go?" Connor asked.

"Yep."

At the sound of car tires on gravel, they turned to see a car pull up next to the SUV and stop. Julia's heart ricocheted around her chest as Jack climbed out of the vehicle and headed toward them.

"Decided to come for a stroll?" Connor asked.

"You could say that." Jack looked at Julia for a moment before glancing away. "I'll take point."

He strode into the forest.

"Stubborn jackass," Julia muttered.

Connor chuckled. "Yes, he is, but at least he's here."

Jack set a fast pace, and they quickly reached the opening to the Elven Forest and walked through the shimmering waves of light. An hour later, they were walking into McHenry's courtyard.

Clanking sounds came from the workshop.

"McHenry!" Connor yelled.

Moments later, McHenry appeared in the doorway and gaped at them. The surprise on his face morphed into pure joy when he saw Jamie.

Julia blinked back tears when the huge man hauled Jamie against his chest and kissed him on the head. He pushed him back and looked him over.

"Are ye okay, son?"

Jamie nodded.

He looked at Julia. "You couldn't send a man a message first? You just took years off me life."

"It was Andrew's doing. He wanted to surprise you."

McHenry turned to his other nephew. "Did he? Well he'll be payin' for that." He reached out and pulled Andrew into an embrace, slapping him on the back.

Then he turned to Connor and Jack, shaking their hands. "Thank you."

He looked at Julia last. Reaching for her hand, he brought it to his lips and kissed her knuckles. "And thank you for bringing my boys home to me."

Julia smiled. "I made a promise to you."

"So you did." McHenry clapped his hands together. "A celebration is in order. I want to hear everything that happened."

He walked toward the house with his two nephews in tow. Julia glanced over at Jack. His face was an emotionless mask. Was he reverting back to the old Jack because of her reaction when he kissed her?

She couldn't let that happen. Not again. She was going to tell him how she felt, tonight.

Two hours later, Julia had eaten too much food and heard too many stories. Now she went in search of Jack, who had slipped out some time ago after barely eating anything. She practiced what she would say to him as she searched the forest.

Julia found Jack several yards from the house, sitting on a stump.

She walked up behind him. "Jack, we need to talk."

He didn't acknowledge her.

"I know you're probably upset about the way I reacted to your kiss the other day, and I want to explain, if you'll let me."

She waited, but he didn't turn around. She reached for his shoulder.

"Jack?"

His shoulder was burning hot. She rushed around to face him and knelt in front of him. His skin was pale and he was soaked with sweat.

"What's wrong?"

He blew out a hard breath. "I don't know."

Her heart slammed in her chest. "Wait here. I'll be right back."

Julia ran back toward the house, yelling for help. Connor and McHenry stormed through the woods moments later.

Connor grabbed her arms. "What's wrong?"

"It's Jack. He's sick."

She led them back to the stump, and Connor looked Jack over.

"Can you tell what's wrong with him?" Julia asked.

"No. Where's your closest healer?" Connor asked McHenry.

"Hours away," McHenry said.

"Then we'll bring someone in." Julia's hands shook as she pulled out the phone Giz had given them. "I'm calling Devin. They can get here before the sun goes down if they hurry."

Julia wrung out the cloth over the bowl next to the bed and turned to mop Jack's face with it.

"I'm fine, Julia, stop worrying," Jack grumbled.

"I'm allowed to worry, Jack Dawson. You can't order me around."

"They're here, Julia!" Connor yelled from downstairs.

Jamie walked into the room. "I'll watch over him. Go on."

Julia ran down the stairs and into the yard. Alex and Devin were there, along with Sheila and Charlie.

"Holy Fates, I didn't tell you to invite the entire knitting club, did I?" McHenry roared.

Before Julia could think of a retort, Alex plunked her hands on her hips. "I've been hollered at by all levels of supernaturals. You don't scare me, McHenry."

"Another feisty one. And you are?"

"Already taken," Devin growled.

"Possessive men, the lot of you," McHenry said with a smirk.

Darcinda entered the courtyard with Giz. She wore camouflage pants, and a green top featuring Kermit the Frog with a speech bubble over his head saying, "I'll pick a faery over a pig any day of the week." Her hair was lime green to match Kermit, and her lace-up work boots were deep purple. Julia couldn't imagine how many animals she must have scared away during her trip through the forest.

McHenry turned and caught sight of Darcinda, and all traces of his smile disappeared. "What's a faery doing here?"

"She's the healer here to help Jack."

He scowled. "We don't need her kind of help."

Shocked, Julia glared at his red face. "I'm not going to argue with you about this. She stays."

McHenry glowered back. "Only until your wolf is on the mend."

Julia took Darcinda upstairs to Jack, and then the faery promptly kicked her out of the room. Now she waited on the front porch with Alex and Sheila while the men milled around in the courtyard.

Finally Darcinda joined them. From the look on her face, Julia was sure she was not going to like what she had to say.

The men walked up to the porch and Darcinda stopped in the middle of the group.

"How is he?" Julia asked.

"His wolf is gone."

Connor bent over double, and Devin and Charlie grabbed him to keep him upright.

"What does that mean?" Julia asked as Alex gripped her hand.

"Jack's wolf is like a vital organ to him. He can survive for a short time without it, sometimes even weeks, but eventually his body will shut down."

Julia shot to her feet. "No!"

"Julia." Alex reached for her, but Julia stepped out of reach.

"This doesn't make any sense. Maybe his wolf isn't gone."

"What do you mean?" Darcinda asked.

"Do wolves just die without their hosts?"

"Normally, no."

"So then where did his wolf go?" Julia pushed.

"There wouldn't be anywhere for him to go," Darcinda replied.

A crazy idea formed in Julia's head as she looked at Connor.

"Werewolves channel emotions for each other, correct?" Julia asked.

Connor nodded. "Yes. If we have a connection with the person, we can help shoulder some of that worry or pain for them."

"And with you and Jack, the connection is even more powerful. You can actually sense each other's emotions, and talk to each other psychically."

"We used to be able to do that. Where are you going with this, Julia?"

"When Jack was shot, you turned into your wolf and protected him. You also more than likely absorbed his pain."

"Yes."

"What if you absorbed his wolf, too?"

"That's crazy."

"Is it? You pulled his wolf to you while he was shot, which could be why you lost control in your own wolf form. Then when he was out of danger, his wolf went back to him again."

"Then why is he sick now?" Devin asked.

Sheila stood. "Because he was tortured and forced to relive the shooting over and over again, so maybe the wolf finally severed his connection with Jack and jumped back over to Connor again."

Connor shook his head. "Not possible. Besides, Darcinda examined Jack days ago, and said she could still sense his wolf."

Julia frowned. "She did, but you were in the room, Connor. Maybe she was sensing him in you."

Darcinda held up her hands. "There's one way to see whether this is speculation or not. Julia and Connor, come with me."

They walked upstairs into a bedroom across from Jack's room. Darcinda apparently had set it up as her healing room, since vials, bottles, and books sat on the dresser. She grabbed several vials.

"I have a spell that will tell us how many spirits Connor has inside his body. You should have two—one for you, and one for your wolf."

Julia held her breath while Darcinda poured several different liquids into a bowl. She held the bowl in front of Connor and began to chant.

A light in the shape of a small ball rose from the

bowl in front of Connor's chest. It hovered there as the glow intensified. The ball vibrated slightly, a high-pitched sound emanating from it as it split in two. Julia watched closely, too afraid to blink and miss something important. A few seconds later, the ball split again. Three lights spun in a circle in front of Connor.

"Holy shit," Connor blurted.

Darcinda's eyes widened. "Well, I'll be. Julia, you're a genius."

Julia's eyes filled. "So we haven't lost Jack's wolf."

"No."

"Then how do we put it back?"

Sometimes love requires an addendum.

CHAPTER 36

Julia joined Connor, who stood on the porch looking out over the darkening courtyard. Darcinda was working on a treatment, and the rest of the team was in the house preparing dinner and giving them space.

"Are you okay?"

Connor shook his head. "I should have felt something. How did I not know I had Jack's wolf?"

"You two are twins. Genetically you're each half of what started as a whole. I think the same can be said for your wolves. If your wolves are anything like you and Jack, they would die to protect each other. I bet your wolf has been hiding Jack's wolf from you.

"No more feeling guilty, Connor. We've all been carrying guilt around for too long. Let it go. We need to be ready when Darcinda comes up with a plan."

Connor pulled Julia in for a hug. "You're a wonderful person, Julia. And you are great for my brother. He needs you."

Julia rested her head against Connor's chest. "I need him too."

Connor set her away from him and looked down at

her. "Thank the Fates. Once his wolf is back, you two need to sit down and have a long talk."

"I agree."

The front door opened and Darcinda peeked outside. "There you two are. I've got an idea."

Darcinda led them back upstairs and explained her plans to Julia, Connor, and Jack...who stared up at the healer like she was crazy.

"My wolf is in Connor?"

"Yes," Darcinda answered. "I'm going to be the magical conduit between you and Connor. That way, your wolf can move back to your body, and we can stop your human half from failing."

"Is it dangerous?" Julia asked.

"I've never tried it before, so I can't be one hundred percent positive, but we should be fine."

"That's not very reassuring," Julia said.

"I think you should leave, Julia," Jack said.

"Oh, here we go," Connor groaned.

"I'm not going anywhere. While you three are connected, I should stay here in case something goes wrong."

"And do what?"

"I don't know. Darcinda, is there any way I can stop the connection once it starts?"

"Yes, you can touch us with iron. My magic will be disrupted."

"There you go." She opened the door. "Charlie, can you go get a piece of iron from McHenry?"

Jack tried to sit up. "Who else is in the hall?"

Darcinda smiled. "The whole team. I told them they couldn't all be in here, so they're hovering out there."

Jack laid back with a huff.

Julia looked down at him with her hands on her hips. "They love you, Jack Dawson, and want to help."

At a knock on the door, Connor opened it and accepted a strip of metal from Charlie.

"We're going to start the spell. Have everyone stay in the hall unless we call to you," Darcinda said.

Charlie nodded and shut the door.

Darcinda circled the bed and positioned each of them. Connor stood at the side, Darcinda at the foot, and Julia next to Darcinda.

"Everything will be fine," Julia promised.

"Says the woman with the iron post in her hand," Jack mumbled.

Darcinda held up her hands, palms together, and began speaking in a language Julia couldn't understand. Light peeked out from around her fingers and began to grow as she separated her hands and cupped them to form a large ball of light. She pushed the light toward Connor and Jack, and it stopped between them.

Beams of light shot outward from the ball and penetrated Jack's and Connor's chests, causing them both to jerk as if they'd been shot.

Julia gasped.

"They're okay, Julia," Darcinda whispered before beginning to chant again. As more light poured from the ball into the twins, their skin began to glow.

A shock wave of power shot through the room, throwing Julia to the floor, where the iron post rolled away from her. She blinked to clear the spots in front of her eyes from the flash.

When she was able to focus again, she saw Connor and Darcinda lying on the floor unconscious. The entire room was inside a bubble of light, and she heard muffled pounding and shouts from the other side of the door. She sat up to see if Jack was okay. Sitting on the bed was a large, gray wolf.

Jack.

She looked at him in wonder, until he bared his teeth, then growled and stalked toward her.

She scrambled backward as best she could, until she bumped against the wall.

Jack looked down at her, his wolf eyes glowing a brilliant blue.

"Jack?" she whispered.

Julia held her breath as he leaned over her and sniffed her neck for a moment and then nuzzled against her. She reached up to touch his face, but before she could touch him, Connor groaned. Jack's wolf jerked back from her at the sound.

Julia reached for him again. "It's okay, Jack. You're going to be okay."

Connor struggled to sit up. "Jack. It's me. You're safe. Let me in."

Jack snarled and snapped at his brother's outstretched hand.

Connor yanked his hand back, his face white.

Jack stared at her for a moment more before diving through the window, glass breaking.

Connor crawled toward her. "Julia! Are you okay?"

The light bubble melted away, and the bedroom door flew open as Charlie and Devin burst into the room. Charlie dropped down next to Darcinda, who was trying to sit up, as Devin rushed over to them.

"Careful." Connor helped her to her feet and then looked out the window. "*Damn* it!"

"What happened?" Devin asked.

"If I had to guess," Connor said, "I'd say that his wolf has been hidden away for so long, it wants to be in charge."

"He'll turn back, right?" Julia asked.

Connor didn't answer her as he continued to stare out the broken window.

"Connor?"

He turned back to face her. "I don't know."

"You need to go after him."

Connor closed his eyes as if in pain. "I don't know if he'll listen to me."

"Why not? You're his twin!"

"You saw him. He tried to bite me. Right now his wolf believes I was trying to capture him. That I separated him from Jack."

"That's crazy! You were protecting him. You didn't even know his wolf had jumped to you."

"It doesn't mean his wolf understands. He won't come back until his wolf feels secure."

Devin stood next to them. "So we form a search party."

"We can't capture him. We'll make the situation worse," Connor argued.

"Not capture him. Talk to him. Let him know we're here for him, so he feels safe enough to return. We can't let him go rogue."

Julia turned to Devin. "What do you mean by rogue?"

The two men exchanged a look.

"Tell me, damn it!"

Connor closed his eyes for a moment before responding. "If his wolf won't relinquish his hold, he could stay in his wolf form forever. It happens sometimes, and it's called going rogue."

"And what do your healers do to fix it?"

Connor shook his head. "There's nothing to do. If he doesn't turn back on his own, and the pack finds out Jack has gone rogue, they'll hunt him down and kill him."

"Then we don't let it happen," Julia said. "We bring him back to us." Back to her, because she was through running from Jack and her emotions.

Love doesn't have a fixed set of laws.
It's open to interpretation.

CHAPTER 37

Julia was a fool. It had been two days since Jack's wolf ran off, and the team was still unable to locate him.

The longer he was gone, the more time it gave Julia to think things through. Before this happened, Julia thought the worst thing was not feeling safe again, but she'd been wrong. What if she never felt needed again?

She had been trying so hard for so long to not feel anything at all. If no one was close, she couldn't be hurt again, but she hadn't forgotten what Jack said to her the night he woke her up from her nightmare. He needed to be needed. At first she thought it was an excuse for him to stay with her, but now? Now she realized that being needed was a part of life as integral as taking your next breath.

Jack needed her, and she was not going to let him down. She had been letting herself down for quite some time, hiding from the truth. Now it was time to acknowledge she had feelings for Jack, and whether he had feelings for her or not, she was going to save him. She knew what it was like to let the beast take control.

If she could find herself again after all this time, there was hope for Jack yet.

So, on day three, when five men showed up on McHenry's doorstep, Julia knew this was about Jack without being told, and it was not good news. And she also knew she would fight for him to her last breath.

Connor, Devin, and McHenry stood on the porch stairs, talking to the men in the courtyard while she and the rest of the women joined them outside.

"Has something happened?" she asked.

Devin turned to her with such a grim expression, her legs would have collapsed under her if she hadn't locked her knees.

"The wolf guard is here."

"Why?" Julia asked, even though she already knew the answer in her heart.

The tall man in the front of the group spoke. "I am Counsel Darren. We have been apprised of your situation and are here to offer assistance."

"If by *situation* you mean Jack Dawson, we don't need your kind of assistance," Julia said.

"What do you know of our ways?" he asked.

"I know you plan to kill Jack instead of help him."

The man narrowed his eyes on her. "A wolf has been killing animals in the forest. We believe Jack is responsible."

"What proof do you have that it's him?"

Darren shook his head. "You are a human, and have no right to an opinion about a wolf issue."

Julia laughed, the sound harsh to her own ears.

"You speak as if humans are backward and couldn't possibly understand the ways of the supernatural. Let me share what this human has learned.

"My elf husband was murdered because he had the audacity to fall in love with me and fight for the rights of humans and supernaturals to marry each other." She looked at Alex who gave her a thumbs-up.

"Devin and Alex almost had to relinquish their powers in order to marry each other, since a faery-elf marriage wasn't allowed. Until recently, Sheila's nymph clan didn't acknowledge the rights of women. Now I'm standing in front of you defending an amazing man who has done nothing wrong."

"He's gone rogue."

"We don't know that. His wolf has been trapped and needs his freedom. We have no way of knowing if he can't turn back."

"If he was having issues with his wolf, he should have gone to one of our healers."

"Really? And what would you have done? Helped him, or banished him? He and Connor are already treated like pariahs because they're twins.

"If his own family won't stick up for him, then why would he think his clan would? Now you show up here to *assist us* by killing him. Have I left anything out of my observations, Counselor Darren?"

He glared at her, but that didn't stop her tirade.

"Wake up and smell the bigoted, prejudicial, sexist flowers, people! That's what the supremacists are all about. It's bad enough when you war against other races and those who are different from you, and now you won't even stick up for your own kind! We're going to try to bring him back first, not kill him without giving him a chance."

McHenry crossed his arms. "We'll do what the lass says."

"You don't have a say about wolf law," Darren sputtered.

"You are a guest here, wolf. Don't make me go to your pack leader and the Elf King to deal with you. I have first say of what happens in these Burrows. We will bring Jack back."

Julia stared out into the forest from her perch on a stump. The same stump she had found Jack sitting on four days ago. For a woman with no patience, she'd been waiting a lot lately. She wanted to scream at the forest and demand Jack's return. Still no luck in finding him. The team was sitting down to dinner, and then another shift would go out and look for a few hours before turning in for the night.

There had been more reports of wolf attacks over the past day. Julia wasn't sure how much longer they could hold the pack back from going after Jack. She was running out of ideas.

Leaves rustled ahead of her. She held her breath and watched for any sign of movement.

A flash of fur in the woods in front of her had her standing up.

"Jack?" she hesitated. She should go back to the house and get someone. But a whimper of pain had her walking farther into the forest. She would not risk losing him again if she went back for help.

Another flash of fur convinced her to go after him.

"Jack! Please stop and let me help."

She followed him through the woods until she stumbled into a clearing and found him lying on his side.

She ran toward him. He had to listen to her. He was trying to communicate with her somehow. Why else would he seek her out?

She walked around to get a look at his face. His eyes were closed. Was he hurt? Dying? Before she could take another step toward him, he opened his eyes. His yellow eyes.

Oh, God.

The wolf jumped up and growled. He prowled toward her, saliva dripping from his bared teeth.

She stumbled backward, tripping over her feet, and landing hard on her butt. She scrabbled backward like a crab, trying to get away from the wolf.

He stared at her for a moment before leaping toward her. She screamed, throwing her hands over her head to protect herself. Growling came from her right, and another wolf slammed into her attacker in midair. The wolves rolled on the ground, growling and scratching. They pulled apart and circled each other, the new wolf's blue eyes glowing in the dusk.

Jack!

The other wolf attacked, biting Jack's back leg, and he yelped in pain. Jack lunged for yellow eyes. Snarls and growls echoed through the forest as they fought viciously. Finally Jack jumped on the other wolf's back, gripping the wolf's neck and snapping it between his jaws. He flung the wolf to the side.

The wolf faded away, and a dead man took its place. Julia stared at the familiar-looking man. After a second, his face came back to her. It was the missing supremacist, Brock Turner.

Jack staggered away from her toward the other side of the clearing.

"Jack! Don't go."

She stopped the gasp from escaping when he turned to look at her. He stared at her. His fur was matted with blood, and more was dripping along his back leg and next to his eye.

Had he totally lost himself to his wolf?

But she couldn't think that, believe that. He was still there. He had to be. She couldn't help Thomas in the end, but Jack—Jack she could, and would, fight for.

Pounding feet sounded behind her as Devin, Connor, and Charlie ran into the clearing.

Jack bared his teeth.

She held up her hands. "It's okay, Jack. No one is going to hurt you."

Connor grabbed her arm. Jack growled at him.

"Let me go, Connor. It's okay. I've got to try. Please. It might be our last chance."

Connor let her go.

Julia took a breath to collect herself before deciding what to say. For some reason, her heart told her now was not the time to go soft on him. She prayed she was making the right decision.

"Jack Dawson, you listen to me. You need to come back right now. Your wolf has had its fun, and it's time to tell him who's in charge."

The wolf cocked his head and blinked at her.

"I know you understand me. So, hear this. You and I have a lot to talk about. I've been afraid to move forward, but I'm ready now, and I want you to be a part of my life. If it's what you want."

He took a step toward her.

Devin hissed behind her. "Julia!"

"Stay back. He's not going to hurt me."

"You can't be sure."

She looked into Jack's blue eyes. "Yes, I can. Please, Jack. Come back to me."

Light shimmered around Jack for a moment, and then it faded away.

"It's taking too long for him to change," Connor whispered.

"You can do it, Jack," Julia pleaded.

She wouldn't let fear take over. She willed Jack to change back. After another few seconds, the shimmering changed to a flash. Julia covered her eyes. When the light dissipated, she pulled her hand away.

Jack stood in front of her. As she ran toward him, he collapsed.

"Jack!"

She dropped on her knees in front of him, and Connor crouched beside him and checked his pulse.

"Is he breathing?" she asked.

"Yes."

Charlie rushed over with a medic bag. He examined Jack's bleeding head and leg, and dressed the wounds before covering him with a blanket.

"How is he?" Devin asked.

"He's in shock. We should get him back to Darcinda so she can heal him."

Julia stared down at him. "What about his wolf?"

"I don't know," Charlie said.

"Connor?"

"I don't feel it, but he's unconscious."

Julia closed her eyes for a moment to give herself a pep talk. She had been so confident when she faced him in his wolf form. Now he looked so vulnerable lying on the ground, and her fear kicked in as her overload of adrenaline evaporated.

He couldn't leave her now. She wouldn't allow it.

When it comes to love,
sometimes you have to throw out the rules and start over.

CHAPTER 38

Julia sat in the crowded room with people who were trying their best to suffocate her. Not on purpose, of course, but their concern and hovering made her want to run screaming into the woods. But she couldn't leave Jack.

Darcinda had been in the room with him for a long time. Connor paced on the porch outside. He had wanted to be in the room with Jack, but Darcinda was afraid Jack's wolf might try to jump bodies again, so she relegated him to the porch.

Where he paced by the window again.

"Devin, can you guys go out and see if you can get Connor to sit down, or at least change his pacing pattern? He's making me dizzy."

"Are you sure you're okay?"

"I'm fine. Alex is making me a cup of tea, which should keep her busy for a while. I'll be fine."

And if she said it enough times, could she make it true? She took a slow, deep breath and tried to unkink her shoulders.

McHenry walked into the room.

"How is Jamie?"

"Good. He and Andrew are out in the workshop prepping some projects. They both needed to get back into a routine after what happened. I'll be forever grateful for what you did."

"Darcinda was the one who was able to break the siren's curse."

McHenry frowned.

Now was not the time to dig into his animosity toward faeries.

McHenry looked out the window at Connor, who was now pacing in the courtyard with Devin, Charlie, and Giz walking beside him.

"Your team cares for each other."

Julia nodded. "They're more family than team."

"I can see that. I asked Alex and Sheila to put together some sandwiches. It will give them something to do, especially Alex, since she is a mother hen."

"Yes, she is," Julia agreed. "Her heart is in the best of places."

"I can see that, but it doesn't help you get some space."

Julia looked at him in wonder. "How have you not been snatched up by some deserving woman, McHenry?"

He ignored the question. "Are you and wolfman finally going to admit your feelings for each other?"

"That's the plan. He just needs to be okay. And I need to convince him I'm ready to move on — with him."

McHenry sat down next to her. "He'll be okay. I suggest using this time to prepare your closing arguments, counselor. Get ready to convince him you two belong together."

Julia smiled at him. "Got it."

"I'll leave you alone, then. Think I'll go help the ladies with the food."

She was finally alone. But unlike her previous stance of pushing everyone away so she wouldn't get hurt again, she now knew how truly foolish she'd been. She needed her family and friends, and she needed Jack. Dr. Jennings's words rang in her ears. Thomas would not want her to be alone for the rest of her life.

McHenry was right. It was time to prepare closing arguments, but this time the stakes were raised, because she was fighting to save herself.

Thirty minutes later, Darcinda walked into the dining room where everyone sat picking at their food. The team shot to their feet, and Alex grabbed Julia's hand.

"How is he?" Julia asked.

"He's stable. He's going to make it."

Devin, Giz, and Charlie exchanged high-fives like high school football players, while Alex and Sheila sandwiched her in a hug.

Connor leaned forward and rubbed his hand over his face. He looked up at Julia with shining eyes. She let go of her friends to reach for him, and he pulled her in for a hug. After a few seconds they turned back to Darcinda, Connor's arm still wrapped around Julia's shoulder.

Darcinda continued. "I had to repair some damage from the cuts, especially on his leg. The wound was deep. But he's not just hurting physically, it's emotional as well. His wolf is trying to settle back down again."

"When can we see him?" Connor asked.

"He's going to be okay, but he's exhausted. I've given him a sleeping spell to calm him down, because he kept insisting on getting up. I'll let one person in to see him for a couple minutes, but then he needs to sleep."

Julia looked up at Connor.

"Do you want to see him first?"

He squeezed her tighter to his side. "I do, but it can wait. You go spend time with him."

Her heart thumped up into her throat. "Are you sure?"

"He needs you more than he needs me right now. Tell him I'm going to pound the crap out of him if he ever does anything like this again."

"Got it. I'll tell him you love him."

She followed Darcinda up the stairs to Jack's bedroom. "Keep him calm, and hopefully the sleeping spell will kick in. He's been fighting it."

Julia opened the door and blinked back tears. Jack lay on the bed with his eyes closed. He was still pale, and she wanted to wrap him in her arms and tell him not to scare her like this ever again.

He opened his gorgeous blue eyes and looked at her, and she calmed down immediately. If she was smart, she wouldn't tell him how much power his look had over her.

"Julia."

One word, and she calmed down some more. Oh, she was in trouble with this man. Deep, deep trouble, of the heart-owning variety.

"Jack. I'm so happy you're okay."

"My wolf is back."

"Do you remember what happened?"

"Bits and pieces. I remember being in the forest. There was another wolf after me. He chased me for days."

"It was the missing wolf supremacist, Brock Turner. How did he track you down?"

"He probably scented me when I attempted to tranquilize him during the raid. Did I imagine what happened in the clearing? Were you really there?"

"I was there."

"He used you to draw me out, but I'm not sure how he would have connected you to me. My wolf would have to smell of you."

"When you turned into your wolf you, um, nuzzled my neck."

He tried to sit up. "I didn't hurt you, did I?"

She pushed him back down again and stepped back. "No."

Jack frowned. "Connor and Devin should never have let you get near me in the clearing."

"They tried to stop me, but I refused to listen to them."

"Stubborn woman."

She smiled. "It worked."

"Did you mean it?"

"What?"

"That you wanted me to come back to you?"

She nodded as a tear rolled down her cheek. "I did. I know I pushed you away before, and I'm so, so sorry. The truth is, I was so scared of letting someone get close to me that I believed it was better to be alone than risk it. But here's the thing, Jack. If I'm not willing to risk my heart, then I'm not really living. Thomas would never have wanted that for me."

"I would never try to replace Thomas. That isn't fair to him, or to you."

Julia wiped her cheeks as more tears trickled down. "And that's why I know you're the right person to risk my heart with again."

Jack's fingers ran over the covers in a nervous pattern. "You are so eloquent, Julia. I'm a man of no words. I want to say all the right things to you, but they get stuck in my throat."

"I don't need eloquence. I need honesty. I'm just happy you're whole again."

Jack shook his head. "I'm not."

Julia's stomach dropped as she rushed to the bed. "What do you mean? What's wrong? Let me go get Darcinda. Is it your wolf?" Her questions shot out in rapid-fire bursts.

He held up his hand. "I have my wolf back. But I've realized he isn't enough." He hesitated. "I won't be whole until I have you."

Julia tried to suck in a breath, but the air didn't want to pull into her lungs. Maybe it had to do with the fact that her heart didn't appear to be beating.

She grabbed his hand. "Jack Dawson, don't tell me ever again that you're a man with no words. You're a man with few words, but, boy, do they pack a punch. You have me, if you're willing to go slow."

He squeezed her hand. "I'll be slow as a sloth demon if you need me to be."

"I just need you to be you. We'll figure things out as we go."

He smiled at her, and she had trouble breathing again. Jack's eyes drooped for a second, and then opened.

"You need to rest now. Darcinda's sleeping spell is kicking in."

"I don't want to go to sleep," he said, even though his eyes drooped again.

She rested her hand on his arm. "I'm right here. Not going anywhere."

He patted the bed next to him, and she hesitated for only a second before crawling on top of the covers and lying down next to him.

Jack wrapped his arm around her, and she laid her head against his shoulder. For the slightest moment, panic kicked in. Lying on the bed with Jack was different, but different didn't mean wrong. She placed her arm over his chest, careful not to bump against his injuries.

After a few moments, Jack's breathing evened out. Julia lay there, watching him sleep, and began to wonder what the future held for them. But then she stopped herself. She wasn't going to go into lawyer mode and start running scenarios in her head. She couldn't control the future any more than she could change the past. Which meant living in the here and now.

The door opened, and Darcinda peeked inside. She gave Julia a huge grin and a thumbs-up before closing the door.

Julia closed her eyes and let herself relax for the first time in what felt like...well, forever.

There is no such thing as guilt or innocence
where love is concerned.

CHAPTER 39

Jack and Julia sat next to each other in McHenry's dining room. The group was sharing one last meal with McHenry, Andrew, and Jamie before they left. Everyone was treating Jack like an invalid, so he wasn't allowed to help with the meal. On the plus side, though, he got to sit holding Julia's hand. And even that simple connection made him and his wolf ridiculously happy.

The group finally settled in for the meal, with McHenry telling stories that had everyone laughing. Once he was done regaling the group, small discussions broke out.

Alex turned to Darcinda. "I have a question for you. When I helped pack your bag, I found a bowl that had a ball of light inside. It hovered and then split into two before fading away."

Darcinda stopped eating. "Two?"

"Yes."

"Where were the balls, Alex?"

"What do you mean?"

"I mean, did they stop in front of you and then start circling? And where did they stop?"

"Yes. One stopped at my chest and the other my stomach. Why?"

Julia gasped, and Connor started to choke on his sandwich, to the point where Charlie threatened to do the Heimlich on him.

"What's going on?" Jack whispered in Julia's ear.

"I'll tell you later."

Darcinda gave Julia, Jack, and Connor a quick glare before turning to Alex and smiling at her. "Nothing's wrong. If you're finished with your meal, I'll explain what the spell is about."

Devin frowned at the exchange. "I'm coming with you."

Darcinda's smile widened. "Good idea."

The three left the room, and Connor was out of his seat and around the table in a millisecond, peeking out the door.

"What the hell are you doing?" Charlie asked.

"Shhh! Let me listen."

The group went quiet. There was some murmuring followed by a squeal and then a thud.

"Connor, grab my bag, we need some smelling salts," Darcinda called out.

Connor burst out laughing.

"Is Alex okay?" Julia asked.

"It's not Alex who passed out," Connor called as he left the room.

"Poor Devin."

"Will someone tell us what's going on?" Jack demanded.

"If I'm not mistaken, Devin just found out he's going to be a daddy," Julia announced.

The table broke out in cheers.

A few minutes later, when the rest of the group was

cleaning up lunch, Jack pulled Julia outside and walked with her to the workshop, stepping inside and closing the door.

She turned to him. "What's wrong, Jack?"

"Nothing's wrong. Too many people out there to do what I want to do."

Her eyebrows rose. "And what is it you want to do?"

"I want to kiss you more than anything. Will you let me kiss you?"

"Jack Dawson. You have manhandled me since the trial. Grabbed me, carried me around like a child, told me what to do. And now you decide you have to *ask me* if you can kiss me?"

"Yes. And I want to correct your last statement. I tried to tell you what to do. No one can tell you what to do, Julia Cole. You are a force of nature."

Julia smiled. "Flattery will get you everywhere."

He took a step closer. "That's good to know."

He brought his hand up and ran his fingers lightly along her jaw.

"Are you okay with this? Last time didn't go so well."

"I'm good."

He leaned down and kissed her softly. Her lips were such a temptation that he knew he'd never get enough of them, of her. He kissed her a little harder, not wanting to push her too much.

She sighed into his mouth, and her tongue ran along his lip before she dove inside when he opened his mouth. *Holy Fates!*

A few moments later, she pulled back and grinned at him. "I thought I might move it along a little faster. There's no need to do the sloth demon imitation."

He grinned back. "Got it. Any time you want to move things along, feel free."

"About that..." She bit her lip. "I have to tell you something."

He forced his voice to remain steady. "You can tell me anything, Julia. Whatever it is, we can work it out."

She looked up at him. "I've learned a lot about myself in the past few weeks. I can't let others rule me or my emotions. And shutting myself down so I don't feel anything is an exercise in futility. But you found a way to break down my defenses. At first, I was irritated."

"I remember. What about now?"

She rubbed his shoulders. "Now I think I'm going to keep you. I'm falling in love with you, Jack Dawson."

His heart pounded, and, as he listened, two distinct beats set up a staccato rhythm, until they merged into one. And he realized in that moment that his wolf was in love with her too, that both hearts beat for her now.

"I'll wait for you to catch up, since I'm already in love with you, Julia. Have been for a while now. Thank you for making me whole."

A shout rang in Jack's head, and he flinched.

"What's wrong?" Julia asked.

"My brother just started shouting in my head. He's happy for us."

"You can sense Connor again?"

Jack beamed. "Yes."

"That's wonderful, Jack. But right now, tell him to go away."

"Yes, ma'am," Jack said as Connor's laugh reverberated in his head before he shut him out.

Julia reached up, and placed both hands on his face, pulling him down for another kiss. Nope, he would never get enough of her kisses.

She was a temptation, but she was his now, and, thank the Fates, he was hers now, too.

Law is a written promise,
and love is a chosen one.

CHAPTER 40

A month later

Hell, what was she talking about? Jack paced as best he could in the small bathroom as he tried to link mentally with his brother. *Connor, you there, man?*

Yeah, what's up?

I'm at Julia's, and she's talking crazy. We just finished watching a movie, and she said something about pretending this is our third date. I've seen her every day for the past month. When I told her that, she looked at me like I had grown two heads. What the hell is she talking about?

Connor laughed. *Holy shit, you're an idiot! Third date is a reference to having sex, bro.*

Jack's heart thumped. *Are you sure?*

Yes, now stop talking to me and go get your woman!

Jack dried his sweaty palms on a towel before jerking open the bathroom door. He walked into the living room and sat down next to Julia.

He lifted his hand and ran his thumb along her jaw, and she closed her eyes. "I want to make sure I understand what you want, Julia. Tell me what you meant earlier."

She opened her eyes, her pupils blown. "I knew you wouldn't initiate anything with me, since we've been taking it slow. I was trying to be a little subtle instead of blurting out that I want to have sex with you, but I didn't do a very good job of it."

"You were fine. And for the record, you can blurt out that you want to have sex with me at any time."

She leaned forward and kissed him. "Really? Any time?"

"Maybe not in front of the guys, but any other time is fabulous, stupendous, wonderful." He stood and scooped her up in his arms.

"You like to carry me around too much, caveman."

He kissed her hard on the mouth. "Yes, I do. It feels right, and rule number one tonight is if it feels right, we do it, and if it doesn't feel right, we tell each other."

"Got it."

Jack carried Julia to her bedroom and placed her on the bed, stepping back to take a long look at her. She was wearing a pair of yoga pants and a T-shirt, and he had never seen such a lovely sight.

"What is it?"

"You are so amazing. I don't know how I got so lucky."

She blushed, red running up her neck onto her face. He wondered if she blushed everywhere.

"Come down here," she whispered.

He climbed up her body without resting his weight on her. "Are you sure, Julia?"

"Yes, silly wolf. I'm more than ready."

Jack lay down on top of her, and they both moaned at the sensation. He tucked a strand of hair behind her ear and then kissed her mouth, brushing her lips with his, rubbing his nose against her ear and down her neck, until he found his way back to her mouth. A few minutes later, Jack pulled away from her mouth, panting.

"I want to see more of you. Okay?"

She nodded, and he helped her pull off her shirt and bra, his mouth and fingers exploring every bit of her exposed skin. Her hands tugged at his shirt, and he yanked it over his head before settling back down with her, skin to skin.

Damn.

Within a few minutes, anxious fingers helped divest each other of the rest of their clothes. Jack held on to his sanity by a hair until she wrapped her hand around his length and began playing.

It was time.

Stroke.

Past time.

Stroke.

Time…What the hell did time have to do with anything right now?

He reached for his wallet at the same time she opened the nightstand drawer and pulled out a huge handful of foil packets. "Here."

He gaped at her.

Again with the gorgeous blush. And his question was answered. The pink spread over her entire body.

"I didn't know if you would come prepared, so…"

"So you bought out the store."

"I did not! I just didn't know what kind you like and what size you need…" She looked away, blushing some more. "I'll stop talking now."

Jack placed his hands on either side of her face. "Baby, never stop talking to me, ever. I love that you did this." He kissed along her jaw and over her closed eyelids. "Now pick a condom, any condom, and let's get busy."

Julia burst out laughing. "I love you, Jack."

"And I love you, my bulk-condom-buying sweetheart."

Jack settled down on top of her again, and it wasn't long before he surged into her. He had never felt anything so right before. And as they moved together and then soared, he knew he'd found his home.

When he was able to catch his breath again, he pulled Julia against him. She snuggled up to his side and kissed his shoulder.

"This is a heck of a third date," Jack said, smiling down at her.

She placed her hand on his chest. "I'm sorry I confused you earlier. Next time you want to make a clandestine call in my bathroom to your brother, you might want to turn off the speaker on your phone."

What? "Julia, I wasn't talking to Connor on the phone."

"Yes, you were. I could hear you."

Jack sat up, pulling her with him.

"What's wrong?" Julia asked.

"I was not talking on the phone earlier to Connor, I used my link with him."

"Your twin-speak? Then how did I hear you?"

"You shouldn't have been able to." His heart banged in his chest like a pinball. "Unless you've mated to me."

"What do you mean?"

"Some wolf couples link telepathically."

"But I'm human."

"I know. Let's try something." He opened his mind and spoke to her. *Julia, can you hear me?*

She gasped and spoke out loud, "I heard that."

"Try and talk to me in your head."

"How?"

"Just think something and push it toward me," he said, grasping her hand.

She closed her eyes. *I don't know what to say.*

Jack chuckled. "I heard that, baby."

Her eyes popped open. "Wow."

"Yeah."

"Since I heard you and Connor earlier, do you think I can talk to him too?"

"I don't know."

Jack closed his eyes. *Connor, you there?*

Yeah, man. Why the hell you reaching out to me now? I thought you and Julia were getting busy.

Julia giggled.

Watch what you say, man.

Why?

Because Julia can hear you.

What?

Yeah, she can hear our conversation.

I'll be damned. You mated her, you dog. Have her try to say something to me.

Julia pursed her lips. *Can you hear me, Connor?*

Connor waited for a moment before responding. *I can't hear anything. Did you say something?*

She asked if you could hear her, Jack responded.

Nope. Maybe she can only hear me through you, so she and I won't be able to talk to each other directly. If that's the case, you'll just have to interpret for us, Jack.

Jack groaned. It hadn't been all that long ago that he was on his own, wishing for the voices again. Now he had his wolf, Connor, and Julia to contend with. *Good night, bro. We'll talk to you tomorrow.*

Come on, really? You drop this on me and then you hang up on me?

We'll talk to you tomorrow. Jack shut down their connection.

Julia laughed. "You are in so much trouble now, with both of us in your head."

"You're not telling me anything I haven't already figured out. I'm going to have to find something to distract Connor. He needs a damn hobby or something."

"Or a mate of his own."

Jack shook his head. "You're starting to sound like Alex now."

Funny. I can't believe I can talk to you like this. What does it mean?

"It means we're meant to be together," he answered out loud.

She smiled and rested her head on his chest. "I already knew that."

He lifted her chin and kissed her softly. "I know we said we'd take this slow, Julia, so I think it's only fair to give you fair warning that someday I'm going to ask you to marry me."

She blinked shiny eyes at him. "And I'm giving you fair warning that I'm probably going to say yes."

He laid her down on the bed and gazed into her big, brown eyes. Eyes that gleamed wickedly at him.

He couldn't stop his own smile. Something that had been happening much more frequently lately. "Probably?"

She dipped her hand into the open nightstand drawer. "Yes. I need a little convincing first. How about we play pick a condom, any condom again."

"Best game ever," he murmured as his mouth met hers.

Thanks!

Thank you for taking the time to read *To Have and To Howl*. I hope you enjoyed the third book in the series. Please consider telling your friends about it or posting a short review. Word of mouth is an author's best friend, and much appreciated. Thank you, AE.

The next book in the series is going to focus on Connor. How could it not? Wait until you see who he ends up with! I think this one is going to be a hoot!!

If you would like to know when my next books will be released, please join my new releases email list at www.aejonesauthor.com or follow me on Twitter @aejonesauthor or Facebook at https://www.facebook.com/aejones.author1

If you haven't had a chance to read my Mind Sweeper series about a feisty woman with the ability to erase memories and the merry band of supernaturals who work with her, please see the series list below. And I will also be writing some spin-off stories about other characters in the Mind Sweeper world, so stay tuned.

Please turn the page to find a list of my other books.

Books by AE Jones

Paranormal Wedding Planner Series

In Sickness and In Elf – Book 1
From This Fae Forward – Book 2
To Have and To Howl – Book 3
For Better or For Wolf – Book 4 (coming soon)

Mind Sweeper Series

Mind Sweeper – Book 1
The Fledgling – Book 2 (A Mind Sweeper Novella)
Shifter Wars – Book 3
The Pursuit – Book 4 (A Mind Sweeper Novella)
Sentinel Lost – Book 5

Mind Sweeper Flashback Stories

Forget Me
Protect Me
Trust Me

Find all of AE Jones's latest releases on your favorite
online retailer or visit her website:
http://www.aejonesauthor.com

ABOUT THE AUTHOR

Growing up a TV junkie, AE Jones oftentimes rewrote endings of episodes in her head when she didn't like the outcome. She immersed herself in sci-fi and soap operas. But when *Buffy* hit the little screen, she knew her true love was paranormal. Now she spends her nights weaving stories about all variations of supernatural—their angst and their humor. After all, life is about both...whether you sport fangs or not.

AE won RWA's Golden Heart® Award for her paranormal manuscript, Mind Sweeper, which also was a RWA RITA® finalist for both First Book and Paranormal Romance. AE was also a recipient of the Booksellers Best Award for her book, Sentinel Lost.

AE lives in Ohio surrounded by her eclectic family and friends who in no way resemble any characters in her books. *Honest.* Now her two cats are another story altogether.

CPSIA information can be obtained
at www.ICGtesting.com
Printed in the USA
LVHW011817170119
604290LV00019B/1294/P